# *Best Friends;*
# *Better Lovers*

**Celya Bowers**

Genesis Press, Inc.

# INDIGO LOVE STORIES

An imprint of Genesis Press, Inc.
Publishing Company

Genesis Press, Inc.
P.O. Box 101
Columbus, MS 39703

Copyright © 2011 Celya Bowers

ISBN-13: 978-1-58571-455-1
ISBN-10: 1-58571-455-0
Manufactured in the United States of America

First Edition

Visit us at www.genesis-press.com
or call at 1-888-Indigo-1-4-0

# Dedication

To my mother.

There's not a day that goes by that I don't think about you.

# Acknowledgements

I would like to take this opportunity to thank all of those people who have helped me along the way and have continued to support me in my quest of being a published author.

My family: Darwyn Tilley, Jeri Murphy, William Earl Kenney, Sheila Kenney, Kim Kenney, Sherry Kenney, Shannon Murphy, Yolanda Tilley, Celya Tilley, Rod Kenney, and Kennedy Tilley.

My BFs: Cherry Elder, Erica Black, Roslin Williams, Maria Persuitte, Sharon Hickman-Mahones, Tammy Hill, Eulanda Bailey, Melody Alvarado, Maria Persuitee, Beverly Cofer, Donna Lefear, Eulanda Bailey, Deandra Garrett, Angela Cavener, Diane Kelly, and Lewis Stewart.

My friends: Judy Brown, Pam Washington, Paula Washington, Mattie Washington Johnson, Gail Surles, Lawrence Leonard, Paul Humphrey, Winston Williams, Shirley Washington, Sheila Allen, Melody Alvarado, Shaunette Smith, Darlene Ramzy, Clara Washington, Kerry Elder, Marnese Elder, Kerry Rand, and Vannetta Chapman.

My new Facebook friends: thank you for letting me into your lives.

To my fellow scribes: Diane Kelly, Angela Cavener, Chanta Rand, and Michella Chappell, thank you for all the advice and suggestions. (You know like, yes, you must write every day).

If I forgot anyone, please charge it to my head, not my heart.

Celya Bowers
www.celya bowers.net
celyabowers@gmail.com
www.facebook.com/celyabowrs
www.twitter.com/celyabowers

# CHAPTER 1

Kamryn Hillcroft glanced at her silver watch again. He was forty-five minutes late. She glanced around The Hoop, a popular sports bar in downtown Dallas, looking for her interviewee. No luck. Normally his being late wouldn't be a big deal, but she was on a deadline for her sports column.

Being the first female African-American sports columnist at the *Dallas Morning News* came with a certain amount of pressure, she knew. There were two sportswriters just waiting for her to miss a deadline. But that wasn't going to happen. She always had a plan B. Besides, she knew he would be there eventually. Brayden Allen, point guard for the Dallas Mavericks, was always on his own schedule. Everyone else had to adapt, including her.

She ordered iced tea while she waited. She was on her second glass when she saw him walking toward her, dressed in a Dallas Mavericks T-shirt and blue jean shorts with sandals. He looked like a walking ad for a fashion magazine. She shook her head. It was a shame to be that good looking.

"Hey, Kam," Bray said, settling into the seat next to her. He kissed her lightly on the cheek. "Have you ordered?"

Only Bray could have such an innocent look on his handsome face and not even offer an excuse for his tardiness. Worst of all, he made her forget her irritation. He was six feet, six inches of gorgeous man with a honey brown complexion complemented by hazel eyes, a dazzling smile, and a thin mustache. Women didn't have a chance against him.

"I was waiting on you." She pulled out her tape recorder and notepad. "How about we take care of the interview first, so I can file my column on time, I might add?"

He shrugged off her comment, grabbed the menu, and waved for the server. "I know. I was late."

Yeah, she knew. This was as close to an apology as she was going to get from Bray. Apologies just weren't his thing. Women were his thing. Tiny, beautiful women were totally his thing. The man ran through women like a hot knife through melted butter. "Which flava is it?" Brayden was an equal opportunity playa. He dated women of all races.

"I'm currently between flavas."

"Oh, that's too bad."

"You know how it is," Bray said quietly. "Oh, that's right, you don't date."

"No, I don't." Kamryn was tired of being reminded that she didn't have a social life. "Can we get to the story?"

"Kam, Steve died three years ago. I know you haven't been on a date since he passed away. The only time you go out is when I take you. It's time for you to get back out there. I could hook you up with one of the guys on the team, if you like. I know how you women dig athletes."

He was trying to get her dander up. And he was doing a darn good job. Kamryn counted to fifty before she spoke. "No, thank you. Just because I write about sports doesn't mean I want to date an athlete. I'm happy with my life just as it is. I was married for twelve years. Why waste my time on a playa? I can think of better ways to waste my time … you know, like getting a root canal without Novocain."

He leaned back in his chair and narrowed those hazel eyes at her. "I'm not saying you gotta marry somebody. But a little practice never hurt."

"I think you get enough practice for everyone in the city of Dallas." Kamryn smiled as she noticed the young waitress approaching their table. "Here comes another victim now."

———◦◦◦———

Brayden wanted to make Kamryn eat her words, but who was he kidding? He liked women. No, check that, he loved women and the attention they gave him. After Kamryn ordered a glass of wine and he ordered a glass of tea, he listened as the waitress rattled off the specials of the day.

Ignoring them all, he ordered broiled salmon because he had practice later that afternoon, not to mention the game tomorrow night. He already knew Kamryn's order. "She'll have grilled red snapper with roasted asparagus tips and garlic mashed potatoes."

The young woman smiled at him and left the table.

Kam stared at him with angry brown eyes. Except for the scowl on her face, she looked pretty. Her round face was perfectly made up, as always. Her shoulder-length black hair hung free and loose. She was tall, toned, and men were always checking her out. Most times, men staring at her didn't bother him, but today it was getting under his skin.

She was dressed in a V-neck blouse that showed off her full cleavage. The diamond necklace he'd given her last year for Christmas hung in the valley of her breasts. Brayden couldn't help himself; he found himself looking and wondering how soft her skin felt.

She still wore her wedding rings, he noticed. He made a mental note to talk to her later about taking them off. She'd been promising to take them off for the last year. He knew she was still mourning her husband, but enough was enough. Kam was going to need a nudge back out into the dating world, and he was just the man to do it.

"You know, my parents are flying in tomorrow for the playoff games. Why don't you come to the game? Mom would love to see you."

She shook her head. "I can't sit in the family box. I sit in the press box."

He'd known she'd say that. She always did. Every year he offered her seats in the family section and every year she turned him down. "My seats are better," he said. "Not only that, you and Mom can rag on my social life."

She laughed. "We don't just talk about those groupies you date. We talk about substantial things like spa days and shopping."

"Okay, so what about the seats? Bring your parents."

She narrowed her eyes at him. "You know Daddy is so proud that Dallas is in the playoffs. That's all he's been talking about for the last few weeks. All right," she said, giving in, "I'll take the tickets."

"Great. Now let's get the questions out of the way. Once my food gets here, the interview is over. You know I can't eat and talk at the same time. If we have to finish it another time, you might not make your deadline." He spotted the waitress bringing their drink orders. "You'd better get started, you don't have much time."

Kam nodded and started with the questions. "What do you think the Mavericks' chances are for taking it all this season?" She was trying to be professional, but that wasn't going to work with him today.

"You know the answer to that question, baby. Ask me a real question."

"Like what?"

The waitress placed their drink orders in front of them. Okay, she got them reversed, but he didn't say anything. Neither did Kam. She merely switched them once the young lady left the table.

"Bray, answer my question," Kam persisted.

"You want a good solid quote for your column, I'll give you one. I think we have just as much chance of winning as the other three teams. Better, because we're determined to prove to everyone that we're back. We're on top and plan to stay there. Our offense makes us one of the highest scoring teams in the league. Not to toot our horn, but we're unstoppable."

She scribbled in her notepad. "My, don't we sound proud?"

"Yes, I am. We've come a long way this season. We've made a lot of sacrifices and had some losses. My social life has been the victim."

"Yeah, right." Kamryn knew nothing would come between Bray and a woman, if that was what he wanted. She continued with her questions. "Is the team ready for the playoffs both physically and mentally?"

"With the first game being tomorrow night, we'd better be ready, right?"

"Well, yes. In fact, I know you guys are ready. Remember, at the beginning of the season, I said you guys were going to take it all. I can see the changes in the new team. Free throws are up twenty-five percent and the highest in the league. Assists are up twenty percent and rebounds thirty percent. You guys work together like a well-oiled machine."

He stared at her in amazement. Kam knew more about sports than most of his teammates. Not just basketball, she knew football, hockey, or just about any sport out there. "Damn, girl. I feel like I'm talking to one of the fellas."

"Oh, so a woman can't know sports? I've been watching sports since I was a kid. I didn't know you were a male chauvinist pig. It really doesn't become you."

"You know I'm not like that. It's just different. Good, but different. That's probably why we hang out so much. It's like being with one of the guys, except I have someone pretty to look at." He hoped he tiptoed through that minefield without Kam noticing.

She laughed and he knew the jig was up. "Flattery will get you everywhere, Bray. But I'm sure you already knew that. You aren't Mr. Fast Play for nothing. Seriously, I want to run a story idea by you," she said softly. Her face suddenly turned serious.

He cleared his throat. "Sure, Kam. You know I'll be straight with you." He was dreading the next few minutes, because he knew exactly what she wanted to talk about. It was the same thing most of the sports world was still talking about: Jason Woken's apparent suicide, three months earlier.

Kamryn took a deep breath to clear her thoughts and hoped she wasn't making a big mistake. "I don't think Jason's death was a suicide."

Bray looked at her with those eyes. "Kam, it was officially ruled a suicide. They found his note to his wife telling her how sorry he was. I know you want to help his widow out by proving it was an accident, but Jason deliberately drove his SUV into a cement pillar at full speed and died instantly. I loved Jason like a brother, but he's gone, and we should move on with our lives."

"He was your teammate for three years, and that's all you got? Bray, there's something bigger going on and you want to turn a blind eye to it. I don't think it was a suicide."

"Kam, let it go. You're making more out of this than necessary." He took a deep breath and a bigger swig of tea. He was hiding something. Normally he would never dare talk her out of anything remotely related to a story. "What do you think you know?"

"His wife says he was gambling and he owed someone a lot of money. He might not have had a choice but to drive into that pillar at full speed. Maybe that was his only way out."

"Is Sandra planting all those ideas in your head? Word is all the money is tied up and she's desperate for some cash."

"Bray, I do have a brain. She told me that the bulk of his estate is tied up with his mother. He never changed his will after they married seven years ago. I'm checking out her story."

He looked surprised. "You don't believe her?"

"I didn't say that. As a journalist I have to check out every possible angle. Sandra said she had a policy on him, but, since his death was ruled a suicide, the insurance company is not releasing the money."

He nodded. "So do you think he was gambling?"

"Well, a few things that I don't want to go into here led me on a journey, and I'm going to do a story about it. I think the world needs to know about professional athletes betting illegally, sometimes on their own games, and the dangers of doing so. Talk about the ultimate insider trading."

"You can't do that!"

"Yes, I can," she said, daring him to say otherwise. "This involves athletes, so it's my job to report it. Do you have any idea how much money is being lost on illegal betting? We could build a homeless shelter in almost every major city in the US with that money. We could start organic farms and go green and still not use all the money that's lost."

He smiled and seemed to relax a bit. "Now that sounds like my Kam, the green girl. You'll be stepping on a lot of toes, so just think about what you're doing," he warned. He reached across the table and rubbed her hand gently.

Now he'd made that gesture many times, but today it shocked her, electrically speaking. She tried to snatch her hand away, but he wasn't having that. He gripped her hand tighter in his much larger hand.

"I have thought about it. I don't want to see anyone else get hurt."

"And I don't want to see you get hurt," Bray said. "You know this is a 'heads will roll' kind of thing." He sighed. "Kam, if you think about who did this to Jason, just think what they'll do to a sports journalist poking her pretty nose where it doesn't belong."

"I know, but if no one ever told these stories, what would happen? I don't want to be the person who knew about this and did nothing. I want to be the person who stopped the madness."

The waitress arrived with their food. Bray stared at her for what seemed to be forever. Finally, he released her hand. The waitress quickly placed their food down and left the table.

"Kam, following this story is not a replacement for human intimacy. Why is this so important to you? I don't know why you think you have to help Sandra so much. It wasn't like she was the nicest person anyway."

She opened her mouth to tell him where he could go with that line of questioning, but he simply held up his hand to stop her.

"We'll table this for now, but promise me you won't do anything until we talk. I mean, really talk."

He was worse than a woman. "All right. And when would that be?"

"After the game tomorrow night. You can tell me what you know about this mess that's gotten your engines going."

"We're going to the usual place?"

"Of course."

"What if you guys don't win?"

"We will. I'll wager my social life on it."

—∞—

As Brayden maneuvered his hybrid Cadillac Escalade through busy downtown traffic, he thought about his interview with Kam. Interview? Hell, he couldn't remember anything he said. He hoped it wouldn't come back to bite him in the butt.

From the minute he'd sat down with Kam, his brain had been focused on her. He'd known her for over five years and they'd always been close friends, but today he was thinking about how sexy she looked.

Where had those thoughts come from? Normally his taste ran to petite or slender women, and Kam was anything but tiny.

Maybe it was the fact that she treated him like a person. Not a celebrity, not a walking wallet, but a regular guy. The fame was nice, but sometimes it was also nice that there was one person who could always put him in his place. His cell phone rang, disturbing his musings. He glanced down at the display and smiled. It was his oldest brother, Sean.

"What's up, bro? You know we're getting ready for the playoffs tomorrow. Too bad Boston isn't in the playoffs," Brayden teased. Sean worked in the legal department for the Boston Celtics.

"Ha, ha, not funny. Just makes my job as a sports attorney so much easier. We can concentrate on who to steal from Dallas next year. Ready to come to Boston?"

"No, not yet. I'm glad you called."

"Oh, this does not sound good. I thought Mom and Dad weren't coming until tomorrow. You're not taking those groupies to your house, are you?"

Brayden chuckled. No matter what, Sean was an attorney first and a brother second. "Mom and Dad are coming in tomorrow. I already ordered the car service to pick them up at the airport. Quit tripping. You taught me too well about bringing women to my house. Kam is the only person besides a few teammates and family who knows where I actually live. I still take the honeys to the condo."

"And when was the last time that happened?"

"Have you been talking to Kam?"

"No, the last few times we've talked, you haven't named anyone but Kam. Usually you're naming women off like the ingredients for a recipe, so either you haven't been dating anyone lately or you and Kamryn have finally seen the light."

He swerved to miss a compact car and muttered a curse. "See what you did? Man, I almost hit one of those little tuna cans. Kam, be serious. We're friends and that's all. You know what kind of women I date."

"I know what you used to date: mindless, although beautiful, women who cared more about your money and status than about you. There's nothing wrong with dating someone with some meat on her bones. Based on the few times I've met Kam, I know she's got more going for her than just being beautiful."

"She's like a sister to me," Brayden told his brother. "It would be like dating Emma. That's just sick."

Sean laughed, obviously not buying any of Brayden's claims. "Okay, little brother, let's just test your theory."

"I don't have time to go on the witness stand right now, counselor. I want to talk about something important."

"Sure. Just answer one question."

Brayden gave a dramatic sigh. "Oh, all right. One."

"How many times a day do you talk to Kamryn?"

"It varies," Brayden hedged.

Sean chuckled. "How about today? How many times have you talked to her today?"

"Today was special. She interviewed me for her column."

"All right, good answer. How about yesterday?"

Brayden thought back to the previous day and cringed. "About six."

"And how many times did you talk to Emma yesterday?"

"I haven't talk to Ems in about a week."

"That's my point, Brayden. You and Kamryn are in constant contact. You've never been like that with anyone else. The most glaring piece of evidence is the fact that you refer to her as Kam and she calls you Bray. No one else can call you that. I called her Kam once and she quickly corrected me. Remember when you came home for Dad's birthday a few months ago? You called her, she called you, and we're not even going to discuss how many text messages. She has all of our phone numbers and contact information. You guys are close, Bray. Would it be that hard to make the leap from best friends to lovers?"

"I'm not attracted to Kam like that." Okay, that was a lie. But Brayden couldn't get his head around that at the moment.

"Yeah, right. I'll let you figure that out on your own. What did you want to talk to me about?"

"It can wait. I want to talk about this."

Sean huffed. "Look, it's not that hard. You got a thing for your best friend. And now you need to decide whether your friendship is worth risking the trip into passion."

Brayden thought about his brother's words. "It might be interesting," he said, giving voice to his thoughts. "Once we cross that line, though, could we go back to being friends? The last thing I want is to ruin our friendship for something that might not last."

"So you have thought about it?"

"Yes, I guess I have."

# CHAPTER 2

The next evening, Kamryn sat between Bray's mother, Janice, and her own mother, Colleen, in the American Airlines Center, ready to watch Bray lead the team to the first victory of the semifinals. She was glad Bray had convinced her to take the family seats. Her father, now seated directly behind the women and next to Bray's father, James, was as happy as a clam.

"How about a beer, Kamryn?" Janice waved at the usher, ready to place her order.

Kamryn nodded. "Sure, I'd love one."

"I still can't believe they are in the playoffs. I'm very proud of Brayden. I know he's wanted this a long time," Janice said with a hint of pride of her voice.

The usher appeared and took their orders for nachos with jalapeños, beer, and soda. After the usher was assured he had everybody's orders, he left.

"This is what I love about you, Kamryn," Janice said, patting Kamryn on her jean-covered leg. "You don't try to act like you don't eat. I wish Brayden would find a nice girl that looked like you."

Kamryn looked at Janice. "Why would you say that? You know Bray likes those tiny or super-slender women who look good on his arm. He'd never look at a woman my size. I don't think he's ever dated a woman over a size four."

"Brayden just doesn't know what's good for him. Those stick figures he dates don't do a thing for his soul. He needs someone who's going to keep him grounded, not have him act a fool and try to spend all his money."

Kamryn nodded. In her professional career as a sports columnist she'd seen many an athlete let his personal life take over his professional one and end up broke. She knew Bray wasn't like that, but she didn't see him settling down anytime soon. "Sorry, Janice, I don't know if that will happen."

"Well, at any rate, I'll keep my fingers crossed that one day he'll see the light."

Kamryn switched topics. "How long are you guys staying in town?"

Janice's chubby face split into a wide grin. "Well, my son is confident that the Mavericks are going to the finals, so we're staying until the end or until Dallas loses."

Kamryn laughed. "We all know how Bray gets when the team loses. It's best to stay about fifty miles from him."

"Why don't we do a spa day in between all these games? How about tomorrow? Brayden says the team is flying out in the morning."

Kamryn nodded. "Yeah, the first games are kind of close during the semi-finals. They don't get much recoup time. So we better take advantage of him being gone."

Janice agreed, then returned to her previous comments. "See, if my son would just open his eyes to the pretty women who aren't the size of a stick, he'd probably be married with kids by now."

"I can't see him settling down with a woman of any size," Kamryn said. "He's having too much fun test driving all the sports cars to settle for a sedan."

———

Brayden tried to keep his mind on the game. Every time Dallas was in possession of the ball and they were driving to the goal for a basket, his gaze went to where his mother and Kam were sitting.

He almost got popped in the face with the basketball for his inattention. He also noticed he wasn't the only one looking in Kam's direction. His coach was also looking at his best friend. Now what was really going on?

His teammate and friend, Tyler Rice, yelled something at him across the floor, but with all the other noises in the American Airlines Center, he couldn't make it out. He raised his shoulders, silently asking what he meant. Suddenly, the basketball was hurling toward him at an enormous speed. Bray steadied himself and caught the ball and pumped it in for an easy three pointer. He loved basketball.

When the buzzer sounded for halftime, Dallas was ahead by five points. Brayden and his teammates headed for the locker room, confident that the game was theirs.

Tyler walked up beside him and slapped him on the back. "Man, didn't you hear me?"

"No, I thought you were telling me you were giving me the ball."

Tyler shook his head. "No, I didn't have the ball. In fact, we didn't even have possession at the time. I was trying to tell you the camera was on Kamryn and your mom. They were knocking back some bottled beer like pros."

Brayden shook his head. When those two women got together and alcohol was nearby, Brayden knew they were up to no good. Kam and his mom acted more like sisters. "Sorry, missed it." They walked into the dungeon, as they called it. "I would have loved to see it."

"No worries," Tyler said as they took a seat in front of their assigned lockers and waited for Coach to make his entrance.

Brayden glanced around at his teammates. He knew exactly what Coach was going to say. They weren't playing their best and they would pay for to-night's poor performance once they got to Chicago tomorrow with a practice to the death.

Coach Greg DeMorris, nicknamed Da Money for his winning record, walked into the locker room with two assistants following quietly behind. Dressed in his trademark dark Armani suit, he stood in the center of the room, demanding attention. Coach stood six feet, five inches, and was probably in better shape than most of the men he coached. When he came to Dallas two years prior professionalism was at the top of his agenda. He didn't want any drama surrounding the team and stressed that constantly. He was also one of the best coaches in the NBA.

"Okay, ladies, listen up," he said sarcastically. "We're up by five. By my calculations we should be up by at least fifteen points. Allen, way to make that three-pointer with a loose ball."

Brayden nodded, not having a clue as to what Coach was referring to, but he knew better than to ask.

⊸∞∞⊸

An hour after the Mavericks' first victory of the playoffs, Kamryn sat in her Chevy Tahoe hybrid in the American Airlines Center parking lot, scribbling notes about the game while she waited for Bray to shower and change clothes. It was part of their ritual. For the last three years they had a late night dinner after every victory at a local hole in the wall. Junior's was just that. It was a small diner that seated about fifty people on a good day. The restaurant was situated in a strip mall near downtown. It was the first place she'd interviewed Bray over five years ago when he joined the Mavericks, and over time it had become 'their' place.

She watched the excited fans walking to their cars. It always amazed her how a grown man would cry openly at a game, but not anywhere else. Bray had explained it to her many times, but Kamryn figured it had more to do with testosterone than anything else. She smiled as she noticed the groupies hanging out in front of the AAC waiting for the athletes to come out.

Too bad they didn't know most of the guys had already left through an unmarked exit.

Her cell phone vibrated, and she knew it was Bray. He was ready for her to pick him up. She started the SUV and headed around the building to do so. Normally Bray used a car service to ferry him to and from home games. He claimed he was too tired to drive home. That was also part of their ritual; if he didn't use a car service, she took him home.

He was waiting for her near the exit and smiled as she pulled up. He slid in, filling the SUV with the scent of a clean man. "I told you we'd win," was all he said as he buckled the seat belt.

"By five points," Kamryn said, putting the car in gear. "I can't believe you guys had the lead, lost the lead, then finally came back. I was ready to come down there and rip you a new one for not playing your best."

His laughter filled the interior. "Too late, Coach beat you to it. Like I'd let a mere woman front me out."

"You'd better be glad I'm driving."

Of course he ignored her threat. "You know you like it."

She did, but she couldn't let him know that. "That's not the point."

"Okay. Tell me why you think Jason's death was not a suicide."

"You want to talk about that now?"

"Why not? The atmosphere is not exactly quiet at Junior's." He shifted in his seat and faced her. "Come on, Kam. Tell me what has you bubbling like a first-grader on a field trip."

"I'll ignore the attitude. I've been checking Jason's financial records."

"Can you tell me how a sports columnist has access to others' financial records?"

"Sandra, his widow, gave me some of the information, but I have connections, Bray," she said. "You know, a favor here, a favor there."

"Go on."

"Okay. Sandra thought there should have been more money in their joint account. She said there was only a few thousand in it. She said there had been withdrawals she knew nothing about. Although the money is tied up, she had a policy on him. But, since the death was ruled a suicide, it won't pay out. She thought I could do a little investigative journalism to see what I could do. She doesn't think Jason would take his own life, but the cops will not listen to her."

Brayden nodded. "Yeah, between them finding the note and the rumors about him betting, they've closed the case. And just because Sandra Woken says something doesn't make it so."

She didn't like his tone. "I know most of the guys on the team didn't like her, including the coach, but if Jason was gambling and that was the cause of his death, that would be an amazing story."

"And Sandra could collect her insurance money."

"You make her sound like a parasite."

"Your words, not mine."

Kamryn was getting nowhere fast. So she tried another angle. "His bank records were clean. I couldn't see where the transfers were going. But they were for different amounts at different intervals. He opened an account at another bank in his name only about six months before he died."

Bray sighed. "I have accounts at two separate banks, investment accounts, and stock portfolios. None of my stuff is at one place, per your brother's instructions. I don't see how this adds up to anything but boring."

"How about Sandra knew nothing about this other account?"

"Not so boring," Bray said. "What the heck was Jason doing?"

"I don't have all the dots connected yet, Bray. Sandra doesn't have access to that account. His mother has access."

"Wow," he said quietly. "I thought you were just blowin' smoke about all this mess. But it still doesn't prove it wasn't anything but a suicide."

"Tell me where that money was going." She arrived at Junior's and parked the SUV. "Bray, I don't want to cause trouble where there shouldn't be any, but it's not adding up. He doesn't have kids outside of his marriage, so there's no baby mama out there claiming he was a deadbeat dad. He wasn't gay, so there wasn't a lover blackmailing him for money."

He stared at her.

"Bray, think about it."

"Okay, I'll agree that the transfers are a mystery." He opened his door and slid out of the SUV.

Kamryn was relieved. She reached for the door handle and was shocked to find that Bray had already walked to her door.

"But I don't want you getting hurt. You're very important to me, Kam. Plus, Momma Hillcroft would kill me if let anything happen to you," he said, referring to her mother. He took her hand and led her inside the diner.

They'd been coming there so long that no one gave them a second glance. It was probably the reason that Bray loved coming here after the game. They took a seat at their favorite booth. Kamryn glanced around the busy dinner and spotted the owner walking toward them.

"Congratulations on the win, Brayden," Junior Harris said as he placed two glasses of his prize-winning tea on the table. "I knew you guys could do it. Now just bring home the championship. What can I get you folks tonight?" He glanced at Kamryn and smiled. "Girl, your column was the bomb today. You call it like you see it."

Kamryn laughed. "Yes, I have to. It was the truth."

Junior nodded. "True. A little honesty never hurt no one."

"Very true." After she and Bray recited their orders to Junior, he went back to his perch at the counter. They sat quietly across from each other, looking around. Junior had the best food this side of restaurant row. It was a well-kept secret, and Junior wanted to keep it that way. He always said he made enough money to keep him in lottery tickets, and that was all he needed.

"So what's the next step?" Bray suddenly asked, playing with the napkin dispenser.

Kamryn shrugged. "Well, with you guys going to the playoffs as I predicted, my investigating time is cut in half. But I have a few tricks up my sleeve to get the information."

"Why do you think Sandra's not on the new account? Seems strange to me."

She thought so, too. "I'm not sure. She seemed hurt when she mentioned it. I have some theories about it, but I need to check out some details on the DL."

"You look so cute when you're trying to use street slang. Baby, it's just not you." Bray laughed. "Okay, care to elaborate on the DL thing?"

She quickly glanced around the room. Her reporter's sense of danger had kicked in. "Sandra said that he was gambling and some strange men showed up at their house, wanting to see him."

He shrugged. "Probably the bookie, or at least his enforcers, looking for some money."

She wasn't going to convince him tonight, she knew. She didn't want him worried about her during the game, so she tried another approach. "It's just that something doesn't feel right, and I have a job to do."

"By searching for clues that aren't there. Promise me that you'll be careful. I don't want to get *that* phone call while I'm in Chicago. Okay?"

"All right. I didn't think you'd be such a woman about this," Kamryn joked, trying to lighten the situation.

"I'm all man, baby. I can show you if you want."

"No, thank you. Save it for those girls who believe you."

---

Much, much later that night, Kamryn pulled up in her driveway and noticed a figure in the shadows. Great, now she had a prowler. She reached for her cell phone to call Bray, then halted before she hit the third speed dial option. She had no right to call him. He was just her friend, not her protector.

She started to dial the police but then noticed the figure was waving at her. No robber would have the nerve to wave, right? Her heartbeat accelerated as the figure walked toward her. Okay, she thought, you still need to be prepared. She slowly reached for the nine millimeter she kept under her car seat. She had a permit for the gun and to carry a concealed weapon. It was her father's idea. He made sure both her and her sister were licensed gun carriers. She stopped as she recognized the prowler's slim outline as her younger sister, Kalyn.

She pushed the electronic button to release the passenger window so she could yell at her sister. "Kalyn, I was getting ready to shoot you! What are you doing here at this hour?"

"I'm hungry. I was just getting ready to search for your spare key when you drove up. Where have you been?"

Rather than tell the entire neighborhood that she'd been hanging out with Bray, Kamryn opened her garage door with her remote and pulled in. After her sister was safely inside with her, Kamryn closed it. She entered her house with Kalyn on her heels.

"So where were you? I know it wasn't a date."

"I was at Junior's." Kamryn walked into the kitchen, flipped on the lights, and began pulling containers of leftovers out of the refrigerator. That was the price she paid for living around the corner from her non-cooking sister. "You know, one day you're going to have to learn how to cook."

"That's what I got you for." Kalyn began to open the containers and picked out a meatloaf Kamryn had made a few days before. "This must mean that Dallas won the game."

"Yes, it does. You should watch the games more often. How many times does Dallas make it to the playoffs? They play again in two days in Chicago."

Kalyn put the container in the microwave and punched a series of buttons. "I know it's a ritual and all, but I figured he would be out clubbing and fighting off the groupies since they're in the semi-finals. Why go eat greasy food with you?"

"We always go eat at Junior's after a victory game." Kamryn put the other containers back into the refrigerator. She knew exactly where this conversation was heading, and she had to put a stop to it before Kalyn got started.

Kalyn walked to the counter and leaned against it, staring at her. "Kamryn, you know more about Brayden than any woman he's ever dated. Now you're telling me that he was willing to forego sure-thing sex with some groupie to hang out with you? Are you sure you haven't slept with him?"

She sounded just like an attorney, which, in a sense, was true. Kalyn had a law degree, but worked in public relations as an image consultant. Kamryn shook her head. "You're not going to start this again, are you? Why do I feel like I'm on the witness stand every time we have this conversation? Bray and I are just friends. Besides, I'm thirty-eight."

The microwave dinged and Kalyn walked back to the microwave. "So? Bray just turned thirty-two. What's your point?"

"My point is that we're friends and that's all."

"I have guy friends and they don't call me as often as Bray calls you. You guys talk every day. You even made him the hero in your romance novel. How'd he take the news of being a romance super stud?"

"I haven't told him yet. Besides, I haven't heard from the publisher whether they want to buy it. I'm not going to tell him unless it sells and it's absolutely necessary."

"Do you think he'll be upset? Most men would be proud to be portrayed in a book." She took the food out and grabbed a fork from the drawer.

27

"Written by Synamun Kiss?" When she began secretly writing erotic short stories, Kamryn decided not to use her professional name, but came up with a fun pseudonym. So Synamun Kiss has written the erotic romance novel.

Kalyn scooped up a forkful of meatloaf and ate it. "I think he'll be jazzed just because you wrote it about him and the sex is hot."

"Be serious."

"I am being serious. Brayden will probably want to try out some of those things you wrote about in the book. How funny is it that the heroine in your novel is a statuesque sister? I think this is a case of art imitating life. I think on some level you want Brayden in that way. Kamryn, you're an attractive woman. Men are always looking at you, you just don't notice."

"Are you sure they're looking at all of me?" She laughed. "I think men like women thin like you." Kalyn had definitely gotten the skinny genes in the Hillcroft family.

"Well, some do, some don't. You should be proud of what God gave you. Do you have any idea of how many women would love to have your body?" Kalyn took another bite of her food. "My point is that you guys are close. And I've seen the way he looks at you."

"How does he look at me?" Kamryn had noticed something had changed between her and Bray in the last month, but hadn't quite put her finger on it.

"Remember Mom and Dad's forty-second anniversary party a few months ago?"

"Of course I do, I did most of the work, thank you very much. You were always absent when there was work to be done. I was running around like a crazy person."

"Is it my fault that one of the professional baseball players was involved in a scandal that rocked the state at the same time?" Kalyn took another bite of meatloaf. "Who made you take a break? Who brought you a plate of food? And who told me to quit trying to play matchmaker for you?"

Kamryn thought about her younger sister's question. "I know the answer to two of those questions is Bray. The third, I have no idea."

Kalyn grinned. "Brayden."

"My Bray?"

"Yes, your Bray told me to stop trying to set you up on dates or he was going to hurt me."

Kamryn chuckled. "And just yesterday he was telling me it was time to get back out there and start dating."

Kalyn placed her now-empty container on the counter. She didn't even bother to clean it out or put it in the sink. That was Kalyn. "Kamryn, I want you to be happy, but I agree with Brayden. You married Steve directly out of college and you guys were married for twelve years. But honey, he's been dead for three years. It's time for you start dating. I think Bray might already have someone for you in mind."

"He's not interested in me that way, Kalyn. This time you are dead wrong."

Kalyn shrugged and headed for the back door. "The minute you guys kiss for real, those words are going to pop into your head and you're going to laugh. Then I want you to call me and tell me that I was right. Thanks for the food." She opened the door and left without giving Kamryn a chance to reply.

"That girl is nuts," Kamryn muttered to herself as she placed the empty container in the sink. There was no way Brayden Allen saw her as anything but a friend.

# CHAPTER 3

Wednesday morning, Kamryn awoke to the sound of her cell phone ringing. It was barely six in the morning. Who on earth would be calling her this freaking early in the morning? If it was her editor, she was going to kill him at the next meeting. She reached for it and pulled it to her ear.

"Good morning, sleepy," Bray cooed before she could scream at him for calling at such an ungodly hour.

"What do you want?" Kamryn grumbled. "Don't you have a plane to catch or something? You do know I have a day job."

"That you do from your house," he finished for her. "I just wanted to remind you of the promise you made to me last night."

She shook her head. "How many promises have you ever kept to me?"

"That's not the point," he countered. "The point is that you promised. I know my promises aren't worth the breath I use to say them. It's the playa in me. What can I say? But I know your promises are worth gold."

She smiled. Bray could probably sell snow to an Eskimo in a snowstorm. "All right, I will not investigate further into Jason's death while you're in Chicago."

"Great. When you and Mom go shopping, please don't let her spend all my money. You know where my keys are, right?"

"I have the spare set from the last time they were in town. Janice and I will do just fine for the few days you're gone."

"That's what I'm afraid of." He ended the call.

Now that Bray was safely at the airport, she could actually get some sleep. She'd barely closed her eyes when the phone rang again. She glanced at the display screen. It was her sister.

"What is it?"

"Oh, is that the voice you greet Brayden with?"

"Would you stop already? Besides, it is. He just called."

"Hmm, let's see. He's going out of town and who does he call? His good old buddy, Kamryn."

"Okay, cut the sarcasm," Kamryn said. "Why are you calling me so early in the morning?"

"I got a call from a friend that works in the Securities and Exchange Commission from New Jersey. You wanted me to check Jason out."

Okay, she was definitely up now. She struggled to sit up in her king-sized bed and grabbed a notepad. "What did you find out?"

"Enough to know that we can't discuss this over the phone. I think this is beyond you, Kamryn. Why don't you cook dinner for me tonight and we'll talk about this. I know you and Bray's mom are most likely headed for the day spa and shopping."

Was she really that predictable? Sure, whenever his mom came to town, shopping and the day spa were the order of the day. "We're going later today. You're welcome to join us. Mom is going as well."

"No, thanks, just cook me something nice."

Whatever information Kalyn had must be pretty good if she was asking for dinner. "Since the weather has been so nice lately, why don't I grill some steaks?"

"Oh, that sounds great. See you this evening."

For the second time that morning, Kamryn was on the receiving end of a hang-up. Her day had to get better.

⸺

A few hours later, Kamryn's day had improved. She parked in front of her childhood home and sighed. Bray had been gone only four hours and he'd texted her twice reminding her not to play Nancy Drew, girl detective, in his absence. That man was slowly driving her nuts. She sighed again and got out of her SUV. Using her key, she let herself into the two-story house. Her father greeted her as she closed the front door.

"Hey, baby girl. Your momma is almost finished dressing." He kissed Kamryn on the cheek. "Like the column today. You put it to the team, didn't you?"

She smiled at her daddy. He was her biggest fan. And sometimes he was her only fan. Her no-holds-barred comments about the local sport teams didn't always win her fans. "You always said tell the truth. If we plan on taking it all, we're going to have to step it up. Chicago has just as good a chance as the Mavericks."

"That's my girl. Tell the truth. How's Brayden?" He headed for the living room.

"Driving me crazy," Kamryn admitted, following her father into the room. Rufus, the family dog, was lying on the sofa. He was a black Labrador retriever, and the word *spoiled* couldn't begin to describe him. He looked at Kamryn with his dark eyes, but otherwise he didn't move. She sat next to Rufus and rubbed him gently behind the ears. He rolled over, begging for a belly rub.

"Rufus, you're terrible," Kamryn admonished him. "You know I'm a sucker for those big, dark eyes." She rubbed Rufus until he barked with joy.

Her father chuckled. "You kids always say we spoiled Rufus. It was you all." Her father moved closer to Kamryn and whispered, "Your mother's birthday is next month. Listen for hints."

Kamryn nodded. "Hey, I'm not a columnist for nothing."

Her mother entered the room dressed very comfortably in jeans, a blouse, and sandals, since they were also getting a pedicure later. "You're a good journalist, that's why you beat out those two idiots for your job," her mother announced. "Now what is all this whispering going on down here for?"

Kamryn and her father exchanged glances. That woman could hear a gnat pass gas. "Nothing, Mom. Daddy was giving me some pointers about my column."

"I'm sure." She walked to her husband and gave him a kiss on the lips. "I hope he was asking you some advice about my birthday present. I don't want a repeat of last year's cookware fiasco. See you later, baby." Kamryn's father had made the bad mistake of buying her mother some high-end cookware. Although it was a very expensive gift, her mother had wanted something more personal.

"Bye, honey. I'll make something light for dinner, since I'm sure you'll be too relaxed to eat," he joked. "Don't let her spend all my retirement money," he told Kamryn.

Kamryn stood and walked to her father. "You got it, Daddy. Between you and Bray, I don't know how Mom and Janice buy anything." She kissed her father on the cheek.

Her mother grabbed her handbag and walked toward the front door. "Oh, baby, we don't listen to them. They're men. What do they know?" She opened the door and walked outside.

Kamryn shook her head and looked at her father. He was actually smiling. "That's your mother, and that's why I love her."

She walked to her SUV, wondering if she would ever have a love like her parents'. She'd had that with Steve when she married him, for the most part, but he was taken from her much too soon. Maybe everyone was right. Maybe it was time to get back out into the dating world. She'd never find another love sitting at home.

"What's taking you so long?" her mother asked, standing near Kamryn's SUV.

"Sorry, Mom." Kamryn hit the remote button to unlock it. Once they were inside the car, she started the engine and then asked, "Mom, do you think it's time I started dating again?"

Her mother patted her arm. "Kamryn, only you know the answer to that. Steve died over three years ago, but I know you still miss him."

"I do miss him, but …." Kamryn couldn't find the right words.

"You feel like you'd be cheating on him?"

"Yeah, kind of. I knew when he was diagnosed with pancreatic cancer that he was going to die, but I never imagined in my wildest dreams that he would have go so soon."

"It's not your fault, Kamryn. Just because you weren't home when he died doesn't make it your fault."

She knew there was nothing she could have done anyway. In point of fact, it hadn't been the disease that had taken took her husband of twelve years away from her, but a pharmaceutical mistake, a mix-up in the medications. "I know, but it doesn't make the hurt any less. I guess I've just been thinking about him a lot since Sandra asked me to look into Jason's death." She put the SUV in gear and headed out of the neighborhood.

"I still don't understand why she would ask you."

Kamryn had wondered, but didn't question Sandra about it. "I know the insurance policy isn't paying out because it was ruled a suicide and the bulk of the estate is tied up. I figured she'd have enough money without the policies. Jason played professional basketball about as long as Bray has."

"I'm sure you'll find your answers. You always do. You thought something was strange with Steve's death and investigated. When you found out the pharmacy filled Steve's prescription wrong, you sued the company."

Sure, she got a multi-million dollar payout, but it didn't bring her husband back. "Sandra thinks I'll be able to prove that Jason's death was anything but suicide so she can collect the insurance policy, but something keeps telling me that there's a bigger story here. I liked Jason. He was a nice guy and he loved his daughters."

"What happens if what you find out isn't in her favor? What if it's illegal?"

She knew what her mother was doing. "You and Daddy always taught me to do the right thing. I would turn the information over the police."

"No matter what?"

"No matter what."

<hr>

Later that evening, Kamryn was preparing for her sister's dinner visit. As promised she was fixing steaks, baked potatoes, and salad. Kamryn was known for her cooking skills, but, unfortunately, Texas was known for unpredictable weather. It rained. Kamryn had to cook her steaks on the stove using her very expensive grill pan.

She was just finishing up the steaks when Kalyn knocked on her back door. Kamryn smiled at her sister as she let her inside the house. "You look cute. Date later?"

Kalyn was outfitted in a denim halter dress that stopped just above her knees. "Yes, I'm meeting this guy I met at the gym for coffee."

"Why is it you meet so many guys?"

Kalyn opened the refrigerator and retrieved a bottle of red wine. "Because, my dear sister, I know when a man is attracted to me, unlike some people in this room." She grabbed two wine glasses out of the cabinet and sat down at the kitchen table.

"You're not starting that stuff again, are you?" Kamryn placed the steaks on a platter. "Bray and I are just friends."

"Yeah, yeah, yeah, I've heard that so much my head hurts. I'll leave it alone for now." She poured wine into each of the glasses.

"Thank goodness." Kamryn brought the platter of medium rare steaks to the table. She'd already placed everything else on the table. Now it was finally time to eat.

Kalyn speared a rib eye and placed it on her plate. "I will say that Bray's right in telling you that you need to start dating. Why don't you take him up on his offer of hooking you up with someone? By dating someone that he picks for you, that will prove to me that you have no feelings for Brayden other than friendship."

Normally she wouldn't rise to the bait, but she'd been dared in the worst way. "As soon as he gets back, I'll bring it up."

Kalyn nodded. "Good." She picked up her knife and cut her steak. "This looks great, Kamryn."

"Thanks, Kalyn. Now get to the news."

Kalyn nodded and took a bite of the steak. "Oh, this is so good. It's just right. Girl, you can still burn."

"Thank you. Now can we get down to business?"

Kalyn laughed. "All right, girl. Phillip, my contact in New Jersey, works for the SEC and he ran Jason's name through the computer."

Kamryn stopped chewing on the steak. "And?"

"His accident could have been suicide, but Phillip says they were investigating Jason and about four other players for illegal gambling. They'd gotten an anonymous tip that several professional athletes on the team had been gambling large amounts of money."

"Shut up!"

"I wish, but that's not the worst part. He wouldn't tell me who the others were because they're part of the investigation."

"Do you have any idea about who they might be?"

"Nope. You write about these people. You should know who would be betting."

Kamryn hated when her sister did this. "So he actually was betting on the games?"

"There's no conclusive evidence. Phil says that's the hard part. It's hard to prove they're actually betting until they get in over their heads."

Kamryn thought as she chewed the steak. What could actually be done at this point? If Jason was murdered, why was he killed?

"Kamryn, I know what you're doing," Kalyn said. "You're playing twenty questions in your head, aren't you?"

"Yes," she admitted. "If Jason was betting, and I suspect he was, why kill him? It doesn't make any sense. You'd want to keep your cash cow alive."

"Okay, Miss Sports Columnist, what's your next step?"

"I don't have a step. I'm going to need some more information before I can move on this."

Kalyn cleared her throat. "Okay, big sister, this is real talk here. If you can find out who's placing the bets, it would be a major story. But this story is also going to step on a lot of athletes' toes, and that's your domain. I'm in your corner, but I do ask that you think about it."

She was touched by her sister's concern and her willingness to help. "Thanks, Kalyn. I'll think about it."

———

Thursday evening Brayden couldn't believe his eyes. Was the scoreboard actually saying that Dallas had lost the second game of the playoffs by three lousy points? Worse yet, it was his fault.

He walked with his head hung low into the dressing room with the rest of the players. Tyler patted him on the shoulder. "Don't worry, Brayden. We don't blame you. Everyone has an off night. Coach might blame you, but we don't."

"Thanks, I appreciate it." Brayden sat down in front of the lockers. He'd missed a crucial basket at the buzzer. They could have been up two games in the seven game series, but instead they were tied with Chicago at a game each.

Tyler plopped down next to him but didn't say a word. They were all waiting for Coach to come in and tell them how disappointed he was in them. But after thirty minutes, there was still no Coach. Only the assistant entered the room, telling them they needed to be back early in the morning for practice.

Every man in the room sighed. That practice was going to be a bear.

Soon he and Tyler were left alone in the dressing room. Tyler had been his friend since both had been drafted by the Sacramento Kings over ten years ago. Tyler cleared his throat and spoke. "Look, Brayden, we've been tight a long time and I'm not trying to get up in your business, but something seems to be troubling you. The only thing that I can remember getting you this messed up was the death of your friend's husband three years ago. Is something wrong with Kamryn?"

He shook his head. "No, man. It's all good with Kam."

"I know you guys are close. Why haven't you two ever dated?"

Brayden laughed. "Kam is like a sister to me," he said. "She and my mom are as thick as thieves. Yesterday they spent the day together. We're like family."

"Well, I think Coach has some ideas about your sister. You know he's been divorced a minute. He always flirts with her when she comes to interview him. Lately, he seems to be pulling out all the stops whenever she's around."

Brayden didn't like the sound of that. "It's business, Tyler. She's a sports journalist. She's supposed to talk to him for her column."

"It's more than that, man. You should check them out the next time she comes to interview him."

Brayden didn't hear his friend. His brain was still out on the floor, missing that shot that lost the game.

"Did you hear me?" Tyler rose and grabbed some clothes from his locker, preparing to head to the shower.

"Yeah, I heard you. There's no way she'd go out with Coach." He hoped that was true.

Tyler shrugged. "If you say so, but if I was interested in a certain sports journalist, I would make certain she knew it before someone else took her away."

# CHAPTER 4

Saturday night Bray didn't think the night could get any worse. They'd just handed Chicago their second win in a seven game series. The team just wasn't in sync, missing easy plays and not getting rebounds. Chicago took full advantage by running past the Mavericks 106-102.

Thank goodness they were flying back to Dallas tonight instead of waiting until the morning. Coach was livid, of course. Bray sat quietly with the rest of the team in the locker room, listening to him.

"This has been the worst game I've seen in a long time," Coach said in a voice that was eerily quiet. The fact that he didn't scream made it all the worse. "There was no defense out there tonight. My nephews could have played against you and won, and they're in elementary school."

He took a deep breath and continued. "The plane is leaving at midnight. Practice in the morning is at seven. Our next game is Monday night. We have a lot of ground to cover if we still want to win the semis." He left the room without another word.

Tyler whistled. "I think I'd rather have him yelling at us. This quiet voice stuff freaks me out. You know practice is going to be a monster tomorrow."

Brayden nodded. "Yeah, better get a good night's rest. I'll probably sleep on the plane."

"Before or after you call Kamryn?" Tyler teased.

It would have been funny if Brayden hadn't been reaching for his cell phone to call Kam at that very moment. "I'm not calling her," he lied. "I was checking on my parents. I'm surprised they didn't call the minute the game was over."

"I'm sure your mom will call," he said, gathering his towel and heading for the shower.

Bray shook his head. Who was he kidding? He was about to call Kam when his phone rang. Maybe it was her? He reached for his phone and glanced at the display. Not Kam, but definitely someone he wanted to talk to. "Hey, man, how's it going?"

"I just saw the game and thought you might need a shoulder to cry on," Brian Collins joked. "I haven't talked to you in a minute. Thought I'd come check out game four in Big D. You know the odds are against you guys."

"Aren't they always? So when are you coming to Dallas?" Brayden hoped to be able to see his friend, but with practice, it didn't seem possible.

"I'm flying in Monday for a few days. I need a little break from wifey."

"Oh, sorry, man. Things okay?"

Brian sighed. "Yeah, pretty much, but between marriage and work, not much time for me. Then I realized I hadn't talked to you in a few months, thought I'd kill two birds with one stone."

Brayden didn't believe that for a moment. They hadn't been in touch in over a year. Brian always had something else going on. Maybe he had another woman in Dallas? Who knew? "That's cool. We can hook up Monday before the game."

"Talk to you on Monday." Brian ended the call.

Brayden put his phone away and headed for the shower, wondering what Brian was really up to in Dallas. There was only one way to find out, and Brayden hoped he didn't get caught in the crossfire.

∞

Sunday afternoon Kamryn sat in front of her computer in her home office, contemplating her next move. Sandra had just dropped two more bombs on Kamryn. Not only had Sandra been planning on divorcing Jason, but he had been betting on his own team. Not to win, but to lose.

Who does that? She was at a crossroads. She'd known Jason for three years, ever since he'd joined the Mavericks. He'd seemed like a team player. She'd uncovered more about Jason's other life than she wanted or needed to know.

Kamryn decided to push ahead with the story, not knowing where it could possibly lead her.

She heard the doorbell ring, which signaled work was over. When she heard the hard knock on her front door, she knew it was Bray. No one else was that impatient. She hurried to the front door before he banged on it again.

She opened the door and smiled. Bray was dressed in an oversized T-shirt, some long nylon shorts, and tennis shoes. "Hey, stranger." She hugged him. "Looks like you had quite a workout today." She motioned him inside and closed her front door. "Sorry about the game last night."

He sat on the couch with a thud. "Yeah. Me, too. Coach worked us within an inch of our lives. We had been practicing from seven this morning until now. I mean hard-core practice. I'm so sore."

She sat beside him and patted his very muscular leg. "Poor baby, that's what you guys get for losing such an easy game. I bet Da Money wanted to have your hide."

He looked sideways at her. "You're supposed to be my friend. I can get this kind of support from my parents."

"I know. I watched the game with your mother. Where was your head Saturday night? It was like your stupid, clumsy twin was playing in your place. It's not some groupie, is it? What have I told you about running around with those women during such an important series?"

"Hey, what's eating you? I listen to you sometimes. I'm the one with the crushed ego, remember. Oh, and thanks for not crucifying me in your column today."

"Well, the series isn't over yet, so I can't really crucify you until the fat lady sings."

"Ouch."

"It's my job, Bray. How would it look if I didn't talk about you guys losing like you did?"

"I know. I'm glad you're so into your job. I mean, you talked about us, but it wasn't as bad as some of the other columnists."

"So are you guys ready for tomorrow night?" She turned toward him and carefully inspected his complexion. Except for looking exhausted, he looked perfect.

"I know what you're doing. I'm okay, just a little overheated. I could use a little refreshment, though."

"Gotcha." She rose and headed to the kitchen. She grabbed a bottle of juice and returned to the living room. Bray was stretched out on the couch sound asleep.

She set the bottle on the coffee table and decided to let him rest. As she walked away his hand shot out and grabbed her, bringing her down on top of him.

"Bray! What are you doing?"

He opened his eyes and winked at her. "What do you think I'm doing?"

"Losing your mind." She wiggled out of his grasp and rose.

He sat up and grabbed the bottle of juice, opened it, and chugged it down in just a few swallows. He held the bottle out to her and shook it, silently asking for a second. "I'm not losing my mind, Kam. You act like I'm a stranger, and I'm not. What's up with you?"

She knew why she was so jumpy. "Jason."

He rolled those hazel eyes toward the ceiling and set the bottle down on the table. "Didn't I say to leave that alone?"

"You asked me not to investigate," she clarified. "I didn't. The information was presented to me."

He took a deep breath. "What did you find out from this information presented to you?"

She took the seat beside him on the couch. "I found out Jason was betting."

"So?"

"He was betting against you guys."

"What?"

"According to Sandra, Jason was betting against you guys to get to the playoffs."

"Wow. You think you know people. I would have done almost anything for him, and to find out he was against us …."

"Did you know Sandra was going to divorce him?"

"I knew something was up with them, but he never said and I never asked."

"Why is it men never talk about emotional things? Are the manhood police out there somewhere ready to ticket you for showing your emotions?"

He looked at her. "I tell you what I'm feeling all the time. Guys just don't talk to other guys about that kind of stuff."

She supposed he was right. Her own brother, Keegan, was the same way. He never told anyone in the family that his marriage was in trouble until he filed for divorce. "All right. So it's a guy thing."

"Check."

"Point taken. Back to Jason. Any idea about how he was placing his bets?"

"Baby, that side of Jason I didn't know, and I'm glad I didn't."

In a way she was glad he hadn't known how the betting process went, but that also meant she was going to have to find another way. She was deep in thought and hadn't realized Bray was so close to her until his lips brushed her neck. It sent a delicious shiver through her body.

"Bray, what are you doing?"

"I thought we'd been through all that." He increased the pressure of the gentle kisses.

She didn't have enough willpower to fight off the long dormant feelings coming awake in her body. "Bray, you have to stop," she moaned.

"You need to sound a little more convincing, baby." But he finally did stop and pulled her against him.

She took a deep breath, realizing that it was probably just the stress of the upcoming game that had Bray acting like he had just lost his mind. Although she didn't like being used as a stress reliever, she could forgive him. "I know you're under a great strain, Bray, and things just got a little out of control. It's okay." She rose. "I'm going to fix something to eat. Why don't you take a nap?"

Brayden didn't want to take a nap. He wanted to figure out what the heck he was doing! He'd just kissed Kam! Okay, maybe not on the lips, but he was heading in that direction, making playa moves on Kam. Boy, as if he didn't have enough going on in his life. Thank goodness she'd taken charge of the situation and he didn't have to stumble over an apology.

He heard the familiar noises of Kam in the kitchen and relaxed a little. He reclined on the sofa and decided a nap might do him good.

He tried to close his eyes, but every time he did images of Kam appeared in his head. Images that never ever stood out in his brain were front and center right now. Giving up on a nap, he went to the kitchen to help her cook.

Kam looked up from the cutting board as she cut up some skinless, boneless chicken breasts. "I'm making grilled chicken salad with salsa dressing. How's that sound to you?"

"Great. Can I help?"

"Sure. Why don't you make the dressing while I grill the chicken and mix the salad?"

He nodded and got to work. It was as if the previous episode hadn't happened between them. They had prepared meals together often and he was thankful they could move forward from his earlier blunder.

An hour later they sat down to dinner and Kam began hitting him with questions about Jason. As if she hadn't shocked him enough already, she asked him about the last game Jason played.

"That was the game against Philly, remember?"

"Yeah, I remember that one, Kam. We lost by two points."

She took a bite of the chicken. "Wow, what did you put in this dressing?"

"Too hot?" Maybe he should have held back on the jalapeño.

"It does have a kick to it. But I think it makes the salad pop." She took a long drink of wine, then cleared her throat. "I was reviewing the tape of the game, and I hate to be the one to tell you this, but Jason threw the ball away."

"Buzzer?"

"No, he had about twenty seconds before the buzzer and he could have at least attempted to make a basket and tie the score."

"That makes me look at Jace in a whole different way." He glanced across the table at the one person he knew inside out. "I don't know what to think right now."

She reached across the table and caressed his hand. "Bray, I know it probably hurts right now, but it's best that all this is out in the open. Jason had a problem, and he was trying to fix it."

"Why would you say that?"

"It's the only reason I can figure that he was killed."

"I still think it was a suicide," Bray lied. "After all, there was a note."

"A partly written note that could mean anything," she reminded him. "I know all the information isn't in yet."

"Exactly. Until we know everything that went down the day he died, we have to be careful."

She smiled at him. "I guess this means you believe me on some level that something's not right."

"You know I always believe you, Kam." He knew this was probably bigger than the both of them, but he wanted to protect Kam as much as he possibly could. Hopefully, he wouldn't get killed in the process.

# CHAPTER 5

Monday evening Kamryn sat next to Janice in the family section watching Dallas and Chicago duke it out for game four.

"How about the usual?" Janice waved for the usher.

"Do we dare?" Kamryn's mind went back to all the uber-rich food they had been eating in Bray's absence. "How's your cholesterol?"

"Oh, I'm fine. You're beginning to sound as bad as Bray. Always going on about what I'm eating. You know he called every day he was in Chicago and asked me what I ate."

"I figured he would," Kamryn said, watching the waiter as he approached them.

"Hello, Mrs. Allen. What can I get you tonight?"

Janice smiled. "I'd like two orders of nachos with extra cheese and jalapeños."

The waiter nodded and inputted the information into the tiny handheld device they used for ordering. The expression on his face said everything.

"Mrs. Allen, I'll be happy to bring you the nachos, but Mr. Allen said no peppers and light on the cheese. Also no beer."

Janice shook her head. "My son strikes again," she told Kamryn. "Well, I guess we'll take it."

The young man smiled, obviously relieved. "Thank you, Mrs. Allen. I'll have that right out." He scurried away before Janice could say a word.

"Sorry, Janice. I had no idea that Bray would do that to you."

Janice shrugged. "That's okay. At least I know he cares about my health. Sometimes a little too much, but I know he thinks he's looking out for us."

Kamryn nodded, noticing one of Bray's exes making her way toward her. *Oh, great,* she thought. *Just what I don't need.*

"Hi, Kamryn," Taylor Crest said, extending her slim hand to her. "I thought I saw you sitting in Brayden's seats." She gave Janice the once-over.

"Hello, Taylor. This is Bray's mother, Janice. Janice, this is Taylor Crest. She dated Bray a few months back."

Taylor plastered on her trademark fake smile and shook Janice's hand. "Oh, it's so great to meet you, Mrs. Allen."

"Nice to meet you." Janice was not impressed with Taylor.

Taylor cleared her throat and swung her hair out of her face. "Kamryn, I know you guys are tight. Is he dating anyone right now? I keep calling his cell, but I haven't gotten a return call. He's usually pretty prompt especially when, you know," she said, darting a glance in Janice's direction.

This was the down side of being best friends with a playa. Women were always trying to get the inside track to him. Like Kamryn would even think of betraying Bray to this groupie. "No, I'm sorry, Taylor. He hasn't mentioned anyone specific lately."

"Good. Tell him to call me." She noticed the usher. "I'd better go before they kick me out of this section. Talk to you later." She left before the usher reached them.

"Is that what my son's been dating? Was anything on her real?"

Kamryn laughed. "Not hardly."

⸻

As the end buzzer for game four sounded, Kamryn was relieved that Dallas had been able to pull out a victory. At least now they were still in the running. The series was tied again at two games each. The Mavericks had a lot of work ahead of them if they wanted to take the semis.

She hugged Bray's parents as they prepared to be escorted to the parking lot. She walked to her SUV and slid inside just as her cell phone rang. She knew it wasn't Bray. Unfortunately, it was her boss. Sighing, she pushed the green button and began talking before he could. "Yes, I'll have the story in on time. Just finishing it up now." She pushed the end button. She hated being micromanaged. In the twelve years she'd been at the newspaper, she'd never missed a deadline or an assignment.

She reached under the driver's seat and retrieved her handy netbook. After she turned it on, she brought up the story she'd been working on earlier that day and entered a few last-minute details from the game. She proofed her column and pushed the send button. Now she was waiting on Bray.

Her phone rang again. Much too early for Bray to have showered, shaved, and dressed, she reasoned. She looked down at the display screen. Sandra. Kamryn didn't have any new information for her, but she'd have to tell Sandra something.

"Hi, Sandra."

"Hello, Kamryn. I know the game just finished minutes ago, but I couldn't help myself. Have you had any luck?"

"No, Sandra. I'm afraid not. Without more about who Jason was gambling with, I'm really at a brick wall. Are you sure you can't remember any details?"

"It's not like I was placing the bets for him, Kamryn," Sandra said quickly. "I'm sorry. I don't mean to take it out on you. This whole thing has me wired. Currently I'm at the mercy of Jason's attorney, and he's not very understanding."

"I don't understand, Sandra."

"As you know the money is tied up. His attorney, who unfortunately isn't my attorney, will not divulge any specifics of the will to me. Apparently when Jason promised me months ago that I was the executor, he changed his mind. With the insurance not paying out because of the suicide ruling, I'm kind of at your mercy." She took a dramatic pause. "Just call me when you get something." She ended the call.

That was odd. Kamryn thoughtfully put away the phone. Sandra was definitely leaving some details out of the equation, and she was going to have to find out what to connect the dots. Her phone rang again. This time it was Bray. Before she could say any kind of greeting, he was already talking.

"Hey, baby, I'm ready."

She didn't get to acknowledge his comment because he'd already ended the call. She was getting sick and tired of everyone hanging up on her. She started the SUV and drove around the stadium, determined to give him a piece of her mind when she saw him.

But he wasn't alone. Another man stood next to Bray. He was slightly shorter and was heavier than Bray's healthy, athletic frame. He was dressed in a suit, whereas Bray was dressed in jeans, T-shirt, and tennis shoes. Funny, Bray hadn't mentioned someone would be joining them. *Another reason to set him straight,* she thought.

They both walked to her SUV, but only Bray slid inside.

"Kam, this is Brian Collins. We go way back to Sacramento," Bray said, fastening his seat belt. "He came down for the game."

Kamryn took in tall, dark, and handsome. When Brian walked around to the driver's side of the SUV, she pushed the electronic button to lower the window. "Hello, Brian, it's nice to meet you."

"So this is the famous Kam. I've heard a lot about you. All good, of course. Brayden didn't do you justice. Damn, you're a pretty thing. Might be a little too much woman for me, but I'm sure some men like it." He extended a large hand to her.

She hated this kind of man. He thought he was God's gift to the skinny female population. She took his hand. "It's nice to meet you, Brian. Bray neglected to mention anything about you, but now I can see how he could have forgotten that detail." She felt Bray's hand on her leg, trying to pinch her, silently telling her to be nice.

"Well, it was nice meeting you, Kam. Maybe I'll see you at the next game."

"Kamryn," she corrected. She knew the next game was in three days. "Oh, you're staying a while?"

He shrugged. "Plans are still kind of up in the air."

Kamryn nodded. "Well, it was still nice to meet you." And she took off.

Bray sat in the passenger seat laughing. "I can't believe you said that to him, then sped off like that."

"I can't believe you never mentioned him. Isn't he Hurricane Collins?" She hadn't recognized him at first, since no one had seen him since Sacramento cut him from the team, but once he spoke, it all came back.

"How did you know his nickname?"

Kamryn kept her eyes on oncoming traffic. "Duh, I write a sports column for the *Dallas Morning News*. I know because I've followed sports nearly all of my life. He played only a year, right?"

"Yeah."

She didn't like Bray's short answer, but decided to let it go for now. "You don't have to get your boxers in a knot. It's just kind of puzzling that he's such a great friend of yours and we're supposed to have been best friends for five years but you're just now introducing him to me."

"Okay, you got me. We're not that great of friends. Brian usually breezes in and out of my life before I know what's going on."

"Where does he live now?"

"I think he's in Chicago. He's married, three kids, and he's some kind of consultant."

"Oh, it's good you guys are still in touch," she said, not attempting to keep the sarcasm out of her voice.

"I know that tone, Kam. What is it?"

"Nothing," she lied. That man was giving her some seriously bad vibes, but for once she couldn't relay her true feelings to Bray.

<hr />

Early Tuesday morning Brayden parked at the American Airlines Center, ready for the grueling practice Coach had promised them after their win last night. He grabbed his bag and headed inside.

After changing into his practice gear, he joined the rest of the team on the floor. He noticed Tyler was speaking to Coach on the sidelines. It didn't look too friendly. Brayden decided to practice his three-point shots and stay out of the line of fire. He had barely shot a couple baskets when Coach roared his name.

Brayden trotted over to him and sat down. "Yes, Coach?"

"We need to talk. My office. Ten minutes."

He shook his head as Coach walked to the dressing room. The day had started out with such promise, he mused.

Exactly ten minutes later, he entered Coach's office. "You wanted to see me?"

Coach nodded and motioned for him to sit down. "As you know, I've been in Dallas for two years. I've been interviewed several times by Kamryn, and she's always been good to us in the press. She's always been fair to the team, never taking pot-shots as we have struggled to rebuild the team. If she says something, it usually has a ring of truth to it."

Brayden had no idea where this was going, but decided to play along. "Yes, she's a good friend. I trust her with my life."

"And that's all you are, friends, right?"

"Of course. Why do you ask?"

"I don't want anything to distract you from your game. I didn't think Kamryn was your type. Although she is very pretty, I think she's much too practical and smart for you. She needs a man that can feed her soul."

As the information sank into his brain, Brayden could feel his blood coming to a slow boil. He wanted Kam to get back out in the dating world, but Coach was not who he thought she should start dating. He hoped his temper would hold until the season was over. "Was there anything else?"

"Yes. How are you feeling for Thursday night's game? Are you and the rest of the team ready?"

"Yes. I think we can take it."

"I need you to *know* we can take it. Not *think*. Now get out there and practice." He picked up the phone, dismissing Brayden. "I'll be out there in a few minutes."

Brayden nodded and went back to his teammates. All the while they ran drills that morning, his thoughts kept going back to his conversation with Coach. Something was nagging at him. He just couldn't figure out what it was, but he was definitely going to find out.

———

A few hours later, Brayden found out what was nagging him. "What do you mean, you're going to dinner with Coach?" Brayden all but yelled into his cell phone. He'd just left practice and wanted to see Kam. He'd called to try to convince her to take a break from writing her column, when she dropped the bomb on him. Yelling at Kam wouldn't help the situation, only make it worse. He took a deep breath, and then spoke in a softer tone. "Sorry, I just can't believe you would consider dating him."

She laughed. "Look, Bray. First, it's not a date. Not really. Instead of interviewing him at the arena, he might be a little more open in a restaurant. You know how much he likes to eat. Anyway, you told me to get back out there."

She made it sound logical, which meant she was hiding something. "You're going to grill him about Jason and your gambling story, aren't you?"

"I have no idea what you're talking about."

"Don't play me, Kam. I know exactly what you're doing. You're trying to find out who's doing the betting and how. You're stepping on a lot of toes with this story."

"You can't blame me for trying to break a hot story. Next to Dallas being in the playoffs, illegal gambling is a hot topic. If I could break that story, it would be great."

He knew that there was heavy competition for Kam's job. The two male sports journalists at the paper would stop at nothing to take her place. But talent was everything, and Kam had plenty of that. "I know, but you make sure Coach keeps those hands to himself. Why do you think his wife divorced him?"

"Because he was always on the road," Kam said, "though I'm sure some extracurricular activity was going on. But I'm just doing an interview, not going to bed with the man."

Bray still didn't like the sound of it, yet he had to let Kam do her thing. "Call me the minute you get in your car to drive home."

She was quiet for a beat. "He's picking me up."

"What? You're letting that man enter your house? What's wrong with you?"

"Bray, it just makes more sense. I'm working from home on my column, and there was no need for us to take two cars downtown."

He tried to keep his eyes on the busy Interstate 35 traffic, but he was about to blow a gasket. "Where are you going?"

"Bray, you aren't going to cause a scene, are you?"

"Where. Are. You. Going?"

"Brayden Maxwell Allen, I'm not answering you when you take that tone. I'm a grown woman and can take care of myself. I don't need you trailing me on my interviews. Got it?"

"I'm just looking out for you. You don't know what kind of man Coach is, and you're letting him pick you up at your house."

"He's your boss," she pointed out. "If I can't trust your boss, then how can I trust you?"

"Because we've known each other five years and I've seen you nearly naked."

She laughed. "Would you stop?"

"Okay. Just promise me you'll call."

"Geesh! Yes, I'll call you the minute I get home."

"Thank you, Kam." He ended the call before he said something he'd regret later, like, *don't go*.

---

Kamryn shook her head. "Silly man." She resumed typing her column. Game five was Thursday night. This was such a nail-biter already with the series being tied. Dallas needed the win desperately. She was already a nervous wreck. She didn't know how Bray's parents dealt with the anxiety.

A few hours later, she waited for her dinner companion. She had dressed in a black dress that criss-crossed in the front and stopped just above her knees. A pair of three-inch stilettos finished the look. She smiled at herself in the hall mirror. Maybe this was her chance to get back on the dating circuit, or at least get her feet wet.

Greg DeMorris had been Dallas' head coach for the last two years. Not only was he one of the youngest coaches in the NBA, he had made quite a change in the Mavericks since he'd been hired. No longer did player foibles make the front-page headlines every week.

She noticed his Mercedes E-class coupe as he parked in front of her house. She grabbed her purse and waited. Bray's words still rang loudly in her ears. She laughed, thinking of Bray actually being jealous. He was such a good friend.

She opened her front door to quite a different Greg DeMorris. Da Money, as he was called by most of the sports writers across the nation because of his winning record, was dressed in a dark suit, reminding her of an ad in a magazine. She'd interviewed him many times, but never, ever, had he looked like this. His sable skin was smooth and his black hair was cut very short. Unlike most forty-five-year-old men she knew, Da Money still had his hair.

"Hello, Coach," she said, inviting him inside. "Thank you for letting me interview you over dinner." She grabbed her purse. "You look very nice." She inhaled the aroma of his cologne.

He smiled broadly. "Thank you, Kamryn. You look lovely, as always. Please call me Greg."

"Thank you, Greg."

He nodded. "Ready?"

"Yes. Where are we going?" She motioned him out the front door. She followed him and locked her front door.

"It's a surprise." He walked her to the car and opened the passenger door for her.

Kamryn slid onto the leather seat and glanced at him. "So how big of a surprise is this?"

He grinned. "If I told you, it wouldn't be a surprise."

She used the time it would take him to get in the car to calm her nerves. Darn that Bray for planting those insane thoughts in her head. Calm down, she told herself.

"I'm taking you to Paradise," Greg said as he settled behind the steering wheel.

"What?"

"Paradise. Don't tell me you've eaten there already?" He started the car and pulled away from the curb. "It's only been open about a year. They have great seafood."

She laughed. "No, I haven't, but I love seafood of any kind. So Paradise sounds great."

"Good. It's pretty laid back, so we should be able to cover a lot of ground over dinner."

"Perfect." As he drove, Kamryn watched the night lights of Dallas. She had a few choice words for Bray once she set eyes on him again.

Paradise was everything Greg promised. It was laid back, but in an elegant kind of way. She was glad she'd dressed up for the event. It was a seafood restaurant, but it was an Italian seafood restaurant. Her all-time favorite. How on earth did he know?

"Surprised?" he asked, putting his arm around her as he guided her to their table.

"Yes."

After they were seated, the waiter took their wine orders and left the table.

Kamryn focused on the man seated across from her. She really hadn't known this side of Greg. Maybe Bray was right. God, she hoped not. One train wreck at a time.

"What are you going to have?" he asked from behind his menu. "I've eaten almost everything here, and it's all delicious. I've brought some of the players here, too, for meetings and such. I believe Allen has been here a time or two on dates."

*No, he didn't.* "Contrary to popular belief, Bray doesn't tell me all his business," she said, struggling to keep her voice even. "We're just friends."

"Yeah, that's what he keeps saying."

Kamryn cleared her throat. "Can we start the interview now?" The urge to question him about his conversations with Bray was strong, but she tried her best not to think about them having a boy's meeting about her.

Greg studied her. "Sure, let's get the questions out of the way so we can talk about other things."

That remark really didn't sit well with her. "Okay, Greg. Why don't we start with your work? How long have you been coaching professionally?"

Greg took a sip of wine and thought. "I guess you could say I've been in the NBA for the last twenty years."

Kamryn couldn't recall Greg ever playing for a professional team. "How did you get into coaching?"

He took a deep breath. "I took the unconventional route to coaching. I got hurt in my freshman year in college, then I decided to be a high school coach. A year of that and I was ready to move on. I ran into my old coach and he convinced me I was NBA material."

"So how'd you make the leap from high school to NBA?"

"Coach's wife."

She choked on her wine. "Excuse me?"

"I thought that would get you. The coach's wife's brother was an assistant on a national league team. He put in a good word, and the rest is history."

---

It was after midnight when Greg dropped her off. They'd had an enjoyable dinner and exchanged a great deal of information that she would never have gotten in his stuffy office. She'd been able to interview him with the minimum amount of fuss and he'd given her solid, complex answers. She hated when the interviewee gave one-word answers and she had to pull information out of them. Greg was quite the opposite. He was confident the Mavericks could make it to the finals.

They'd gotten so wrapped up in talking about basketball, time had slipped away. Before they knew it, the place was closing and they were politely being asked to leave.

She entered her house and took a deep breath. Thank goodness nothing had gone the way Bray had predicted. She was going to give him a piece of her mind.

"How was dinner?" a very masculine voice asked from the darkness of the living room.

How could someone have broken in her house without the alarm going off? Her heartbeat thudded against her chest. She fumbled inside her purse for her cell phone, but then remembered she hadn't taken it, fearing Bray would call all night.

She wanted to scream, but the sound was stuck somewhere in the back of her throat. If someone was in her house, where could she hide? Suddenly, bright light flooded the living room and relief flowed freely through her veins. "Damn it, Bray. I could have shot you!"

He was seated on her chaise lounge dressed in a pair of jeans and a T-shirt. "No, you wouldn't." He rose from the lounge and walked toward her. "How can you shoot me if the gun I gave you is under the driver's seat of your SUV, which is parked in your garage?"

"You searched my car?"

"Please."

"How do you know where my gun is?"

"I found it by accident last year. By the looks of it, you hadn't moved it since I gave it to you. How was dinner?"

After her heartbeat returned to normal, and she could think clearly again, she answered him. "Dinner was wonderful. I hear it's one of your favorite restaurants."

"What are you talking about?"

Since he'd scared half the life out of her, she felt a little teasing was in order. "Greg said you take your dates to that Paradise restaurant."

Those hazel eyes looked thoroughly confused. "Greg?"

"Coach."

"I know his first name. You guys are on a first-name basis now?" He closed the distance between them. "What exactly went on in that dinner meeting?" He grabbed her hand and pulled her to the couch. "Tell me exactly what happened!"

# CHAPTER 6

"Nothing happened." Kam sat down on the couch and crossed her legs. "I'm wishing something had so I'd deserve this cross-examination, Perry Mason. Am I allowed to have counsel present? Should I call my brother?"

Bray paced the area in front of Kam. She was playing this really cool, and that was driving him nuts. Kam and Coach are on a first-name basis? What was going on?

"Bray, you're really losing it." She patted the area beside her. "Sit down."

He complied. "Okay, sorry for getting crazy. I just don't like the idea of you and Coach getting chummy."

"Bray, I was doing my job. Greg is part of my job. You're part of my job."

"Oh, that hurt."

"Sorry, I didn't mean it that way. But you're going to have to realize that I have a job to do and I'm going to do it. It took me a long time to get here, and I don't have any plans to leave my job."

Okay, he'd come on too strong and now he was paying the price for it. "I don't know what's going on with me lately. First, I almost wrecked my SUV coming over here and now this."

"What?"

"A car came out of nowhere and was coming right at me on the freeway." He shook his head, still not believing it. "Probably just some crazy kids with nothing else to do but terrorize drivers on the road," he said, hoping to ease the news of his near accident.

"Are you sure you're all right?" She caressed his face. "Why didn't you call me?"

"You were on your date," he said, trying to keep the sarcasm out of his voice. "Remember, you said not to call you."

She opened her mouth to spout what he suspected would be some independent woman dribble, but good sense must have prevailed. She instantly closed it.

A minute or two passed before she opened her mouth again. "What's wrong with us?"

Well, at least she'd noticed it, too. "I don't know, Kam. Maybe we're under a strain with the playoffs and all. You know how bad I want this."

"I don't think that's it. Maybe it's time for me to spread my wings, too. You're right, Kalyn's right, Mom's right. I should get back out there and start socializing."

"So what brought this on?"

"Since Steve died, after every Mavericks' victory, we go to Junior's and talk about the game and whatever else is going on in our lives. I don't want you to curtail your social life just because you've got a friend who can't let go of her dead husband."

He so didn't like the way this conversation was going. "So you don't want to hang out anymore?"

"No, I love hanging out with you. You let me be me and you don't judge the fact that sometimes I don't wear makeup or I don't feel like doing my hair, or sometimes I just want to hang out at the house or that I like to eat."

He should have known where she was going with this conversation. Damn that Taylor. "Mom told me about Taylor last night. I'm sorry. I don't mean for all my exes to track you down and put you on the spot."

Kam, being Kam, wouldn't take his apology. "Don't worry, Bray, I've been doing this for a few years. It's going to take more than a few of them coming to me when you've cast them aside without so much as an explanation."

"I can't change who I am," he admitted.

"And I'm not asking you to. It's part of your charm. You don't offer women apologies or explanations and they don't expect it from you. I want you to know that Greg asked me out to dinner tomorrow night for a real date and I accepted."

"You don't have to tell me who you're dating, Kam." *Lie.* "I'm glad to see you getting back out there," he said, forcing himself to remain calm. He rose quickly and faced her. "Now that I know you're safe and at home alone, I'll talk to you later. Have fun on your date."

He was happy for her. Wasn't he? So why did it feel like someone had just kicked him in the gut? He made his hasty exit before Kam could say another darned word.

———

After Bray left her house, Kamryn sat on the couch wondering what was really going on with him. Why was he so upset about her going on a dinner date with Greg? If anything, he should have been happy that she took his advice about dating.

After about thirty minutes she realized that she wasn't going to get any work done and decided that a glass of wine would round out the evening. She had just taken her first sip when there was a knock at her back door.

She greeted her sister. "For once I'm glad you don't cook." She ushered her sister inside. "I need to talk."

"You never need to talk. This must involve Bray." Kalyn walked to the fridge and inspected the contents. "No doggie bag?"

"No. The food was excellent, so I ate it all."

She pulled out the makings for a sandwich and piled the ingredients on the counter. "You're not supposed to eat like a pig on a date, no matter how business-related it is."

Kamryn laughed as she handed Kalyn the loaf of wheat bread. "You know I don't roll like that. Not anymore. I did that while I was married."

Kalyn nodded. "I know you weren't happy with Steve."

"I was happy. He liked things a certain way, and that's what I did. Not that I regret the life I had with him, but I'm not going to lose myself again."

Kalyn nodded. "I wondered why you sold the house you guys had and bought this one. It makes sense now. You were starting over."

"Yes, I was. Didn't you ever wonder why I used my maiden name when I started writing for the paper?"

"Well, yeah, but I just figured it was one of those artist's thing."

"No, it was a Steve thing. He really didn't want me working, and especially being a reporter. So that was our compromise."

"I'm sorry, Kamryn."

"Don't be sorry. I did love him and he loved me. But that part of my life is over, and this time I'm living for me."

"That's my sister," Kalyn said, clapping her hands. "I've waited three years to hear that."

"By the way, I have a date tomorrow night."

"Get out!" Kalyn exclaimed. "Brayden finally stepped up to the plate?"

"No, I took your challenge. I told you Bray wasn't interested in me like that. Greg asked me for a real date after our interview and I said yes."

Kalyn stopped making her sandwich. "You mean to tell me that you're going out with his coach? Girl, you're playing with fire."

"Am not. Bray's glad I have a date."

Kalyn continued making her double-decker sandwich. "And of course Bray told you this." Kalyn had two slices of everything on her sandwich: ham, turkey, provolone cheese, tomatoes, onions, peppers, and she topped it all off with spicy deli mustard.

"Yes, he did."

Kalyn sat at the table and narrowed her gaze at Kamryn. "What are you not telling me?"

She debated not telling her sister about the kiss, but figured Kalyn would find out anyway. "Bray kissed me Sunday."

"Back up."

"He came over Sunday after practice. He was really down about them losing and he was exhausted. It wasn't anything, he was just stressed. He just nibbled on my neck. We agreed to just forget about it."

"Kamryn, you're drowning and don't even know it. Brayden kissed you, but it had nothing to do with stress, the games, or anything else. That man wants you. He just doesn't know how to tell you because he doesn't know how you'll react."

"I don't believe that for one second. Bray and I don't have any secrets. Besides, one of his friends is in town, but that guy gives me a bad vibe. I just didn't like him."

"Is he as cute as Brayden?"

"No. It was Hurricane Collins."

Kalyn gasped. "How on earth does Bray know that guy?"

For those being raised in the Hillcroft household, *Sports Illustrated* was the most-read thing in the house, next to the Bible. "Bray said they played together when he played for Sacramento."

"There's your story, Kamryn. Find out why he left the league, what really happened. There's always been a cloud of suspicion around him."

Kamryn wanted nothing to with that story. "No, thanks. Hopefully he'll be gone after Thursday's game."

"He must really be bad if you want him out of town." Kalyn took a bite of her sandwich. "I'm sure Hurricane will blow out of here as fast he blew in."

Kamryn sighed, wishing and hoping that would be true. "I think it's going to be more like there'll be devastation everywhere."

〜〜〜

After driving around Dallas for almost an hour, Brayden finally went home. Why was he so upset? Kam was a grown woman and could make her own decisions about her social life. Why did he care? He parked his SUV in the garage and entered his house. Of course his mother was waiting for him in the kitchen.

"Mom, what on earth are you doing up?"

His mother was seated at the table drinking a cup of tea. "I'm up because my son is acting strange and I want to know why."

He sat at the table and smiled. "You know me like a book."

"I know you like my son. Now what's going on with you?"

"I wish I knew," Bray admitted. "Things have been weird these last few weeks. Maybe it's the playoffs."

"What has that got to do with you and Kamryn?"

He shot a look at his mother's plump face. She was smiling. Not a good sign. "What do you mean?"

"She called here, worried and looking for you. Now would you like to explain what's going on?"

"Nothing, Mom."

"Is that why you were camped out at her house? I raised you better than that. I know you care about Kamryn. She's a nice girl and will make some man very happy."

"That's just it. She's dating my coach."

"Good for her. Coach DeMorris is one hot cookie."

"Mom! That's my coach, and she's my best friend."

"He's still a nice looking man and Kamryn is beautiful. It's time someone appreciated her for the woman inside. I know she loved her husband, but he's gone now. It's time for her to move on."

"Yeah, she was saying the same thing tonight. I just don't have to like it."

"Have you noticed that since he died, Kamryn has been happier, more at peace with herself, and enjoying life? Haven't you noticed it?"

"Yeah, now that you mention it."

"So why are you upset that they're going out on a date? I don't see you running up asking her for a date."

"We go out all the time," Bray reminded his mother. "You even hang out with Kam."

"But I'm not the one jealous of her dating my coach. I suggest you talk to Kamryn and tell her what you're feeling. And the next time you kiss her, don't tell her it was an accident."

Surely Kam hadn't blabbed. "Who told you about that?"

"You just did." She rose and took her cup to the sink. "Honey, I see how you greet her. You kiss her on the cheek, no matter how many times you've seen her that day. I know what you're doing."

"And what's that?"

"You're trying to slip inside Kamryn's defenses on the sly. That's not going to work, not with Kamryn. If you're doing this for all the right reasons, you're going to need to give up those playa ways. She's not one of your groupies. Kamryn is independent, smart, and needs someone who will truly appreciate her for the woman she is. Can you do that?"

Not waiting for an answer, his mother left the kitchen.

He hated when she did that.

# CHAPTER 7

Brayden had a lot to think about.

Was his romantically inclined mother correct? Did his feelings run deeper for Kam than he was willing to admit? Why did the thought of her going to dinner with Coach make him want to throttle the man?

Cooking always helped him relax. Even at two in the morning when he had practice at seven. He had to cook something. He looked in the refrigerator and decided on a frittata for his parents to eat for breakfast.

As he chopped the vegetables for the dish, he calmed down and could focus on what was important. He wanted Kam to be happy, and if, for some strange reason, it was with Coach, who was he to stand in her way?

Apparently, he thought as he mixed eight eggs with some heavy whipping cream, he was exactly the man to stand in her way. The very idea of Kam dating Coach infuriated him to the $n$th degree.

He just needed to figure out if it was because he was developing feelings for her or because he didn't want Coach to have her.

He poured the egg mixture over the vegetables and waited for the mixture to set. He loved being alone in the kitchen in the wee hours of the morning. With his parents being there during the playoffs, he didn't get to do much cooking. Once his mother arrived she claimed the kitchen as her domain, and he never argued with his momma.

His cell phone rang as he slid the eggs into the oven. After he closed the oven door, he unclipped his phone and pulled it to his ear. "Hello?" He half-hoped it was Kam. Unfortunately, it wasn't the one person he wanted to talk to.

"Hey man, I can't believe you're up," Brian drawled.

"Yeah, I had a snack attack," Brayden said, not knowing why he was lying to Brian. "Where you at? Sounds like someone is having a good time."

"Some club in North Dallas. Why don't you come join us? We could always use another man here. Man, it's loaded with women!"

"Sorry, I have practice early in the morning. Maybe another time."

"You're missing some sweet-looking women. You've been hanging out with Kamryn too long. You forget what a good woman looks like."

"Kam is my friend and not a topic of discussion. Keep her name out of your mouth."

"Okay, man. No need to get crazy. I didn't know it was like that. I've just never known you to be with a big girl."

"There's a lot you don't know about me." Bray ended the call.

The next morning Brayden walked into practice, determined not to lose his cool with Coach. Today was date night. The last thing he needed was to lose his temper with the one person who could ruin his chances with Kam.

Whatever they were.

He changed into his practice uniform and went out to join the team. He had barely shot a few shots when the coach yelled his name. "Allen!"

Brayden trotted over to Coach. "You wanted me, sir?"

"Yes, Allen," Coach said. "You've been under percentage on your free throws lately. Practice those until I tell you otherwise." He bellowed someone else's name, effectively dismissing Brayden.

He knew his stats weren't down, but this was most likely for punishment. For what, he had no idea. Maybe it was something to do with Kam.

After three hours, Brayden thought his arm was going to fall off. He could probably make a free throw in his sleep. He took a deep breath and shot another one. Yep, he was paying for something, he just didn't know what. His entire body relaxed when he heard the whistle signaling that practice was over, at least for now. He headed to the dressing room, thinking about sitting in the whirlpool to ease his soreness. Then he realized he wasn't alone.

"Allen. My office."

Brayden followed Coach to his office. He waited for the invitation to take a seat, but it didn't come.

"Allen, since you and Kamryn are friends, I'm sure she told you that we have a date tonight. I really want to make a good impression on her. What's her favorite restaurant?"

"She likes seafood." Brayden turned to leave the office.

"Hold on, Allen. What's your hurry?"

"Did you need anything else?"

"Anything off topic with her? What's going to make me strike out?"

Like he'd help another man get to Kam. "She's pretty laid back. Sports never hurt."

"All right. I'd liked to talk about something else besides sports when I'm on a date. You can leave."

Brayden nodded and went to the dressing room. Tyler was sitting on the bench talking on his cell phone. When Bray sat next to him, he ended his call.

"Is it true? Does Coach really have a date with Kamryn?"

"Yeah." How did Tyler know?

"That's all you got to say?"

"Man, Kam is a grown woman. She makes her own decisions."

"So you're just going to let her?"

"Ty, you know how it is. If I say don't go, that will make her go all the more."

"Yeah, I know. You still should take a stand." He walked to the shower.

Brayden shook his head at his friend. Everyone in his life seemed to know what he was feeling except him. He needed to talk to Kam, but he'd have to wait until tomorrow to do it. If he unloaded on her now, she'd never speak to him again.

After sitting in the whirlpool to relax his arm muscles for hours, he finally made it to the shower. He was the last person to leave the dressing room. He laughed at himself. There was a time when he'd be the first person out of there, ready to hook up with one of his many ladies for an evening of hot sex. Now the one woman he wanted to see couldn't see him because she had a date with Coach. Life was funny.

After saying good night to the maintenance manager, he headed to his SUV in the parking garage. The elevator delivered him to the floor where the athletes parked their cars. He looked at his black Cadillac Escalade hybrid and smiled. Kamryn had talked him into getting a hybrid. She had convinced him that the hybrid was so much better for the environment. He unlocked his SUV and started to get in, but someone stopped him. He turned around to face two men who didn't look like fans. They were both about six feet tall. The older man was burly, and the other was pencil thin. If this turned ugly, Brayden could handle them.

"Look guys, here's my wallet, the keys are in the ignition. I don't want any trouble."

"And we ain't here to rob you. We've already been paid. We want you."

"For what?" He had no idea what these guys wanted. Was this some kind of crazy plot to hurt Dallas' chance at winning?

"You ask too many questions." The older burly man took a swing at him.

Brayden dodged the punch by mere millimeters. He moved to his left and hit the slender, younger man with a right hook Brayden's dad would have been proud of.

Brayden was shaking the pain from his hand when he saw flashing red and blue lights illuminating the entire parking level. The older assailant said, "We'll be back." He helped his buddy to his feet and they scurried away on foot before security arrived.

Brayden shook his head and looked down at his red, swollen hand. He needed some ice quickly.

"Mr. Allen, are you all right?" The security officer got out of his vehicle, gun drawn, looking around for the criminals. He radioed in the direction the perpetrators were running.

Brayden nodded. "They came out of nowhere. They said they'd be back."

The officer nodded. "Did they take anything?"

Brayden shook his head. "That's the crazy thing. I offered them my wallet and the keys to my SUV, and they didn't take it. Said they'd already been paid."

The young officer scratched his head. "That's weird. I've never heard of anything like this. There've been a few muggings after games, but nothing like this and never on the players' level." He looked down at Brayden's hand. "Mr. Allen, that hand doesn't look good. Why don't we go back to the Center so you can put some ice on it? I'll call the team doctor."

He wanted to say no, but his hand was beginning to throb something awful. He could barely make a fist without the pain increasing about tenfold. "Yeah, I'll go back downstairs." He closed the SUV's door and headed for the elevator.

⸻

Kamryn marveled at her date. Greg was much different from the night before. He didn't want to talk about basketball at all. Every time she brought up the subject, he effectively switched the subject to something about her. He wanted to know about her. The restaurant was excellent. Next to seafood, French cuisine was her favorite. La Maria's was the most elegant French restaurant in Dallas and worth every penny of the dinner she'd ordered: slow roasted beef tenderloin with potatoes, carrots, onions, and leeks in red wine. Her thoughts went to Bray and his culinary skills. If she described it to him, he could probably cook it.

"You know, you could at least pretend to listen to me," Greg teased. "Where's your head?"

"I'm sorry, Greg. I was just enjoying the food. What were you saying?"

"I was asking you if you could cook."

Odd date question, she thought. "Of course I can. Not to brag, but I'm pretty good. Can you?"

"Not much. I've always been on the road so much I never really got into it. There's just something morally wrong about a straight man cooking and enjoying it."

"Better not tell that to the chefs that are on those cooking channels. They'd hurt you." She also thought of Bray. Most of his teammates had no idea that he could cook so well. It was a shame he couldn't be his true self around his teammates.

Greg seemed to be outdone at that statement. "Okay, maybe not those guys, but other guys."

She smiled. "You tripped over that one pretty well."

"I know. You know what I mean. I deal with super egos on a daily basis. I can't imagine any one of my team cooking a gourmet meal. Could you?"

"I don't know, Greg. A person's private life is always the opposite of what you think it is."

He nodded. "True."

"Take Jason, for instance." She saw her segue and she took it.

"Okay."

"Did you know he was betting?"

"I knew he was up to something. We'd had a few meetings about his personal life in the last few months with him and his high-dollar attorney. His committing suicide saved me from cutting him from the team and kicking him out of the NBA."

"You were cutting him?"

"Yeah, I can't have mafiosos hanging around the Center looking for one of my players. He was detrimental to the organization. We were in the process of getting rid of him when this happened."

Kamryn's heart beat erratically at the news. How many skeletons could one man have? "Could you describe the guys looking for him?"

"Of course." His cell phone went off and he looked down at the display. "Crap."

"What's wrong?"

"Team doctor. This can't be good." He pulled the phone to his ear.

Kamryn watched his expression. He went from angry to furious in about two seconds. "Was he injured? How bad? I'll be there in thirty minutes." He ended the call. "Sorry, Kamryn, we're going to have to cut this short. One of the players was injured in a robbery attempt. I need to determine if he'll be able to play in tomorrow's game."

If the pain in her heart was any indication, she knew exactly who it was. What she couldn't figure out was why Greg would deliberately not tell her. "Who?"

He opened his mouth and then shut it. He took a deep breath and said, "Allen."

She didn't need to think about it. He'd been there for her countless times in the last few years. He'd stayed at her house after her husband died and made sure she rested. When everyone else was offering generic platitudes about losing her husband, he'd stayed with her and listened to her cry until she fell asleep. "I'm going with you."

Greg sighed. "You don't have to. His hand is bruised, that's all. I'll take you home."

"You can do that. But nothing will keep me from seeing Bray. I do know how to drive. So it's your choice. You can either take me with you or I'll drive to the arena on my own." She dared him to deny her.

He threw two one-hundred-dollar bills on the table and rose. "It's not really my choice, is it?" He helped her out of her chair and they left the restaurant.

# CHAPTER 8

Two hours after the incident, Brayden sat on the examination table in the team doctor's office, listening to the one-sided conversation Julian Serriano was having with the coach. With his right hand submerged in a bucket of ice, he could only hope that he would be able to play in the upcoming game.

Julian walked to the table and lifted Bray's hand out of the ice. "How's it feeling?"

"Frozen."

Julian smiled. "Good. Good. At least you're feeling something. Was it a robbery? The security guard wasn't very forthcoming with information." He carefully inspected Bray's hand. "I think you might be able to play tomorrow."

"That's good news," Brayden said. "No, it wasn't a robbery."

"Don't thank me yet. You'll get to play, but I don't know how long. Once the swelling goes down, I'll be able to make a better determination." He narrowed his brown eyes at Brayden and put his hand back into the ice bucket.

"What?"

"Tell me what happened," Julian said in soft voice. "Coach is on his way. What's going on with you, Brayden?"

He wished he knew. Julian was staring him down waiting for some kind of explanation, ready to do damage control if necessary. "I was the last person to leave this evening, and when I walked to my ride, two guys attempted to jump me. I thought it was a carjacking, I offered them money, but they didn't want it. My SUV, either. Then they tried to rush me, but they didn't know what they were doing and I was able to overtake them."

Julian nodded, taking in the information. "They don't sound like the brightest crooks, do they? Coach should be here in about thirty minutes." It was standard protocol when an athlete was injured during playoffs for the team physician to contact the head coach, no matter what time, no matter how minor the injury.

"Any other pain?"

"No, just my frozen hand," Brayden said sarcastically. "Can I take it out of the ice now?"

"Give it about thirty minutes. Then I'll check the swelling." He walked into his office.

Brayden sighed. For all the trouble those idiots caused, he should have hit the little one a lot harder. Now, odds were he wasn't going to be able to play in the game very much.

About thirty minutes later, Kamryn burst into the examination room. She looked gorgeous in a light blue dress that hugged her curves, and she was wearing stilettos. She headed straight for him. As if he knew where she going, he spread his legs apart.

"Oh, my God, Bray," Kam said walking in to the vee of his legs and hugging him tight.

Her body was pressed against his. It felt so good to have her nestled against him. He had to hug her back. Without giving his injured hand much thought, he pulled his hand out of the bucket and wrapped her in an embrace. He laughed as she jumped when his cold hand touched her. "Just some idiots. I'm fine," he said, trying to sound reassuring.

She caressed his face. "Are you sure?" Her big brown eyes were focused on him. Tears pooled in her eyes and she sighed. "Damn you." She pulled him down for a kiss.

It was just the stress of the moment, he told himself. Kam had kissed him on the lips many times, but it always had a friendly undertone. This time, however, there was nothing friendly about the kiss. Tongues were involved.

Slowly Kam ended the kiss and put a few inches between them. "Sorry, Bray. I was just so worried and I guess it just got to me." She pulled a moist wipe out of her purse and wiped his face. "Lipstick." She stepped out of his embrace to the nearest mirror and cleaned up her face.

He nodded. It wouldn't look right if Coach walked in and saw his face, or hers, for that matter, slathered with the remnants of Kam's lipstick. "You're always a step ahead of me."

She shook her head as she threw the wipe in the trash. She reapplied her lipstick, then walked back to him and sat by him on the table. "Not this time. I didn't know I was going to kiss you like that until I saw you sitting on the table. Greg was downplaying the accident all the way here, so I didn't know if he was just being a man and not telling me that you were clinging to life, or he just didn't want me to come see you."

Brayden knew a playa move when he saw one, but he couldn't tell Kam that. Coach had no intention of Kam being anywhere near the Center, but Kam most likely hadn't given him an option. "He just wanted to protect you."

"Bray, you don't have to cover for him. I know he didn't want me to come and I know why. He's talking to Julian right now."

He watched her closely. "Kam, if you don't want to talk about the kiss, we don't have to. We will have to talk about what's brewing between us and why at some point."

She let out a sigh. "Good. Why don't we make it for later?"

He picked up her hand with his uninjured one. "Okay, Kam." He noticed Julian's voice was unusually loud outside the closed door and laughed. The door also wasn't closed earlier. Julian must have walked in on them while they were kissing. "Here they come. Are you ready?"

She shot him such a look. "I'm not doing anything wrong." She slid off the table and straightened her dress.

He thought about the situation and tried to reverse it in his brain. How would he feel if he were in Coach's shoes? He'd be ready to hurt somebody for messing up his game. "You're right."

The door opened slowly, with Julian entering first. "Everything all right?" He walked to Brayden and took another look at his hand. "Looks promising. I'll get some more ice." Julian hurried out of the room.

Brayden looked from Kam to Coach and back to Kam. She hadn't looked at Coach once since he and Julian entered the room. Her eyes were on Bray. The silence was deafening.

"How did this happen, Allen?" Coach inspected the swollen hand for himself.

"I think it was thugs trying to make an easy mark. I don't know what they were after. I offered my wallet and the keys to my ride, but they refused. I got in a few good hits and they were off before the security guard got there."

Coach nodded. "Since you didn't scream bloody murder when I picked up your hand just now, I know it isn't broken. Think you'll be up for the game tomorrow?"

"You know nothing would keep me away. But this is Julian's show." He tried to make a fist, but it was next to impossible.

"I know that. Hopefully, the swelling will have gone down by tomorrow's game. I want to you go home and relax until tomorrow. I'm sure your mother will look after you, right?"

"Yeah, my parents are still here."

Kam cleared her throat. "I'll drive Bray home. He's hardly in a condition to drive with a banged-up right hand. Do you mind, Greg?"

Bray knew that it wasn't a question, and probably so did Coach. He watch as Coach looked from him to Kam, studying both of them intently.

He took a deep breath and said, "No, Kamryn, I don't mind." He kissed her lightly on the forehead. "Seems like a good idea, considering the circumstances. Julian will examine him again in about thirty minutes and you guys can be on your way."

He narrowed his dark eyes on Brayden. "Julian will be at your house in the morning to examine your hand again and give the final determination. Are you filing a police report?"

"No use bringing more publicity to this than necessary." Bray also wanted whoever was behind the hiring of those thugs to show their hand.

Coach nodded. "Good thinking. We're in a good position and can take the lead in the series. We don't need any negative press."

Brayden already knew this. It was how Coach rolled. He wanted everyone associated with the team to be professional at all times. No scandals, no run-in with the police or anything else to mar all the hard work he'd done getting the team in shape. "Got it."

Coach stared at him, then looked at Kam. "Can I speak with you outside?"

"Sure, Greg." She followed him out of the examination room.

Bray wondered what was being said. He was tossing around the idea of going to Kam's rescue when Julian walked in with a bucket of ice.

"I'm supposed to keep you here thirty minutes, but honestly, I've done what I can and stopped the swelling. It's up to you and your healing capabilities. I'll come by and check your hand in the morning. My guess is you'll be able to play some of the game, but probably not all. I'm sure he'll want to save you for Saturday's game in Chicago."

Brayden had figured the same scenario. "It's okay, Julian. I don't blame you."

Julian laughed, reaching into one of the cabinets. "I appreciate that, Brayden."

Julian wrapped his hand quickly. "Leave this on tonight, take it off in the morning. I'll see you later."

Brayden was left alone with his thoughts. The kiss he and Kam had shared earlier was at the front of his brain. He knew Kam felt what he felt, but what was that?

He knew what he felt for Kam was stronger than the bounds of friendship. But she wasn't anything liked the women that he'd dated in the past. He would have to have a whole new game plan when it came to her. Was he ready?

He would use the drive home to figure it all out.

⸻◦⸻

An hour later Kamryn and Bray were headed to his house. She was seated behind the wheel of Bray's SUV and trying to concentrate on the road. She looked over at him several times. In all the time she'd known him, he'd never been physically hurt. He was fidgeting in the passenger seat but said nothing. "Are you hurting?" She rubbed his arm. "Do you need me to call Julian?"

"No, I don't need you to call Julian," he snapped.

"Calm down. You just seem uncomfortable, that's all."

"Sorry, Kam. I guess I am uneasy, and the fact that I'm starving isn't helping matters."

"We're about twenty minutes from the house. I can fix you something when we get to your place, or I can pull into a drive-thru. Which would you prefer?"

"You know what I want."

He didn't like fast food. No matter what he ordered, he said it was always wrong. He told Kamryn that was the reason he'd started cooking. "Okay. I hope Janice hasn't been too worried."

"I forgot to call my parents."

"Brayden!"

"Oh, I know that tone. Everything just happened so fast."

Kamryn shook her head. "Janice is going to kill you." She laughed. "I can't wait to see this show."

When Kamryn parked at Bray's house, she realized she had no way home. Bray certainly couldn't drive her, and she wouldn't dare ask his mother to drive her home. Sure, Janice would volunteer to do it, but she wasn't that familiar with Dallas and would probably get lost on her way back. She'd call her sister to pick her up after she got Bray settled.

"Why don't you stay here tonight?" he asked, getting out of the passenger seat. "Before you say you're not that kind of woman, just hear me out."

Kamryn clamped her mouth shut and joined him as they walked inside the house.

"My hand will be better in the morning. If not, Mom will be able to drive better in daylight." He hesitated. "It's not like you haven't stayed here before. You can stay in your room. I promise not to touch you."

She knew she was being silly. They were two adults and had been friends for over five years. They'd slept over at each other's house numerous times over the years, always in separate rooms, of course. Tonight shouldn't be any different, except everything about this night was very different. "Okay, Bray, I'll sleep in my room."

"Good," Bray said, walking into the kitchen and turning on the lights.

She took a deep breath, hoping she hadn't just made a big mistake. "Now that that's settled, let's see what I can fix for you." Kamryn opened the fridge and saw the makings for a turkey sandwich. "Turkey okay?"

He nodded. "I'll go find Mom."

"No need," Janice said from the doorway of the kitchen. She was dressed in her silk bathrobe. "Your coach called about twenty minutes ago and told us what happened." She hurried to the table and hugged Bray, being mindful of his swollen hand. "Are you okay?"

"Yes, Mom. My hand just got banged up a little."

"Thank goodness Kamryn was there to help you." She looked in Kamryn's direction. "I hope your date wasn't ruined." His mother looked in Bray's direction, but his thoughts were a million miles away.

"Not really. We're going to have a make-up date later." Kamryn sliced up tomatoes, onions, and pickles for the sandwiches. She hoped no one could tell how much her heart wasn't in that statement. If tonight told her anything - and it had told her plenty—it was that she was not attracted to Greg. "Janice, would you like a sandwich?"

"Oh, no, dear, I was just waiting for you guys to get here. I just had to see him for myself." She yawned. "I'm going to bed. See you in the morning." She left the room without another word.

Kamryn finished preparing the sandwiches, wondering why Janice had not asked her how she was getting home or when.

⟠

The next morning Kamryn woke to the sound of light tapping on her closed door. Before she could invite the knocker inside, the door opened and Bray walked into the room. He was dressed in knit shorts and a T-shirt.

"Hey, sleepy," he said sitting on the bed.

She pulled the comforter closer to her body. "What time is it?" There wasn't a clock in her appointed room. Luckily, there had been a nightshirt that she'd left there the last time she stayed over.

He pulled the comforter away from her body, ignoring her pleas not to. "We both know you got on that excuse for a nightshirt, so I know I'm not going to see any skin," he teased.

She laughed at his pouty expression. "You're a mess. Has Julian been here already?"

He nodded. "About an hour ago. I've been cleared to play for a little while, anyway. There's still some swelling, but Julian told me to relax until game time." He waited a beat. "That's not why I'm in your room."

"Why are you in my room?"

"Mom said breakfast is in thirty minutes." He rose from the bed, gazing down at her.

"Okay, I'll be down right after I shower and dress."

"Need any help?"

He always pressed the right buttons, no matter how things were between them. "No, I don't need any help. What I need is some privacy."

"My way sounds more fun." He leaned down, kissed her on the forehead, and left the room.

After she was assured that Bray had left the room, she pushed back the covers and went to shower. While the hot water soothed her tired body, Kamryn thought about the last twenty-four hours.

In one day her simple life had turned upside down and sideways. She'd gone from dating one man to the arms of someone that had been in front of her for years. What on earth was she thinking, kissing Bray like that? Well, it was too late to do anything but go forward, she told herself. She turned off the water and got out of the shower, determined not to look back at what she couldn't control.

∞

Bray drove Kam home after breakfast, hoping that they could finally talk about the kiss that rocked his world. Kam sat in the passenger seat fiddling with her purse. "Okay, Kam, we need to talk about last night."

"I know."

"What are you feeling?"

"I don't regret it, if that's what you mean." She took a deep breath. "You know I wouldn't just do that on a whim, Bray. I guess on some level, I have been looking at you differently."

"Same here, baby. Now what are we going to do about it?"

"Nothing."

"Nothing?"

Kamryn sighed. "Bray, it's no secret that you love women."

Okay, she had him there. "I can change, Kam. You'll see. I've been thinking about us for a minute, and I think I'm ready."

"Bray, I know you think you want me in that way. But, like most of your affairs, this, too, will pass. I was married once. When Steve died, it tore me apart. Some days I didn't want to go on without him. I don't have enough room in my heart for you to *think* that you're ready. I refuse to be one of those women that you have cast aside like a piece of wadded-up newspaper when you're tired of me."

"Understandable. First, I would never do that to you in a zillion years." She opened her mouth to respond. "Let me finish before you start your 'I am woman' speech."

"Of course, continue." She looked at him with those big brown eyes. "I can't wait to hear this."

He ignored her sarcasm. "You're not the only one dealing with some new emotions here. This is new and scary territory, Kam. Why don't we take this one day at a time? I'll show you what I feel."

She mulled over his words and then said, "What's the second?"

"What?" He was totally confused.

"When one mentions a first, there's usually a second."

"Oh, I was listing the ways we can take our friendship to another level," he said. "The second reason is that we do know each other, Kam. We can't have anything between us but the truth."

"You can't change who you are. I think we've both gotten carried away. I was worried about you last night, and my emotions got the best of me."

"Kam, you know I don't get carried away." He parked in front of her house and looked at her. "You're coming to the game, right?"

"Try and stop me."

At least there was Junior's. "We still gonna hang afterwards?"

"It's going to take more than a few seductive tongue kisses to stop me." She got out of the SUV. "Now go relax before the game, because if you guys don't win, then we can't go to Junior's." She hurried into the house without looking back.

# CHAPTER 9

After she was sure Bray had safely left her neighborhood, Kamryn went upstairs to change into fresh clothes. Her mind was buzzing with too many possibilities. Was she really contemplating a relationship with her best friend? Kalyn was at work and useless at these kinds of questions, so she decided to go with plan B. Her mother.

She drove to her parents' home and entered the house. It was mid-morning, and her father was already in his favorite chair taking his morning nap. Rufus was on the floor next to her dad.

Most likely her mother was in the kitchen, either cleaning up the morning dishes or preparing lunch. Kamryn took a deep breath and walked into the kitchen. She was half right. Her mother was using her new laptop to look for recipes.

"Hi, Mom," Kamryn said, kissing her mother on the cheek. "I saw Dad and Rufus taking their morning nap."

Colleen smiled. "Yeah, those two couldn't protect a fly. You came in the house and they both slept right through it. Shameful."

"But they look so cute sleeping."

Her mother nodded. "I never said they weren't cute. Your father claims it's my cooking that keeps him sleepy. He says I make too much, but since it's just us, he has to eat it all."

Kamryn shook her head. "Leave it to Dad to rationalize it that way."

"So what brings you by this early in the morning?"

Since she worked on her column from home, everyone in the Hillcroft family knew Kamryn didn't normally get up until lunchtime. "Actually, I wanted to talk to you about Bray."

Her mother rubbed her hands together. "Oh, goody. Janice and I were just saying what a cute couple you guys would make."

"Oh, no. You and Janice haven't been talking about this to Bray, have you?" That would explain his kiss.

Her mother closed her laptop and moved it to an empty space on the table. "And when was the last time a grown man listened to his momma?"

"Point taken. It's just that with everything that has happened in the last few days between Bray and I, it would have seemed a logical explanation to the events."

Colleen was totally focused on her daughter now. "Oh, honey, you must share."

She took a deep breath. "Well, it all started on Sunday. Bray kissed me. We chalked it up to stress."

"Honey, that wasn't stress. I like Brayden. He's been wonderful for you, and he helped you through your grief when Steve passed away. He's always willing to help any of us out, and that's because he cares about you. If that man laid those lips on you, it was on purpose. Whose idea was the stress theory?"

"Mine," she said, feeling like an idiot.

"I thought so. It's okay, Kamryn, if you're not ready. I've seen that man look at you like a piece of prime rib. I think he'll wait you out."

"That's just it, Mom. I kept telling him that it would never work between us then last night when I was on my date with Greg, Bray was attacked and the team doctor called Greg to tell him."

Her mother held up her hand. "Don't tell me. The minute you looked at Bray you rushed into his arms."

Kamryn stared at her mother. "Were you hiding at the American Airlines Center?"

"I don't have to. It's written all over your face. You haven't stopped smiling since you sat at the table. I knew something had happened between you, I just didn't know what."

"So you think I should pursue a relationship with him?"

"Only you know the answer to that. Did I ever tell you how I met your father?"

"Yes, I've heard the story a million times. You met him at church when you were seventeen and he was nineteen."

"Well, there's a little more to the story than that," her mother said.

"Okay, Mom, I'll bite. Tell me the story."

Colleen smiled broadly. "Well, I met your father when a group of friends and I went to dance at the center. When I laid eyes on him I knew he was something. Back then men wore suits everywhere, not like now. Anyway, he asked me my name and told me his.

I was seventeen and getting ready to graduate high school the next summer, so my mind was on college. He told me he wasn't going to college and was working in a factory. Well, I didn't want nothing to do with a man who didn't want more out of life than working at a factory until the good Lord called him home."

Kamryn's brain buzzed with the new details. "But you guys are married now and Dad just retired as an accountant," she couldn't help pointing out to her mother.

"This is my story, dear."

"Sorry."

"To continue. After that I didn't see him for about three months. He started showing up at my church. I think you guys would call that stalking these days. He told me he wasn't giving up on me. I told him that I wanted to be a teacher and I needed a professional man. I didn't want to have kids with a man with no future."

"Oh, Mom! You were one of those women?"

"Not really. It was the times we were living in, honey. What kind of future would we have had if we didn't dream big?"

"Dad always says you have to envision the impossible to make it possible."

"I didn't want to lead him on, so I told him that if he went to night school, I would go out with him."

"Mom!"

"He promised that he would, and he did. We started dating the next week, and when I graduated from high school we got married."

"But when did you go to college? Dad?"

"Honey, every relationship has compromises. We made a deal that I would go to college full time and he would go part time. Our parents helped out when you kids started coming along, but we finished college, got our respective degrees, and look at us now. We've been married forty-two years and I love him more every day. There's nothing I wouldn't do to please him."

Kamryn stared at her mom.

"My point is, baby, that in every relationship, there are things about the other person we don't like. If they're worth having, then there's a compromise for both of you. Your father was a whiz at math, and that's how he became an accountant. But if he hadn't been so persistent with me, he would have never known that. Sometimes we all need a push."

---

Thursday evening Dallas won in a runaway game against Chicago 120-105. Kamryn scribbled notes in her pad while she waited for Bray to exit the side of the building. He didn't start, but he played from the second quarter until the coach took him out a few minutes before the buzzer.

It was a record night. The Mavericks were now leading the semifinal series 3-2. Bray had hit a season high of thirty-five points. It was an amazing game, she thought. Her cell phone buzzed. It was Greg. She let her voicemail pick up the missed call. He'd wanted to meet after the game, but she already had plans with

Bray and those were unbreakable. Greg didn't understand, and she'd have to make it up to him later. Tonight was for her and Bray.

He walked out of the building, looking around for her SUV. Once he spotted it, he walked toward it. He was dressed in jeans, a golf shirt, and tennis shoes. Kamryn was half expecting Brian to emerge from the shadows. He didn't, thank goodness. She smiled as Bray opened her passenger door. She inhaled his cologne as he slid into the seat. He always smelled wonderful.

"Hey, baby," he said. He leaned over and kissed her on the mouth.

Kamryn should have objected, but his lips felt too good against hers. He was definitely bringing his A-game when it came to kissing. Finally, he pulled away. "Sorry, I don't know what came over me." He winked at her.

"P-Parents," she said attempting to put the SUV in gear.

"My parents are on their way to my house. They took a car service to the game tonight. Dad said he'd be too keyed up to drive home. You know this."

Yes, she did. She had already had the same conversation with Janice earlier that day. Somehow Bray's tongue had sucked out all of her thought processes and apparently her memory as well. "Yes, I know, I just forgot for a minute."

He chuckled. "Are you going to drive us to Junior's or what? You want to make out like high school students?"

"No," she said. "I do not want to make out with you."

"Says you."

---

Finally, after giving him "the look" for about a minute, Kam started the SUV. So much between them was up in the air; he wanted to know where he stood with her, but it wasn't the right time. He had enough going on with his parents in town for the playoffs and trying to make sure they had enough to do to keep them out of mischief.

He now understood what his older sister, Emma, meant. Being the middle child, she was the only one still in their hometown of Glasshill, Iowa, and she often looked after their parents. Although his parents were still relatively healthy and active, he still worried about them. His older brother, Sean, an attorney for the Boston Celtics, also worried about their parents. Brayden often thought of returning to their small hometown, but he didn't think he could live there now.

He'd changed too much to enjoy the small town as much as he once did. He couldn't imagine living anywhere without Kam. He shook his head, trying to dislodge the thought, but it was too late. It was already there. He was falling in love with his best friend.

They arrived at Junior's and Kam parked the SUV. Brayden hurriedly got out and went to open Kam's door. She was surprised, to say the least. He helped her out of the vehicle.

"Thank you, Bray."

He closed the door. Bray nodded, grabbed her hand, and they went inside the restaurant. Junior met them as they sat at their booth.

"Good game, Brayden." He looked down at Bray's swollen hand. "Need some ice for that hand?"

He looked down at his hand. He'd forgotten about the incident. His brain was so focused on his family and Kam, he hadn't felt the dull thud that was now coming to life in his hand. "No, Junior, it's okay. I'll take something when I get home."

Kam shook her head. "Men. Heaven forbid you show a sign of weakness." She dug inside her purse and pulled out a small bottle of aspirin. "Can you bring a glass of water for Mr. Basketball?"

Junior laughed. "You got it, Kamryn." He glanced at Brayden. "Good thing this woman is taking care of you." He left the table.

Brayden took the bottle from Kam. "You know I could have taken something when I got home. You trying to punk me in front of Junior and the boys?"

"Please. If you don't take care of your hand, you won't be able to play and win the game. I'm just trying to protect my job."

He laughed. It wasn't like Kam needed the money. He knew about her payout from the lawsuit, but she still worked like she needed the cash. Maybe that was her therapy after what she had gone through with her husband.

"Okay, what's wrong?"

"Nothing," Brayden said, watching the waitress approach with two glasses of water.

The young girl placed the glasses on the table and smiled at him. "That was an awesome game tonight, Mr. Allen."

"Thank you."

The young girl nodded and left the table. Kamryn cleared her throat. "Are you going to answer my question or drool over the pretty young thing?"

"Jealous? I like that in a woman."

"You wish."

"You know you want me."

"Sure. I want you to tell me what's got you zoning in and out tonight. Is something wrong with Janice? Is that why you screened her food order tonight?"

"No, there's nothing wrong with Mom, and I mean to keep it that way. She's been eating rich, fatty foods since she and Dad got here. I had to put the brakes on it, especially not knowing how long they're going to be here. Dad just lets her have her way and doesn't say or do anything. Was she pissed?"

"Oddly, no. She thought it was sweet. I did, too. There's something sexy about a man who cares for his mother."

At least that was something. His hand started throbbing more and more. He opened the pill bottle and took two tablets. He chased that with most of the water. "So when's the next big date with Coach?"

"Why don't you tell me?"

Brayden didn't like the line of questioning. "What are you talking about?"

Kam shrugged. "I thought maybe you guys were having another boys' meeting about me and you might have discussed strategies."

He was simmering. "Are you trying to make me *act a fool* in public? There's no way in hell I would tell Greg DeMorris anything about you. Why would I help a man get to you?"

"I-I-I just thought …."

"Well, you thought wrong."

"Maybe I did."

The waitress returned and took their order. Brayden was going to have to do something to lighten the mood at the table. But one thing was still in his mind. "So when are you seeing Coach again?" *Never* would be the best answer, he thought.

"I don't know. He wanted to get together tonight, but I told him that we have a ritual. I'll talk to him tomorrow."

"Kam, I appreciate you not wanting to miss our ritual and everything, but what about Coach?"

"Bray, we've only had one real date. It's too early to tell where it's going. It's nice to be able to talk about sports and not feel self-conscious about it."

"We talk about sports all the time," Bray couldn't help saying. It was what he loved about being with her.

"I know and I appreciate it. You let me be me. You don't mind that I love food, and you don't make big girl jokes."

"Kam, you're a beautiful woman and you love life. Never hide that from me."

She smiled broadly. "Thank you, Bray. You always know the right thing to say."

As usual, Brayden enjoyed his celebratory meal with Kam. Most of the team had wanted him to party with them, but too much was riding on the next game. He was afraid if he broke the ritual, they wouldn't win the semis and go on to the finals.

"How's the gambling story going?"

She shrugged. "Hit a wall. Jason was a very complex person, which no one knew. Everyone knew a different Jason. Did you know that he was in danger of getting cut from the team?"

Bray played with his water glass. "I knew something was going on, but Jason would never say so. He was in Coach's office almost every day during practice the last few weeks before he died. Then when those guys showed up at practice one day and refused to leave, that was it. Next thing I knew there were rumors about a trade in the near future. Jason died before anything could take place."

Kamryn wasn't surprised at the information. She nodded. "It's always sad when a professional athlete's private life takes over his professional one."

"True. Most of the guys I started playing with aren't in the league anymore due to some kind of scandal, bad judgment, or just plain stupidity."

She looked at him for a heartbeat. "You want to talk about us, don't you?"

"Well, yeah." He noticed the waitress bringing their food. "As soon as I eat." He was starving, having been too nervous to eat before the game.

"You don't have to tell me," she said, smiling at the young girl placing their orders in front of them. "You know I love to eat."

"And I love that about you." He took a bite of his burger before he said anything else he was going to regret.

Kam, being Kam, laughed. "Don't worry, Bray. I know what you mean. It's refreshing."

"Oh, baby, you mean everything to me." He reached for her hand across the table.

To his surprise she didn't snatch her hand from his. "I know you mean that, Bray."

"I do."

They ceased all conversation and continued eating their oversized hamburgers. After they finished, they headed to Bray's house. On the quiet trip home, Bray tried a little experiment as Kam drove. He placed his left hand on her leg.

"I know what you're doing, Bray, and you need to stop."

"What?"

"If you're seeing if you can unnerve me before I get to your house, you win. But there's nothing I'm going to do about it. You have to get on a plane in seven hours and play a game in thirty-six or so hours. You have to save your strength. In the event I was willing," she amended.

"Hope springs eternal, Kam."

⊷◦⊶

Thursday evening the Hillcroft siblings gathered at Kamryn's house to watch game six. Keegan, the oldest and only male in the house, took his place on the sofa nearest the food. He politely folded his six-foot-three-inch frame on the sofa and waited for all the festivities to begin. As was their tradition, Kamryn cooked. Keegan would clean up the mess and Kalyn ferried the food into the living room.

"I love when you cook, sis," he said, munching on a hot wing. "You always have enough for a man to eat. Not that cutesy food too small to fill a brother up."

She laughed as Kalyn brought in platters of nachos, buffalo wings, fried cheese sticks, pizza pockets, accompanied by beer and wine for everyone. Kalyn handed an imported brew to her brother, while she and Kamryn each had a glass of wine. "I'm sure there's a compliment in there somewhere." She took a seat beside him and patted her brother on the knee. "Thanks for coming over."

He took a swig of beer. "I would have just been going over some legal briefs anyway." Keegan was the only practicing attorney in the family and newly divorced. "Heard from that publisher yet?"

"No, not yet. It's a good thing since I've been really busy with this other story I've been working on." She grabbed a hot wing and ate it.

Keegan looked at her with that 'oh no' face. "What is it? Will I be bailing you out of jail while Bray is out of town? You know he'll flip his lid if something happens to you."

She looked sideways at her annoying brother. "Why would you say such a thing? Bray and I have been friends for five years, and that's all we are. He does not rule my life."

Keegan shrugged. "Yeah, right. You don't sneeze without him knowing."

"What are you talking about?"

"He calls me before he goes out of town to let me know, just in case something jumps off in his absence."

"Seriously?"

"Seriously. He wants to make sure you're protected," Keegan said, smiling.

"But I don't understand. I'm not his responsibility."

"In his eyes, you are. Because you're his best friend in the universe. His words, not mine."

Kamryn sat there dumbfounded. What was Bray doing?

---

Exactly three hours later, Kamryn, Kalyn, and Keegan looked at the TV screen, not believing what they saw as the final score. Had Dallas really lost the easiest game in history? Now the series was tied once again at three games apiece?

Kamryn was the first to speak. "Did I see that right? Did we really just lose like that? It was like they couldn't find their groove and get in sync with each other. Bray never plays that badly."

"They can't be awesome all the time, Kamryn. Unfortunately, this is the playoffs. I bet Da Money is going to yell at them all the way back to Dallas. When are they coming back?" Keegan asked, then drained the last of his third beer.

Kamryn rose and started stacking the empty dishes for Keegan to wash. For three people they sure ate a lot of food, she mused. Nothing was left. She was going to have to start using that treadmill she bought last year if she kept eating meals like this. "Since they lost the game, I'm sure Greg is going to bring them back tonight."

"Greg?" Keegan stood and began gathering empty beer bottles. "Who is Greg? Does Bray know he has competition?"

This was what she got for letting her family get in her business. "For the last time, Bray and I are friends. Greg is Da Money, the coach."

"You're on a first-name basis with the coach?"

"We had a date the other night. We had to cut it short when Bray got hurt."

"What happened?"

"Some guys jumped him in the parking garage. Funny thing is, Bray offered them his wallet and the keys to his Escalade, but they didn't want either. Said they'd already been paid. He was able to hold his own and they ran off."

Keegan shook his head. "I'd say it sounds like they were doing a job. Who on earth would want to harm Brayden?"

She couldn't imagine anyone wanting to harm Bray. He didn't have any drama unless she counted those groupies. Kamryn didn't think they would be smart enough to hire someone to hurt him. "Bray didn't think it was anything to worry about, so he didn't file a police report. But he's had some strange things happen to him in the last week. He's almost had a wreck twice."

"Umm," her brother said as he headed into the kitchen.

Kamryn hurried into the kitchen and put the dirty dishes in the sink. "What are you thinking, Keegan?"

He shrugged, putting the beer bottles in her recycling bin. "If it was anyone besides Brayden, and if he wasn't one of my clients, I'd say that he owes somebody some money. I'd also say the person is tired of waiting for him to pay. I see this a lot in my line of work. It's really common with athletes, both minor and professional. I hate to say this, Kamryn, but they're easy marks for gambling professionals. Rich guy starts gambling and loses his shirt, borrows or bets more than he can get his hands on. The enforcers show up to break something to show they mean business."

"But Bray doesn't bet. You know how he is about blowing money. Don't get me wrong, he likes to have a good time, but in moderation. He's very diligent about having a back-up plan."

"Yes, I know. That's why I said if it was anyone else but Bray, the scenario might be believable."

"Instead of my story getting easier, I keep coming up with more possibilities."

"That just means this is gonna be one hell of a story when you get all the pieces together."

Kamryn was beginning to think Bray had been right last week. This story might get her killed.

———— ∞ ————

The plane arrived back in Dallas at two in the morning. There were no fans waiting. Officially the team wasn't supposed to come back until Sunday afternoon since the last game was Monday night. But Coach had been furious after the game, so they had to pack up and leave. They needed the win. It was do or die.

Bray grabbed his bags and headed for the car service stand. After such an awful game, he just wanted a good night's sleep so he could be ready for practice in the morning.

After he was settled in the backseat of the car and the driver was on the way to his house, he relaxed. He glanced at his watch. She might still be up, he thought. He took out his cell phone and pushed the first speed dial option.

"This had better be good, Bray," Kam said into the phone. Then, "I'm glad you called."

He smiled. "I just wanted to hear your voice. I know you saw the game, so I won't give you the awful details. We have practice most of tomorrow. Maybe we can hook up on Monday before the game?"

"No way, buddy. You have a very important game that you guys very much need to win. So I want you to get all the rest you can. We can celebrate after you guys are semi-final champs."

That sounded promising. "You mean we can have an actual date and talk about how much I can change?"

"It means we're going to Junior's when you guys win."

———————

Monday night, game seven, Kamryn sat alone in the family section of the arena. No one dared accompany her to the game tonight. Her father, who loved sports more than she did, told her that his heart wouldn't be able to take the pressure of the game, plus he didn't want to be near the Center in case things didn't go well.

Kamryn had to be there; it was her job. Well, technically. She wrote a column, so she wasn't really reporting on the game. But she wanted to be there for the highlights. Someone had to be there for Bray, no matter the outcome of the game.

Her gaze went to the sidelines. She noticed Greg, but he was too intent on the game, and rightly so. Funny, she thought, he hadn't called her since that night. They never did reschedule their date. Maybe destiny took care of her ending it with Greg so she wouldn't have to.

Each minute of the game seemed to take hours, but finally they were in the fourth quarter. Dallas was down by five points. Every basket Dallas attempted got blocked by the Bulls. Kamryn was on the edge of her seat, trying to remain composed, but once Tyler had control of a loose ball, she was up on her feet like the rest of the crowd. He made the three-point shot easily, bringing the Mavericks within two points. There were still three very long minutes left to play in the game. How was she going to survive until the game was over?

# CHAPTER 10

Looking at the scoreboard, Kamryn couldn't believe her eyes. Dallas had won the game by two points. The sold-out crowd went crazy. Strangers were hugging strangers, grown men were weeping unashamedly in public. Kamryn wiped away her own tears as she headed to the parking lot.

"For the first time in franchise history, the Dallas Mavericks are headed to the NBA finals." Kamryn typed on her netbook in the privacy of her SUV. She could barely keep her heart from jumping out of her throat. She was excited, Bray was excited. The whole Dallas-Fort Worth metroplex was beyond giddy with the prospect that Dallas could actually take it all.

Her cell phone rang. She figured it was Bray giving her the all-clear signal, and she was correct. She answered the call, and she could hear all the craziness that was going on in the dressing room. She could barely make out what Bray was saying. "What?"

"How's this? I'm in Coach's office."

"Better. Now what were you saying?"

"Give me thirty minutes. Damn reporters just left."

"I could catch an attitude from that last statement, but I know you're excited over the win and I will ignore the jab about my fellow reporters. Congrats."

"Thanks, babe. You're what I'm excited about." He ended the call.

Okay, that was cryptic, she thought. Best not to focus on it for the moment, she told herself. Her cell phone rang again. This time it was her editor. He'd been texting her during the game, wanting her column immediately after Dallas won the semi-finals. Like she didn't know how to do her job. She hated when he tried to micromanage her.

"How much longer, Kamryn?"

She gave a dramatic sigh. "Barney, you are killing me," said Kamryn, exasperated. Did the man think she just pulled the stories out of her behind? "I'm finishing it up right now. Another ten minutes. Promise. I've never missed a deadline, and don't intend on starting tonight." She hit the end button on the cell phone and continued typing.

She'd had a feeling Dallas was going to win and she'd written most of her column earlier that day, but there was no substitute for being in the American Airlines Center and watching Dallas actually win the semi-finals. She finished her column and read it again and again, searching for any typos or sentence fragments. Every word sounded like pure gold to her, but she was biased. She had loved the Mavericks even before Bray joined the team. She emailed her column to her editor, then called him to make sure he got it.

"Barney, I just sent it to you."

"Yeah, got it. Reading it right now. Sounds great." He ended the call.

Kamryn laughed. Men! Barney was never one for saying 'thanks for being a team player.' That was understood from the minute she'd taken the job as columnist seven years ago. She'd clawed her way to columnist and wasn't going to let anyone take that away from her.

Since she had a little time to kill before picking up Bray, she took out her notebook with the notes on Jason. So much about him didn't make sense to her. Why was he betting? Was he really in financial trouble? Hopefully, a door would open soon and she would have some answers. Her phone buzzed at her. She had a text message. She sighed. If it was her boss, she was definitely changing her cell number. It wasn't her boss. It was Bray and the message only had one word. "Ready."

She laughed, started the SUV, and headed around the corner to pick him up. He was standing outside the building with one of the security guards. Since his attack, a guard had been ordered to escort him to his vehicle. Bray slid inside the car and kissed her quickly on the lips. "I'm feeling so good that I might eat two hamburgers tonight, with some onion rings."

"Are you sure about going to Junior's?"

"Of course, we can't stop now. It might jinx me."

Any other person and Kamryn would have laughed, but she knew this man was dead serious. They had to keep the tradition of going to Junior's for a late dinner after a victory.

"Okay, Bray. Junior's it is." Kamryn put the SUV in gear and they were off. As she drove, Bray was quiet. She wondered where his head was. Was he thinking about the week ahead? According to NBA rules, there has to be at least seven days between the end of the semi-finals and the beginning of the finals. "What's on your mind, Bray?"

"You."

She was going to have to stop asking him what he was thinking about. He always told her. "Bray, we said we'd take it a day at a time. Right now you need to concentrate on winning the championship."

"You do agree there's something between us?"

"Yes, but there's no rule that says we have to act on it this second."

He was quiet for a heartbeat, probably weighing his options. He wasn't Mr. Fast Play for nothing. "All right, Kam. I don't want to ruin tonight."

"Me, either." She parked in front of Junior's and glanced around the small parking lot. Usually after a game there would be maybe ten cars in the parking lot, but tonight it seemed the lot was overrun with cars, trucks, and SUVs. Could be just a coincidence, she thought. It wasn't exactly a secret that she and Bray ate there.

They went inside and the place was packed. It was standing room only, except for their table, which was vacant, due to the large 'reserved' sign on it. As they walked through the crowd men shook Bray's hand and slapped him on the back, congratulating him on the win. It felt like home.

Junior met them just as they sat down. "Good evening, Brayden. Man, you almost gave me a heart attack at the end, but it was worth every cuss word I was screaming at the TV. Dinner's on me tonight, guys."

"Thank you, Junior," Kamryn said, still not believing the size of the crowd. "This is amazing."

"Hey, this is the first time Dallas has gotten this far." He left the table without taking their order.

"How's he going to know what we want to eat?" Kamryn asked.

Bray laughed. "Baby, we always eat the same thing when we come here. Just relax."

---

Brayden leaned back in his chair, watching all the festivities going on around him and Kam. Although Junior's was small and packed to capacity, he felt at ease. The liquor was flowing freely, but neither Junior nor Kam would let him have so much as a sip of beer. No matter how many patrons offered, Kam gave them that million-watt smiled and told them no.

"You have to stay in top physical condition for the championship," Kamryn reminded him as she drank a beer.

"There are other ways to stay in top condition that would involve just the two of us. I guarantee that you would break a sweat, and I'm better than any workout."

She choked on the beer. The exact desired effect, he thought.

"Bray, we said we'd wait."

"Oh, did that also include talking about sex, too? You take all the fun out of everything. So I can't tell you how many times I'd make hot, steamy sweaty love with you in one night? Or how you would be too tired to move from the bed, or any other flat surface you happen to land on."

"Brayden Allen, I will leave you right here and you'll have to find another way home if you don't cut out all this sexy talk."

He was getting to her, just like she'd unknowingly gotten to him in the last few days. "All right, I'll stop saying it, but you can't stop me from thinking about it."

She wadded up a paper napkin and threw it at him. "You're doing this on purpose."

"Of course I am. I'm a man, it's inborn."

She opened her mouth to speak, but the waitress was bringing their food. After the young girl distributed the food and praised Brayden for his basketball skills, she left and Brayden focused his attention on Kam.

———

The next morning Kamryn rolled over in her king-sized bed, glanced at her bedside clock, and cursed the day Bray was born. It was after ten in the morning. She had an article and a column due in five hours! Darn that Bray! Because of him and his sexual talk, she hadn't gotten much sleep.

Every time she closed her eyes, all those sexy images he kept referring to kept popping into her head. Couple that with the fact that she didn't get home until the wee hours of the morning, she was tired. But she still had a job to do. Resigning herself to the fact that she had to get busy, she got out of bed, took a shower, and dressed.

She went to the kitchen to make some coffee. As the aroma of hazelnut crème-flavored coffee filled the room, Kamryn felt her creative juices starting to flow. Her boss wanted her to write an extra column about the Mavericks making it to the finals. Her brain buzzed with possibilities.

Her doorbell rang, breaking the spell. As she walked to her front door, the bell chimed a second time, then a third. She knew exactly who it was. Bray. No one else was that impatient. She opened the front door and there he was, dressed in a knit exercise outfit. "What on earth are you doing here?"

He leaned down and kissed her on the cheek and then on the mouth. "Well, it's good to see you, too." He stepped inside the house, causing her to step back. "I had to come see the sportswriter everyone in Dallas is talking about." He walked into the living room.

She closed the door and followed him. "I haven't read the column yet. How did it sound?"

He sat down on the couch. "You know it was the bomb. Don't play. You know it was all that."

"I know what I turned in, but I haven't read what actually got into the paper. Editorial usually chops an inch or two off just because they can. Now it's almost the afternoon and I still have a column to write and a story to investigate." As much as she'd love another kiss from his golden lips, she had responsibilities. She stood in front of him, hoping against hope that he'd leave.

"You said we'd talk." He grinned at her. He patted the space beside him.

"I didn't mean now. I meant later."

"This is later, Kam." He crossed his muscular arms across his well-defined chest. "I want to talk about us now."

Since she had one determined man on her hands, she might as well as get it over with as soon as possible. She sat down at the end of the sofa. "Okay, talk."

"You're not going to make this easy, are you?"

"Of course not," she said. "That's not my style. Now, you were saying?"

"Okay, I get it. I need to bring it. So I will." He took a deep breath and said, "We've been friends a long time, Kam, but lately something has changed between us. I don't know how or why, but I see you in a totally different light. You're a beautiful woman, Kam, and I want you."

"And you're a playa. I should say king of the playas. Bray, I'm not the woman you think I am."

"Will you let me find out? Or am I supposed to take you at your word?"

No matter how good those lips tasted, this was a bad idea. "Bray," she said slowly, "you're used to a different kind of woman."

"Baby, I know you. I've seen you nearly naked, so stop all the 'my body' crap. We've shared a bed before, so stop all this crazy talk."

What was he talking about? When had he seen her nearly nude? She was always careful not to show more skin than necessary, and he was always the perfect gentleman with her. She couldn't recall a time when the unthinkable could have happened. After a moment's thought, she gasped. She'd forgotten. It seemed like a lifetime ago. It was those early days right after her husband had died unexpectedly. She couldn't sleep, work, or eat, whether from guilt or grief. She'd called Bray, just hoping he'd talk to her until she fell asleep, but instead he came over in the middle of the night and held her in his arms. Snuggled against his big muscular body, sleep finally claimed her. When she awoke the next morning he was still nestled against her, sound asleep. "Okay, I'll give you that point. You date a lot of women, and I don't share."

"Name a woman I've dated in the last six weeks," he challenged.

"Is *date* the operative word here?"

He smiled. "I'm a man, but yes, date is the operative word."

"Natasha, Bambi, Tiffany, Taylor, and the crazy one, Heidi."

"See, you don't know me like you think you do. I haven't dated Natasha since Valentine's Day, which was about two months ago. Tiffany, the week after. Taylor was months ago, and Heidi, I never dated. She was why I had to replace my backup cell phone. Girl was blowing up my phone and leaving all kinds of crazy messages. You were right on that one."

"I guess you mean my suggestion that you have a separate phone for your social calendar many years ago was correct."

"Yes, that was a good idea," Bray admitted. "That saved me a lot of headaches. When I don't want to be bothered with the honeys, I just leave that cell at home."

"You're welcome."

He rolled his eyes toward the ceiling. "Yes, thank you for recommending it, Kam. You're always looking out for me."

Kamryn nodded. "So you're telling me you don't have a little something-something on the side with anyone?"

"Yes, that's what I'm telling you. I can't help it that women like me."

"Bray, look at me."

He did.

"Why do you want me?"

He stared at her. "Do you find me attractive?"

She couldn't believe her ears. "Yes, Bray, I think you're a very attractive man. So does every other woman in Dallas. I wasn't thinking about physical, I'm thinking more about whether we have a real connection."

"Kam, I'm not stupid. I know you think I'm a jock, but I do have a brain and I love talking to you. We talk about everything, not just sports. You have keys to my house. You hang out with my family when they come to town. You've been to my hometown in Iowa, and my mom thinks you rock."

She knew he was right. Over the years, they had interacted with each other's families. Her father thought Bray could do no wrong as long as he was wearing a Mavericks' uniform. "What's your point, Bray?"

"My point is that we've been best friends for a long time and nothing will change between us. This will only heighten our bond."

She didn't believe that for one minute. Things had already changed between them. Should she dare tempt fate by crossing the line of friendship? Could they go back to being friends after this was over?

"I know what you're doing, Kam. Stop it! Listen to your heart, not your head. Your overactive brain will come up with a million reasons why this won't work."

"It won't work, Bray."

He shook his head. "I can't believe that you're going to turn your back on what's happening between us. You're running away from what you're feeling. Baby, every time I kiss you, it's like someone threw a match on my soul and it turns into an inferno. Yeah, I'd like to run, too, but that's not an option."

She grabbed his hand and pulled it to her face. "You don't understand. I'm not running, but my brain is on overload right now. I have a deadline, and I'm not going to make it sitting her talking to you about this."

He threw his head back and sighed. "Okay, I'll leave you alone until you get your work done. Why don't we go out to dinner tonight?"

She wanted to say no, but not only was her heart not listening to her brain, neither were her lips. "That sounds good."

He smiled, pulled her onto his lap, and wrapped his strong arms around her, locking her in place.

She knew he was going to give her one of his trademark kisses that made her blood boil. She prepared her mouth for a kiss, but nothing happened. She heard him clear his throat.

"Baby, I need to ask you a question."

"Now?"

"I want your undivided attention."

She wiggled a little in protest with little success, except for waking up his erection. Not exactly what she was meaning to do, but she wouldn't complain. "Okay, you have my attention."

"Good."

She waited a beat. "Are you going to ask me or what?"

"All right. Have you kissed Coach?"

"That's none of your business." She made a move to get up, but again she failed.

"It's all of my business. I need to know."

"Well, I'm not telling. I don't ask you who you have kissed."

He ran a hand down her back, waking up every inch of her skin between her neck and her hips. "I'll have to kiss the information out of you."

"I thought you were leaving," she said.

"Nah, just wanted you to relax your guard so I could do this." He kissed her softly.

"Not fair," she whimpered against his lips, but she couldn't resist kissing him again.

"Only way I play, baby."

---

After kissing Kam within an inch of her life, Brayden left her house before they got in a lot of trouble. Once in the security of his SUV, he made a call to his accountant.

"How's my favorite client?" Kyle Forrest asked in his Texas twang.

"I need to see you. Now." It wasn't a request.

"Sure, Brayden. You on the way to my office?"

"Yeah, I can be there in about thirty minutes."

"See you then."

Brayden ended the call and headed to downtown Dallas. Kyle had been his accountant since his arrival in Dallas. He liked his money to be managed by someone in the same city. Kyle had come highly recommended.

He reached Kyle's office in the Hallsburg building, which housed attorney and investment firms. Most Dallasites referred to the six story gold building as the Money House. Brayden took the elevator to the fourth floor and was greeted by Kyle's young assistant, Melba. He disliked Melba.

"Hello, Mr. Allen," she said in her cheerleader voice. "Amazing game last night. Sometimes I can't believe that I know you."

Brayden sighed. If there was a downfall to Kyle being his accountant, it was this girl. Not only was she Kyle's college-age niece, but she talked about fifty miles a minute. "Thanks, Melba."

"He's waiting for you."

"Great. Nice to see you." Brayden headed down the hall before she could reply.

Kyle met him at the doorway. "Sorry about Melba."

"It's all good. She's good for the ego, in small doses."

"Come on, let's talk." He ushered Brayden into his corner office. After they were both seated, Kyle asked, "What's up?"

Brayden took a deep breath. If he gave this a voice, then it was as good as done, but it was time. "I'm thinking about retiring after the finals."

Kyle coughed. "Are you serious? You're one of the best point guards in the country. This is your time."

"Yeah, but I've been doing this ten years. I'm seriously thinking of calling it quits. My contract is up after this season." He was so tired of everyone treating him like a piece of meat or only thinking of how much money he could make them. "What I need from you is my financial position. If I don't work another day in my life, what would happen?"

Kyle nodded. "I can see you've thought about this a minute, huh?" He began typing on his computer. "Just a second and I'll have this printed up for you."

A few minutes later, Kyle handed Brayden a thick stack of papers. He flipped through them, then asked, "So, Kyle, how am I looking?"

"You look great. You purchased your parents home eight years ago and paid cash. Since then the house's worth has almost tripled. Your investments are doing well. If you didn't play another season, you'd be fine financially. You could maintain your current lifestyle for a very long time."

"I'm most concerned about my parents' position."

Kyle nodded. "Worst-case scenario?"

"Yes."

"Okay. You need solid numbers. In your parents' account there's a little over two million, so they should be fine if you never work another day in your life."

"Great." He looked at his portfolio accounts. "I just want to make sure they will be provided for, no matter how much longer that is."

"Understandable. You know, not all professional athletes think like you do."

"My parents are special to me."

"You're good, your parents are good. When you get time you can read those reports and let me know if you want to move any of your money around or change anything."

Brayden stood and shook Kyle's hand. "Thanks, Kyle. I appreciate you seeing me on such short notice."

"No problem. It's what I'm here for."

"Thanks. This is confidential for now. I haven't even told my agent yet, so keep this to yourself."

"Gotcha."

Brayden left the office feeling much better about the future. He just had to convince Kam that his intentions were sincere.

---

"Brayden finally kissed you? I mean really kissed you, tongue and all? You guys are finally getting this party started," Kalyn said much later that afternoon. She was leaning against Kamryn's kitchen counter, eating a sandwich.

Not that she had done much work since Bray had left her house earlier. Those kisses had burned a hole in her brain, and now she needed to hear the voice of reason. Too bad it wasn't from her sister. Kalyn was ecstatic about the news of the kiss. Kamryn listened to her sister as she fixed lasagna for dinner. She had just started assembling all her ingredients when Kalyn showed up looking for food.

Kamryn finished assembling her killer lasagna and shoved it in the oven. "I wouldn't necessarily say it was a party, but I guess I'm willing to explore it a little." She still got hot flashes thinking about all the ways his tongue had mated with hers.

"Whatever you're calling it, I'm glad you're doing it. I brought the full report about Jason with me. I wasn't able to find out much."

"Great, we can look at it after dinner."

"You're kidding, right?" Kalyn walked to the fridge and got a soda. "I bet you money Bray is going to have all your attention after dinner. You won't be able to look at it. I can give you a quick overview while you're putting the finishing touches on dinner."

"Okay," Kamryn said.

Kalyn walked to the kitchen table and opened her drink. "The day before he was killed was an odd day, even in Jason's crazy life."

"How odd?" Kamryn joined her sister at the table. "Do I need my notepad for this?"

"Not really." Kalyn took a sip. "Jason's day started about ten. He withdrew a hundred grand from his joint checking account."

Kamryn nodded. "Yeah, I know about that account. I just can't tell where it is, or how much is in it. It's buried pretty deep. Sandra doesn't even have access to it. She didn't even know about its existence until I told her about it."

"This sounds like something off TV, Kamryn," Kalyn said. "You couldn't make this stuff up. Talk about split personalities."

Kamryn shook her head. "Kalyn, I don't know who Jason was. Nothing is making sense. This started out as a simple favor to a friend and now it's morphed into this thing. Now I don't know how to stop it."

"You could always walk away from it. This isn't part of your job, Kamryn. You were going to do a story, but it's not your column."

She weighed the options of quitting. No, that would be the coward's way out and she wasn't a coward. She couldn't let Sandra down, and she couldn't let herself down. After all these twists and turns, she had to know the truth. She smiled at her sister. "Thanks, Kalyn."

"You're welcome. Everyone needs a little push every now and then."

She hadn't doubted that for a second. "I know it's morbid curiosity, but I'd like to know what actually happened to this guy."

"Me, too. I don't know why he was moving so much money around. It would be interesting to see where all this leads to."

Kamryn sighed. "As long as it doesn't lead to me getting hurt, I'm all for it."

<hr />

The doorbell sounded later that evening as Kamryn slipped into her dress. It was just like Bray to be early the one time she needed him to be late. She was nowhere near ready for him. She hadn't finished putting on her makeup. It was barely seven. She'd been counting on him being at least thirty minutes late. The bell sounded again. And again. She decided she'd let him in, then resume getting dressed.

She answered the door, but it wasn't Bray. It was his friend Brian, who she thought had left town. Dressed in grungy jeans and a T-shirt, he looked like five miles of bad road. The well-dressed man she'd met at the game was gone. Someone or something had worked him over pretty good.

"Brian, what are you doing here?"

"I was looking for Brayden. I tried his cell, but it went to voicemail. I don't like leaving messages. I was wondering if you knew where he is at the moment."

There was something about this guy she didn't like, so she didn't take the safety chain off her door to let him in. "Well, he's not here, either."

"Any ideas where he may be?"

"Brian, he's a grown man. I don't keep track of his every move. I thought you were going back to Chicago days ago."

"Not right now. It's a little hot in the windy city right now." He looked at her. "You're not going to let me in? Where's all that Texas hospitality? I'm Brayden's friend. Doesn't that rate me something?"

"That's the only reason I'm not calling the police. Bray is not here and I don't know where he is." It was the truth. "If he happens to come by or I talk to him, I'll be happy to give him your number."

"Never mind."

Kamryn wondered why he was still in town and if Bray knew. She watched him limp down her walkway and into a small compact car. He screeched the tires as he pulled away. Maybe Kalyn should be running a report on Brian. Something about him smelled like trouble. She hoped it wasn't contagious.

Forty-five minutes later, Bray rang the doorbell. True to form, he was late. Kamryn was glad because she'd had time to finish dressing. She glanced at her image in the mirror. Perfect. She slipped on her stilettos and went to answer the doorbell as Bray rang it a second time.

She had been planning to tease him about being late, but all those thoughts left her brain when she opened the door to let him in. Bray was dressed in a suit! He was dressed in a dark blue suit that was obviously made for his athletic body. He looked like a decadent piece of her favorite cake, triple chocolate.

"These are for you." He leaned down and kissed her, then handed her a crystal vase with two dozen of her favorite yellow roses. "So can I come in or what?"

"Yes, you can." She inhaled the aroma of the roses. "These are lovely. Thank you." She kissed him. His lips tasted sweet, like something she should sample a second time. So she did.

"What are you trying to do to me?" He closed the front door. "I'm trying to show you how good I can be and you're tempting me like this."

She stepped back and grabbed his hand, leading him into the living room. "I have no idea what you're talking about."

He sat down on the couch. "You know exactly what I'm talking about, baby. We've known each other a minute, so it's not like we're strangers. We don't have to do all that unnecessary chit-chat."

"So this is like an express date?" she challenged, standing in front of him.

Instead of him saying something sharp or even comical, Bray pulled her on his lap. "You might as well accept the fact that you're not going to get rid of me. So if you have to keep rationalizing it in your brain, that's fine." He kissed her slowly and thoroughly to prove his point.

"I have to get dinner on the table." She made a move to get up.

"I'm not really that hungry. At least not for food." He kissed her softly, teasing her mouth open and letting his tongue do his talking for him.

Kamryn moaned, trying to find a scrap of willpower against those sinful lips and Bray's ever-moving hands. "I spent the afternoon cooking, Bray," she said against his lips. "I spent hours getting ready for tonight."

"Later," he whispered against her lips as his hands settled on the side zipper of her dress.

In the recesses of her mind, she heard the sound of her dress being unzipped, but there was little she wanted to do about it at the time. She was going to go with the moment.

His hands were inside her dress, touching her hot skin intimately. Every place he caressed seemed to start an inferno inside her body. She wrapped her arms around him and caressed his freshly cut hair. He smelled wonderful, and it seemed to fuel her responses to his wet, hot, soul-sucking kisses.

When they came up for air, Bray said, "Okay, Kamryn, we got two choices. We can make love here or we can make love upstairs. I really can't guarantee I can make it upstairs if you don't hurry."

A nervous laugh escaped her kiss-swollen lips. Was she really contemplating making out on the couch? "Upstairs."

"Got something?"

"Shouldn't I be asking you that?"

"So you are interested?"

She wanted to kiss that smirk off his handsome face. "You wouldn't be here otherwise."

He kissed Kamryn long and hard. "Now Ms. Hillcroft, time for dessert."

# CHAPTER 11

Brayden took a deep breath once he and Kam entered her bedroom. He was nervous and didn't know why. Well, yes, he knew why, but there was little he could do about any of it now.

He struggled out of his jacket, letting it fall to the floor. Kam sat on the bed watching him. They were both nervous about the large and monumental step they were about to take. He sat beside her on the bed. "Changing your mind?" God, he hoped not.

"No," she said softly. "Just thinking."

"Well, stop it," he said, leaning down and kissing her. He helped her out of her dress. Her body was beautiful and lush. She wore a black lacy bra and matching French-cut panties. "Do you have any idea of how sexy you look right now?"

She looked down at her body as if seeing it for the first time and smiled at him. "Thank you, Bray. Your turn." She motioned for him to take off his clothes.

That was one of the downsides of dating your best friend, he thought. With Kam there was no room for anything but real talk. No tired playa lines were allowed. Besides, she could tell when he wasn't being honest. "You look sexier than any woman I have ever seen. Why did we waste so much time?"

"Now who's doing all this thinking?"

He took off his shirt and let it fall to the floor. He stood and slid off his slacks, leaving on his silk boxers. He moved next to her on the bed, determined to kiss away every doubt she had.

As their tongues fought a battle their bodies had yet to fight, Brayden's hands glided over her body. He unsnapped her bra and threw it the floor. For a minute he forgot to breathe. He stared at her. She took his breath away. "Oh, baby," he whispered. He leaned down and kissed her breasts, letting his tongue play with their delicious peaks. Easing her down on the bed, he opened his mouth wider to get as much of her breast in his mouth as possible.

"Bray," she said, a little uneasy. She ran her hand over his head, bringing him closer to her body. "I don't know how much more I can take."

"I'm just getting started." He began suckling her breast, letting his tongue toy with her erect nipple. After he was sure he had her full attention, he moved to her other breast and repeated the process. He chuckled against her perfumed breast as he heard a gasp of pleasure escape her mouth.

She started to writhe under him, fully getting into the game. She wanted more. She moved her hips in invitation, silently begging to feel more of him. "Please, Bray," she panted.

He ignored her pleas and, as he drove her out of her mind, his free hand worked her panties down her legs until she kicked them aside. Now she was ready. He kissed her on the mouth again before rising, taking off his boxers and locating the condom in his slacks.

He shook the gold packet at her before he set it on the night table.

He stared at his best friend, lying naked on her king-sized bed, looking sexier than any model. All the lustful fantasies he'd had since that first real kiss couldn't compare to the woman stretched out before him.

Kamryn took a good look at all of him and sighed. He was larger than Steve and she was a little worried about logistics. Tight skin pulled over bulging muscles and one very large, very thick, erect penis. "I don't know about this, Bray." Her eyes roamed over his ripped body. She'd seen him without a shirt on before, but this was somehow very different.

"Don't worry, baby." He sat on the bed and pulled her into his arms. "I got you." He kissed her lips. "You trust me, right?"

"You wouldn't be here if I didn't."

"I know." He reached for the condom and slipped it on.

He positioned himself between her legs and entered her slowly. Kamryn gasped at the invasion. He slid the tip of his penis inside, then pulled almost completely out. He repeated the process several times, each time deepening the penetration before pulling out. Kamryn thought the anticipation was going to be her death. He was definitely all man.

He leaned down and kissed her, wrapping her in a tight embrace as he pushed again, this time harder, longer, not pulling back. When Kamryn felt her body tighten in defense, she closed her eyes and forced herself to relax.

Bray was patient. His slow, easy strokes relaxed her in a way that defied description. He dropped light kisses on her face and neck. When his tongue darted inside her mouth, she prepared herself for the pain that was to come once he was fully inside her. But the pain didn't come. She did.

Kamryn couldn't believe it. She'd finally had an orgasm. After twelve years of marriage without one, she'd given up on ever experiencing having an orgasm. She thought she was one of those women who just didn't have them. Now with Bray, she had had an orgasm almost instantly. She couldn't believe she'd just shared such an overpowering emotion with the absolute last person she'd thought she'd ever have sex with. Kalyn was right. The world did move. She let out a sigh of contentment.

"I must be good," he chuckled, wrapping his arms around her and surging forward. "Just wait, baby, you'll be reaching for the stars and begging me for more."

Kamryn had to agree. He was that good. She lost herself in his lovemaking. Each powerful thrust took her farther than the last. Bray pulled her closer and increased his tempo, she knew he was about to climax and held on for the ride. "Kam!"

They lay in bed breathing hard, and looking at each other with goofy smiles on their faces.

She caressed his sweaty body. Her fingers glided easily over the flat planes of his stomach. This man made her feel like the prettiest woman walking on the earth. He had relieved any fears she had and replaced them with sexual confidence. "Bray, you were excellent. To be honest, I wasn't sure about logistics, but you were so gentle. You're much larger than Steve."

"He couldn't bring you to an orgasm?"

"How did you know?"

"Because one of those times you were screaming your head off, you said so." He pulled her on top of him. "Honey, don't ever be embarrassed to tell me anything. If I do something that you don't like, all you have to do is tell me."

"That's no problem. Ready for round two?" she challenged.

He laughed. "I think I created a monster. But I like it."

Kamryn watched him with amazement as he whipped off the condom and replaced it with another one. As he lay on his back, he guided her on top of him. She gasped as he filled her body with none of the gentleness from earlier. His hand rested on her hips, guiding her movements. As they settled into a rhythm that satisfied them both, he pulled her down for a kiss, nestling himself deep inside her body.

Kamryn didn't know which sensations were sending her over the cliff of no return. Was it the feel of her body rubbing against his, electrifying her soul, or was it those kisses that took her breath away? She decided she didn't care and just enjoyed the ride.

Later, when they were both spent, she lay on her side and watched him as he slept. Who knew he had that kind of magic? Okay, now she realized there was enough room in her heart to care for two men. She hated when Kalyn was right all the time.

"I hope I put that smile on your pretty face," Bray said, looking at her with sleepy eyes.

"You know you did," she answered honestly. "It was also something Kalyn said a few weeks ago about you."

"Share." His hands wandered down the front of her body, lingering on her breasts.

She shivered at the feel of his long fingers gliding over her body. He knew exactly where to pause and where not to.

"She said it was good to be friends first. Now I know what she was talking about. I should have been shy about baring my body to you, and in the beginning I was, but right now I'm not embarrassed in the least. So thank you for that."

"You always had it in you. It just took me to bring it out. See, you were worried for nothing." He studied her. "Seriously, the only person I'm concerned with is you. How do you feel about what we've done this evening? Do you regret it?"

"I feel fine about it. I don't regret anything I do with you. I've told you that. We've been friends for a long time. As you said before, we know each other better than some couples. Bray, I'm almost thirty-nine years old. I know when I want something."

Hazel eyes mocked her.

"Okay, sometimes I do need a little push. But if I didn't want this to happen I wouldn't have let you in my house."

"Yeah, right. You know I don't give up."

"Yeah, I know."

147

He pulled her closer to him. "How about a nice long shower and then we eat that wonderful dinner you made?"

She didn't want to leave the cocoon of the bed. It was so serene lying in bed cuddled up with him. It was the stuff romance novels were made of, and it seemed now she was a card-carrying romantic. "Why can't we stay here just a while longer?" She moved closer to him and rested her head on his chest. "This just feels so wonderful. I don't want it to end."

"Me neither, baby."

---

The next morning Kamryn woke early from a very good night's rest. They had never gotten up and eaten dinner last night. Maybe it was because they had been too busy having sex. She yawned, stretched, and gazed at Bray as he slept peacefully. Slipping from the bed, she took one last look at him. The sheet barely covered his body. He was some kind of fine. Quietly, she went into the bathroom and closed the door.

The hot water jetting from the tropical rain showerhead soothed her tired and achy muscles. Each way she turned under the hot water, her body complained at the action. But she hadn't felt this good and rested in years. So this is what Kalyn was always talking about, she mused.

She was definitely going to sleep the rest of the day, just as soon as Bray left her house. Then it hit her. His parents were going to know he hadn't come home the night before. She hoped his mom wasn't worried and didn't call the police thinking something had happened to Bray.

"Janice is going to kill me," she said to the steamy room.

"Why is my mother going to kill you?" Bray asked as he stepped inside the shower. He wrapped his arms around her and kissed her on the neck. "You feel good," he whispered against her ear.

Kamryn was amazed at two things. First the fact that she hadn't heard Bray enter the bathroom, and secondly, that she wasn't embarrassed being totally nude in front of him. It was as if they had been doing this for years instead of this being their first time underwater, so to speak. Bray looked very sexy with the shower raining down on him. It was hard to remember what she was thinking about. "You didn't go home last night. What must she think?"

He turned her so that she was facing him. "I'm a grown man, Kam. Besides, she knows I was having dinner with you. That's all she knows. Okay, well now she might have put two and two together and come up with sex." He guided her against the nearest wall and kissed her, slow and easy.

As Kamryn got lost in his kisses, she felt his hands roaming her body. When he headed south, she knew she was a goner. With a little encouragement she widened her stance and sighed as two fingers entered her. She had never done anything this wicked with Steve. Bray was introducing her to a whole new world, and she planned to enjoy every minute of it.

Slowly his fingers went back and forth, driving Kamryn out of her mind. His kisses kept tempo with his amazing fingers. She didn't know how much more she could take. Just one more thrust, she promised herself, then she'd make him stop. But her body wasn't having it. Each time Bray surged forward and pulled back, Kamryn couldn't wait for the next one. Bray lived up to his reputation with the ladies. After such an exhilarating night with him, she had another orgasm.

"Wow, Bray," she said, trying to catch her breath. "I've never done that before."

He smiled, releasing his hold on her. "I aim to please."

She leaned against the wall for support. "You aimed very well."

"Ready to test that theory in bed?" He turned off the water and opened the shower door.

Kamryn stood and watched him march to her linen closet and grab two of her prized bath sheets. He wrapped one around his waist and then handed one to her.

"You're kidding, right?" She wrapped the towel around her.

He looked down at his very noticeable erection. "No, I don't think so. Unless you're tired and can't handle any more." He winked at her.

"Don't you have practice?"

"Yes, I do, much, much, later this afternoon. Plenty of time for me to get my strength back. Are you covering the game on Saturday?"

She shrugged. "Most likely. Barney had the two sports writers handling the games in the semi-finals. They were moaning because I didn't have to cover any of them."

"They still making noises about you having the column?"

"Yes, but I don't want to talk about work right now. We have a much more pressing item to discuss." She took his hand and led him back to the bed and showed him exactly what she wanted and how many times.

---

After making love to Kam, Brayden couldn't sleep. He was too excited. He looked at her as she slept and smiled. She might have fought him all the way, but it was a good ride. Though they were friends, sex wasn't as awkward as he'd imagined it might have been. He hadn't imagined that it would have been so off the chart. In all his experiences with women, he'd never felt so many emotions rolling through his body as he had when he was making love to Kam. Boy, was he in trouble.

He knew he needed to leave, but he couldn't hasten the moment. He wanted to stay and make love with Kam all day. Unfortunately, that wasn't an option. He had responsibilities to the team and to his family. There was a basketball championship ring out there with his name on it. He sat up and took a deep breath. He grinned in satisfaction as he took in the scattered clothing on the floor. He spotted his boxers lying next to Kam's underwear. He rose from the bed, careful not to wake Kam, scooped up the boxers, and headed for the shower.

After he finished he slipped on his trousers and went downstairs to fix Kam a breakfast she wouldn't forget. French toast with scrambled eggs and bacon sounded good, he thought as he entered her kitchen.

Unlike most of the women he normally dated, Kam had a hearty appetite. He loved that about her. Why had he wasted all that time with the wrong women?

He started making coffee. Since he'd been at her house countless times, he knew where everything was. He located the package of hazelnut coffee. He wasn't a flavored coffee fan, but it was Kam's favorite. Maybe there was compromise in there somewhere.

He was combining eggs, milk, vanilla, and cinnamon for the French toast when he heard a faint knock at the back door. He glanced at the kitchen clock. It was barely eight in the morning. Who could it be at that hour? He hoped it wasn't Coach. That would be a sticky situation.

Curiosity got the best of him and opened the door. He grinned at Kam's little sister. "Hi, Kalyn, what are you doing here?"

She had on makeup and was dressed in a dark business suit. She reminded him of Kam without all the curves. Kalyn walked inside the house and closed the door. "I could ask you the same thing." She winked at him. "I thought I smelled food cooking." She glanced in the direction of the stove.

"You smelled coffee. I haven't started cooking yet."

"You cook?"

"Yes. I'm pretty good."

Kalyn walked to the table and took a seat. "Well, Kamryn never mentioned you could cook. I'm going to need a sample to see if you're as good as Kamryn."

He knew Kalyn often showed up at Kam's for meals at all hours, as if Kam operated a soup kitchen. That would definitely have to change now that he was in the picture. He shook his head. They had slept together only one night and now he was acting like a dictator, trying to run Kam's house as if it were his. What was going on in his head?

"So can I get some food or not?"

"How about I make you something to go?"

"Ah, the morning after," she said slyly. "I can take a hint. Tell Kamryn to call me." She rose and left as quickly as she had come.

He shook his head. He must be losing his mind. Here he was already making 'those' kinds of plans in his head with Kam. His cell phone buzzed in his pocket interrupting his thoughts. "Hello?"

"Brayden."

"Brian?" He had assumed that his friend had left town days ago.

"Yeah, man. Kamryn didn't tell you I rolled by her house yesterday?"

"No, must have slipped her mind." Not that he'd given her many opportunities for conversation. "You're still in Dallas?"

"Yeah, something came up. I need to talk to you. In person and alone."

Not even Brian could make him leave Kam right now. "I have practice this afternoon. Why don't we meet after that? I'll call and let you know when I'm done."

"Why not sooner? This is important," Brian persisted.

He noticed Kam standing in the doorway, dressed in a bathrobe with a smile on her face. Nothing that Brian had to talk about could compare to Kam. "Something important just came up. Later." He pressed the end button on his phone and put it back in his pocket. "Good morning." He walked to Kam and kissed her. "Last night and this morning are beyond description, baby."

"For me, too," she whispered. "What's for breakfast?" She glanced at the mixing bowl on the counter.

"French toast and my version of scrambled eggs and bacon. How's that sound?"

"Sounds great." Kamryn walked to the coffee maker and poured a cup of coffee. "Do you want the griddle or the skillet?"

"Already taken care of," he said over his shoulder. "I'm just letting the butter melt on the griddle."

Kamryn nodded and sat down at the table. "Feels strange that I'm not cooking. It's nice for a change."

"Sometimes it's good to let people wait on you, baby. You're always cooking for your sister, or me, for that matter. You need someone to cook for you."

She took a sip of her coffee. "You're telling me that person is you, right?"

"Right."

# CHAPTER 12

The minute she saw Bray's Escalade fade from view, Kamryn went back inside the house, heading straight for the spare bedroom. Her bedroom was a wreck. She'd never be able to fall asleep in all that chaos without changing the sheets and cleaning the room, and that was so not happening. The room had too many memories of the previous night and earlier that morning.

She walked into the spare bedroom, pulled back the covers, and slid between the sheets. Her last conscious sight was the bedside clock as it read ten-thirty.

"Kamryn, get up," a voice demanded.

She ignored the voice and turned over on her side. Even her stomach muscles were sore, she thought.

"Girl, you know I'm not leavin' without some details."

Kamryn didn't bother opening her eyes. She knew exactly who had invaded her house and her personal space. "Kalyn, shouldn't you be at work? I thought you had some big case to work on this morning," she mumbled, pulling the pillow over her head. "I thought that baseball player was in divorce court this morning." Kalyn's job as an image consultant often had her acting like a professional hand-holder to the über-rich.

"I've been to work. Idiot thought the judge would be lenient with him if he had written statements from all the charities he'd volunteered at. Like being caught with three strippers in a motel would just disappear from everyone's minds."

"What did the judge say?"

"That adultery was still wrong, no matter how many charities he'd volunteered at, gave money to, and helped with their fundraisers. It probably would have looked better if he'd done any of that before getting caught with those women."

"Like you told him months ago," Kamryn muttered.

"Exactly. And now I'm here wanting to know what happened last night. I thought I was being nice, letting you off the hook this morning."

Okay, that had her attention. Kamryn lifted the pillow and looked at her sister. "You must be crazy. You weren't in my house this morning, and I just laid down a few minutes ago."

Kalyn plopped down on the bed and hit Kamryn on the leg. "For your information, I came by this morning. I kept smelling food cooking when I was out walking Sapphire. She left a little something on your lawn, by the way. Brayden let me in and he was fixing your breakfast. Now I know you don't let everybody cook with your pricey cookware, so I'm assuming he can burn. He had the nerve to offer me some food to go. Clearly, he was ready for round two and trying to get rid of me. And if you look at your clock, you'll see that it's now six o'clock in the evening."

She did as her younger sister suggested and, sure enough, it was a little past six. Where had the entire day gone? Surely she hadn't slept for over eight hours. She struggled to sit up, wincing as she did so. She was getting too old for marathon sessions of sex.

"Wow, Bray must have really put it on you if you're that sore," Kalyn said in her wisdom.

"No, it's just been a while. I've been a widow over three years, you know."

"I'm surprised you still knew what you were doing."

"Why are you here?"

"You know why. I want details. Was he worth the wait? What is your status now? What time did he leave? Does this mean I get some free tickets now?"

"Slow down, Kalyn," Kamryn begged. "I don't have answers to any of those questions. We didn't get to talk because he had practice. The first game of the finals is Saturday."

"So? I don't see what one thing has to do with the other. He could have said something before he left, since he was doing the morning after breakfast thing."

"Well, we didn't get to talk." Kamryn's head was spinning, partly due to Kalyn and her onslaught of questions, mostly because she hadn't eaten since breakfast. Was Bray still at practice? What was she supposed to do now?

"Did you hear anything I just said?"

"No, Kalyn. Sorry. What did you say?"

Kalyn stood and placed her hands on her slender hips. "I told you in honor of you finally getting some I would treat you to a steak dinner. You probably need the protein anyway. Bray looks like he could make you see stars and the moon."

"And then some." Kamryn got out of bed, realizing she was still in her nightshirt.

"This is too much. It's almost bedtime again, and you're in your nightshirt. I'm so telling Mom."

"Shut up." She walked across the hall to her bedroom, knowing Kalyn would follow her. She hoped Kalyn didn't freak out when she saw the mess in the room.

"Oh, my God! Looks like somebody really got their groove on up in here. I've never seen this place in such disarray. Wow, you guys must have been throwing clothes off the minute you got upstairs."

"I'm not going to dignify that with a reply." Kamryn walked into her closet and grabbed some jeans and a blouse. "I'll be dressed in a few minutes."

Kalyn shook her head. "I need some details."

"Over dinner," promised Kamryn. "I'll be able to recall more if I have food in my stomach."

———

"Brayden, are you all right?" Tyler asked, hovering over him on the basketball court.

"Yes, just tired." He was lying on the court staring at the ceiling. Practice had been over for at least an hour and most of the other players had gone home already. "Didn't get much sleep last night, and Coach didn't let up today. I'm spent."

Tyler sat beside him and let out a moan. "Yeah, you got that right. I'm exhausted myself. I'm going home and sleep until practice in the morning. I guess he really wants us to be ready. You know he considers us a challenge, since we've never come this far before."

"Yeah, I know. I would like to have a championship ring before I retire, too."

"You're thinking about hanging up your tennis shoes?"

Brayden had been tossing the idea around in his head since his meeting with his accountant. Basketball was such a physical sport. It took more and more each season to stay in shape. "Yeah, I have. We're running up and down the court for forty-eight minutes, and we don't have any protection. We've been lucky, Ty, no real injuries. I don't want to press my luck."

Tyler nodded. "Yeah, I've been thinking about it, too. I like Dallas, but what on earth would I do?"

Brayden and Tyler had been friends a long time. So they had few secrets between them. Tyler was a closet artist. "You could paint."

Tyler shot him a look. "Man, how would it look?"

"Sometimes you have to say damn the consequences. We've given ten years to a grueling sport. We deserve to do something relaxing in our free time."

"So you're going to cook and I'm going to paint?"

"I've really been thinking about it. My brother's an attorney, and he's been checking out properties for me here in Dallas. I mean, I want to make sure my parents are set and everything, but I'm seriously thinking about retiring."

Tyler laughed. "Wouldn't have anything to do with Kamryn, would it?"

"Possibly." Brayden couldn't hide that stupid grin on his face.

"I know that look," Tyler teased. "I've just never seen it on your face."

He sat up. "What look?"

"The 'I'm hanging up my playa shoes' look." Tyler stood and extended his hand to help Brayden up. "It's great to see the good ones fall."

---

"What do you mean you want to look at Jason's wrecked car?" Kamryn looked down at the succulent rib-eye steak on her plate. Kalyn had had hare-brained ideas before, but this one was too much, even for her carefree spirit.

"Because all the events on the day he died just don't make sense. I mean, it would probably be better for his widow if it was an accident, since that would double the insurance policy. But something isn't adding up."

"He was gambling," Kamryn reminded her sister. "Maybe he was in over his head and couldn't pay."

"Come on, Kamryn. You know how those kind of people roll. They would have roughed him up a little, but not killed him. How would they ever expect to get paid? They would need him alive."

"I thought about that. Sandra said something had been troubling Jason, but he wouldn't tell her about it. She was also getting ready to divorce him."

"Why?"

Kamryn had always thought Jason and Sandra looked happy when they were out. Perhaps it had just been an act. "I would assume his gambling problems."

"So can we go check out his car?"

"What exactly are you looking for?"

Kalyn cut into her steak. "Who knows? On those crime shows when it's something like this, it's usually the simplest explanation."

"True. Remember Bray's friend who came in last week?"

"The one that made your skin crawl?"

"He's still here. Worse, he showed up at my house yesterday."

"What? How did he know your address?"

"I didn't get a chance to tell Bray last night. I've got a feeling that Bray doesn't know he's still here. He's hiding something. I don't know what, but I have a feeling it involves Bray."

"You know, guys aren't like us. They don't really talk like we do. They have man codes and stuff. Maybe he's staying at Bray's condo downtown and driving his car."

"No, his parents are driving his BMW while they're here and he's driving the Escalade. Brian was in an old, beat-up car when he came to the house."

"Your dull life is anything but that now, isn't it?" Kalyn took a bite of steak. "This place always has the best food."

"It's delicious. We should bring Mom and Dad here for their next anniversary. Dad would love it, and no one would have to clean up."

Trust Kalyn to find a loophole, Kamryn mused. "Back to this mess. What do you want to do first?"

Kamryn wanted the Jason issue out of her life as soon as possible. "Let's look at the car in the morning. Maybe we should bring Dad, since neither of us knows much about cars. He'd be able to spot something quicker."

"Great idea."

---

Brayden waited for Brian at The Hoop for an hour, but he never showed. After drinking his third vodka and cranberry, minus the vodka, he decided to head to Kam's. They hadn't talked about the events of the night before. He had to know everything was fine between them before going home to bed.

He laughed as he got in his SUV. There once was a time when he would have been thinking about which honey he was going to take back to his condo for a night of sex, but those days were gone. Was he losing his mind? Was he really ready to settle for one woman?

Twenty minutes later he parked in front of Kam's house. Her living room light was on. He hoped she was up working. He took a deep breath and rang her doorbell. A few minutes later, she opened the door and smiled at him. It made every problem he'd had that day fade away. She was dressed in lounging clothes, and her hair was up in a ponytail. The very casual appearance made her look ten years younger.

"Hi, Bray," she said, inviting him inside.

He kissed her as he closed the door. "Hey, Kam."

She grabbed his hand and led him into the living room. They sat on the couch. Now came the awkward part. Bray studied her; she looked refreshed and rested. "I wanted to talk to you about last night."

"Why?" Kamryn gazed at him in confusion. "Isn't that my line?"

"We didn't really talk about it since I had to leave this morning for practice. I wanted to know how you feel about what we did."

"I don't think I'm following you, Bray." She eased onto his lap. "If you think I'm regretting it, I don't. I'm not going to run to the media and claim you defiled me. I didn't think I'd see you because of the practice schedule."

"So we're good?"

"Why don't you be the judge?" She kissed him slowly, teasing his lips apart and engulfing his mouth with hers. "Any questions?" she whispered against his lips.

"No, not a one," he said, kissing her in return. "I could stay like this all night."

"You have practice tomorrow," she reminded him as the kisses continued.

Bray sighed. "Yeah."

Slowly she ended the kiss and slid off his lap. "You need to save your strength."

He knew she was right, but darn it, he wanted to explore more of those kisses. "So let's talk."

She rolled her eyes toward the ceiling. "Bray, everything is fine. I'm not going to cry when this is over. I'm a big girl. I know what I'm doing."

"Why do you think it's going to end?"

"Bray, we're two different people. You're used to a bevy of women, and I don't share. The novelty of this is going to wear off, and I know that."

"You think I'm playing you?" Bray stood abruptly and started to pace the room. "You know I couldn't do that to you, Kam. There's too many good years between us for me to play you. Why don't you think I can be happy with one woman?"

"I'm just being realistic. I know you won't intentionally hurt me, but I've known you five years. You've never dated one woman at a time. I've seen you juggle five women at once, and we won't even talk about last summer. Settling down to one might be too much of an adjustment for you. You might feel stifled in a monogamous relationship. I just don't want our friendship to be the victim of this."

She sounded so practical when she stated her case. And yeah, most of it was true. "Kam, it's not like that."

"Tell me what it's like then."

"I don't know," he said simply.

"Exactly. We don't know what the future holds for either of us. So we'll take it one day at a time."

It sounded so simple. Why did it feel as if she didn't have faith in them as a couple? "Okay, one day at a time."

She sighed.

"What is it?" Bray sat by her and took her hand. "What can I do to help?"

"First, your friend Brian came by here yesterday. Did you give him my address?"

"No. He called me earlier wanting to meet after practice, then he stood me up. That's why I was late getting here. What did he say?"

"Not much. He was looking for you. He was in an old, beat-up car."

Okay, that was weird, but the look on Kam's face told him something worse was coming. "What else?"

"Kalyn, Dad and I are going to look at Jason's car in the morning. I did some checking and I found out which wrecking yard has it."

"Why?"

"Kalyn has a bug up her butt about the incident. Since Dad is going with us, you don't have to worry."

"Well, I am worried. About all you guys. If I didn't have practice, I would come with you, just to see the look of disappointment on your pretty face when you don't find anything incriminating the Mafia."

"I don't think we'll find anything, either, but if I can eliminate something, it will get me closer to ending this mess."

"I'll be happy when it's over, too."

"I didn't know you were overly concerned about Jason."

He pulled her in his arms. "I'm not. I'm overly concerned about you. Now kiss me so I can go home and get some rest."

# CHAPTER 13

The next morning Bray walked into the American Airlines Center expecting to see the rest of his teammates, coaches, and trainers out on the floor. Instead, he saw Kelly Patterson. She was dressed in tight jeans and a tighter blouse that left nothing to his imagination. She wore too much makeup and her hair was perfect.

She walked toward him with an exaggerated swagger in some high-heeled shoes that made his hips hurt. He shook his head as one of the trainers took his bag from his hands.

"Coach is in his office. He wants to talk to you before practice." The young man walked away.

"Brayden, you haven't returned any of my calls," she whined in that voice he'd once thought sexy. Now it sounded like nails on a chalkboard. "You weren't at the club last night, either. I saw some of the other guys from the team there. Where were you? I've even been by the condo, but you're never there."

"Hey, Kelly. I don't have much time. I haven't called you in a few months. Why are you showing up now?" He knew, but didn't really care. Kelly made her way around the professional athlete circuit, and it looked like she was back at the top of the list. The reason she hadn't been in touch with him was because

CELYA BOWERS

she'd been dating a football player. The affair must have fizzled, and now she was back.

"I wanted you to call me. I wanted you to miss me."

He knew that was a lie. "I guess you'll be waiting a long time for that call."

"You don't think I look good?"

He looked her up and down. Kelly couldn't look bad if she tried. "I didn't say that. You always look good. But I'm not interested in you anymore."

She actually looked surprised. "Men would kill to be in your position."

"I don't doubt it for one minute," Bray said honestly. "I found someone else and am no longer on the market. So go find another playmate."

She stood with her hands on her narrow hips, tapping her stiletto-clad feet. "You can't do this to me!"

"Look, Kelly, I have practice now. Either leave or I'll call security."

She thought about her options and headed for the exit. "You haven't seen the last of me, Brayden Allen."

Brayden ignored her threat and walked into the dressing room. Man, what was he thinking getting involved with her? He knew exactly what he was thinking with, and it had landed him in an empty affair with an empty-headed woman who treated their dates like a business transaction.

"Allen, glad you could join us!" Coach called as he entered the dressing room. The rest of his teammates were seated. "Now that Cinderella is here, we can do this."

167

He hated being on the receiving end of Coach's comments. But Greg DeMorris won championships, and that was the name of the game. "Sorry, Coach."

Coach waved off his remark and pointed to the vacant seat. "Sit by your girlfriend."

Brayden stiffened at the remark. Everyone knew Tyler wasn't gay, and neither was he. It was one of those remarks an outsider could take the wrong way. After he finally took a seat next to Tyler, Coach started.

"Okay, ladies, our first game is in two days. Practice yesterday was horrible. It was like watching my nephews play ball, and they're in elementary school. We've got to pick it up if we want to win. I need you focused and ready to play some basketball Saturday night. So whatever problems you have going on at home, with wives, girlfriends, or new friends, you need to keep that on lock for the next ten days. Got it?"

"Yes, Coach," everyone said in unison, military style.

"Allen, see me before you head to the floor. Everyone else, out in ten." Coach left the room without another word.

Brayden knocked on the closed door a minute later. "Come in."

Coach was seated behind his massive mahogany desk and working at his computer. Brayden took a seat and let out a tired breath. "You wanted to talk to me."

Coach turned away from his computer and focused all his attention on Brayden. That was never a good sign. "Allen, I know how things are with women and professional athletes. All they see is the money you make, not how much time you've put into honing your craft."

Brayden nodded. He knew exactly where this little chat was going. Kelly. "Thank you, Coach, but I'm not seeing her."

"Doesn't matter. Women like that are nothing but trouble. She's looking for a meal ticket, and I'm not having that in my house. Like I told you guys when I first came to Dallas last year, I'm bringing back the image of a real professional athlete. We should carry ourselves like professionals at all times, not just when we think the camera is watching. I'm so sick of athletes getting caught doing stupid things because the larger brain isn't doing their thinking. You have a lot going for you, Allen. You can take the world by the tail. Hell, you could end up with my job."

Brayden doubted that. Coach was the man with the Midas touch, turning just about every team he'd work with into champions. "Thank you, Coach. I've taken care of the situation."

Coach nodded. "I told security she is not allowed on the premises while there is practice going on. She was here when I got here this morning. Tried to tell me some bull about being pregnant by you and you avoiding her. I know that's not how you roll. I know you would take care of your responsibilities."

Bray saw the handwriting on the wall. Coach had let Kelly stay until he got there. That was why no one was out on the court when he arrived. "If she's pregnant, it's not mine." He'd had sex with Kelly one time four months ago and he'd used a condom.

"That's what I want to hear. I know you guys think I'm overreacting, but I've seen too many careers end over something just like this. We're on our way to Dallas' first national championship, and I will not let anything or anyone stand in our way. You're an excellent guard, but if this girl is going to be a problem, I'll sit you out so fast your head will spin."

Again, Brayden didn't doubt the man's words. Coach was all business. "As I said, I have remedied the situation."

"See that you have." Coach turned back to his computer, dismissing Brayden.

Brayden walked into the dressing room. His teammates were already out on the floor warming up for the hellacious practice that was to be. He quickly changed into his practice uniform and joined his team.

⊶⊷

Kamryn yawned as she parked at Sinclair Wrecking Yard. She glanced at her companions. Kalyn was seated in the passenger seat. Her parents were in the backseat.

She gave Kalyn a narrowed glance. "See what you started?"

"The more the merrier," said Kalyn. She opened the door and slid out of the vehicle.

Kamryn sighed. This was supposed to be simple. They had been planning to check out Jason's car on the DL. All that was gone by the wayside when her mother decided to tag along. Her dad served a purpose, he knew about cars. What did her mother know about?

She slid out of the SUV, grabbed her digital camera, and led her entourage to the office. With a little sweet talk from Kalyn, they were directed to the area where Jason's car rested.

Her mother walked beside her, glancing at all the wrecked cars. "That one is a pretty shade of blue."

"Mom, this is not a shopping expedition. We're looking for Jason's car. It's a black Range Rover, not a metallic blue Mercedes."

Her mother shrugged. "I'm going to get a new car and haven't been able to decide on a color. Now I think I'll get that pretty shade of blue."

"That's good, Mom."

Her mother looked behind her. "Is that it?" She nodded at a damaged SUV.

Kamryn smiled at her mother. "I'll have to check the license plate number." She pulled the sheet out of her purse and scanned the paper. "No, darn it. His plates were personalized. J-Ball."

Her mother laughed. "Couldn't he be a little more creative?"

"I know," Kamryn agreed. "It made him stick out like a sore thumb." What had that idiot been thinking? She continued walking and there it was, sitting there all alone, away from the other wrecked vehicles.

Her reporter's senses were on high alert. "Dad, can you look around the SUV to see if anything looks odd? The official police report stated that Jason hit the concrete pillar head-on at a high rate of speed."

Her father nodded, taking in the information but saying nothing. He walked around the car, not touching it, but inspecting it. "What was his cause of death?"

"Officially, the police have ruled it as a suicide because the witnesses stated he didn't try to stop. There were no noises of screeching brakes. Most likely the impact of the crash killed him," Kamryn said, wondering what her retired accountant father was leading up to.

He opened the driver's door, then closed it and walked to Kamryn. "They're judging the accident on the fact that he didn't try to stop? Talk about hurrying to put a case to bed. I know the police department is understaffed, but this is ridiculous! I'm writing the mayor!"

"Dad, calm down," Kamryn said, patting her father on the shoulder. "They also found a note he'd been writing to Sandra."

"So there was a note."

"Not really. It was the beginning of a letter to Sandra, but he didn't sign it and the words were vague, not your usual suicide note."

Her father smacked his lips together. "You mean, 'I can't go on anymore'?"

"Yeah, it was like 'sorry it has come to this.' "

Kamryn opened the door and peered inside. "If I was going to end my life and was leaving a note, it would say more than that."

"That's because you're a journalist, baby. You're into the details, because that's your job. Maybe he was just scribbling something."

"I don't think so, Dad. I mean, anything is possible, but it's just not logical to me."

"You said yourself," her father said, "that he had been gambling. Sometimes drastic problems call for drastic measures."

"No, that wasn't the Jason I knew. No matter how much trouble he was in, he wouldn't leave his girls."

"Sounds like a good mystery."

Kamryn nodded. "You got that right, Dad. I just hope I can find all the answers I need."

He let out a tired breath. "I know you will, baby girl. If there's a story in this, you'll find it. Let's pop the hood." Her father went to the front of the SUV and, after a serious struggle with the twisted metal, managed to open the hood.

They all gasped. The engine had taken the brunt of the impact. The engine block was maybe six inches wide now. Kamryn could imagine Jason's last moments before his life ended. "What an awful way to go."

"True," her father said, putting his arm around her. "I hope it was quick. From the looks of this, I don't think he knew what was happening until it was too late, since no one heard his brakes or a horn."

"A horn?"

"Yes. I was thinking if I was in a car and had lost control of it for whatever reason I would blow my horn to warn people. He didn't."

Kamryn thought. "You're right, Dad. No one mentioned a horn or any kind of warning." She sniffed the air. "You smell burnt rubber?"

Her dad inhaled. "Yes, I do. Smells like it's coming from this SUV. Get back," her father barked at her. "Everybody get back!" He pulled Kamryn away from the SUV. They joined Kalyn and their mother behind a row of wrecked Hondas.

A few minutes went by and nothing happened. Kamryn wondered if some animal had died in Jason's vehicle since it had been at the wrecking yard. She was on her feet and headed toward the SUV.

"Kamryn, come back," her father called.

She had a bad feeling in the pit of her stomach, so she decided to take her father's warning. She turned to head back to safety, but she heard a loud thud and someone turned off the sun.

Harding watched in horror as his daughter was thrown nearly twenty feet. He raced to Kamryn as she lay limp against an old Toyota.

"Baby girl, can you hear me?" He patted the side of her face. "Come on, baby."

Kamryn moaned and swatted at his hand. "Daddy!" Slowly she opened her eyes and stared at him. "What was that?"

"Somebody booby-trapped the SUV." He slowly and carefully checked for broken bones and gave a silent prayer to the man upstairs that she didn't have any."

She took a deep breath. "It was her."

"It was somebody." He looked Kamryn over and looked for any signs of trauma. "How do you feel?" The rest of the family joined them.

"I have such a headache," Kamryn said, rubbing her head. She attempted to stand, but it took a family effort to get her upright.

"It's okay, baby. We're going to take you to the hospital."

"Dad, I just hit my head."

"I know, honey. You'll feel better soon. I promise."

"But Dad, I just need to lie down."

"Trust your daddy."

"I always do." She closed her eyes and slumped over in her father's arms.

---

Brayden finished his shower. It had been the most grueling practice in his professional career. Yeah, the first game was two days away, but Coach had run them as if they had already lost. He just wanted to eat and go to bed. The good thing about having his parents visiting during the playoffs was that he didn't have to cook unless he actually wanted to. And his mama could burn when she had a mind to do so.

He slipped on a T-shirt, shorts, and sandals. He dialed his house to see what his mother had cooked, but instead he got his answering machine. His parents didn't go many places without him or Kam with them. His mother claimed Dallas had too many different roads and she was always afraid she wouldn't be able to find her way back to his house.

He tried his mother's cell phone, ready to read her the riot act about leaving the house without telling him, but he got a surprise when she answered. "You're where?"

"At the hospital," she said.

He thought his heart was going to pop out of his chest. "What's wrong? Which hospital? What happened?" And he only thought he was having a run a bad luck lately. "I told you you were eating too much rich food lately."

"Brayden, calm down. We're at Mills Park Hospital."

"The poison control hospital! What on earth did you take? I told you to quit trying to read your medicine bottles without your glasses!"

"If you don't stop screaming at me, I'm hanging up this phone," his mother threatened. "I'm still your mother and don't you forget it, Brayden Allen."

He took a deep breath. *Calm down*, he told himself. It couldn't be that bad if she was talking to him on the phone. Another deep breath. "Okay, sorry. I didn't mean any disrespect, Mom. You just scared the crap out of me. What happened? Is it Dad?" He didn't think he could bear it if anything happened to his parents.

"It's not us. It's Kamryn."

⁓

Thirty minutes later Brayden arrived at the hospital. He couldn't remember how he got there. The last thing he remembered was getting directions from his navigational system. As he entered the building he hoped he wasn't recognized. The last thing Kam would want was publicity about this. Luckily his mother had given him the room number and no other information, so he wouldn't have to stop at the front desk and alert more personnel that he was there. Mills Park was a small hospital located in north Dallas. It had exactly four floors. Kam was in room 450, which meant she was in the critical care unit. This was so not going well. What could have happened to Kam? If she was in critical care, there was a major problem. He really didn't need this right before the biggest week of his life.

Once the elevator opened on the critical care ward, Bray took a deep breath and walked to the nurse's desk. The young woman looked up from her computer screen and gasped. "Oh, my God!"

"Hello," Brayden said, trying to defuse the situation before it got any worse. "Kamryn Hillcroft." Although he knew the room number, he still had to be escorted to the room.

"Oh, my goodness. It's you!"

Brayden waited a beat before asking for Kam's room again. He didn't want to appear rude, but the situation was getting the best of him. He leaned closer to the woman. "Look, I'll sign anything you want, but right now I need to see my friend."

Apparently, his quiet tone filtered through the young woman's brain. "Oh, yes, certainly, Mr. Allen." She paged someone over the intercom system. "Javier will be here in just a moment."

"Thank you. I'll stop by the desk before I leave and sign anything you want."

"I'll take you up on that, Mr. Allen."

Soon a young man appeared. He recognized Brayden instantly, but was not as vocal as the nurse. Brayden followed the orderly down the hallway. A few of the doors were open and he glanced inside looking for his parents, her parents, anybody that looked familiar.

He was about to ask the young man if he was in the right place when he saw Kamryn lying in the hospital bed with an oxygen mask strapped to her face. He pushed the door open further and gasped at the full sight of her looking so helpless in the bed. "Baby!" At that moment he didn't care about the upcoming game. Nothing mattered but Kamryn. He rushed to her bedside and hugged her.

She pulled the mask down so she could talk. "It's okay, Bray." She wiped away his tears. "I'm fine now. They want to keep me overnight because I hit my head and was having headaches."

He wanted to ask her more questions but didn't think she could answer him correctly. "Oh, baby." He kissed her forehead. "I'll stay with you."

She shook her head. "No, Kalyn will stay. You have a game in Canada."

"Screw the game." Had he really said that aloud?

"Not on my watch," she said. "You've waited a long time for this. You have to go. You can't let the team down." She took a deep breath and replaced the mask, effectively closing the discussion.

He watched for a few heartbeats. His entire future was lying in a hospital bed and looking at him with glazed brown eyes. He wanted answers and wanted them now. He turned his glare to five very quiet faces. "Now who's going to tell me what happened?"

Harding cleared his throat. "I guess that should be me." He walked toward Brayden. "Why don't we talk down the hall?"

Brayden took one last look at Kam before he stomped out of the room. Harding followed and guided him to the nearby lounge. After the men took their seats, Harding began.

"We went to the wrecking yard."

"Yeah, I know about that," Bray said. "What happened between you guys getting to the wrecking yard and ending up here?"

Harding looked at him with serious brown eyes. "Brayden, I know you're upset Kamryn got hurt, and I'll tell you what I think happened, but I'm going to need for you to stay calm."

"I'm trying, Harding. That's the best I can do right now."

Harding shifted in his seat and leaned closer to Bray. "I think someone knew we were coming and booby-trapped the SUV. She's getting close to the truth and is making someone very nervous."

"Did anyone call the police?"

"And tell them what?"

"That Jason's SUV was rigged with a booby trap," Brayden said through gritted teeth.

"And how do we explain our involvement in a case they have already deemed open and shut?"

Okay, he had him there. Besides, there wasn't much the cops could do at this point anyway. The main thing was that Kam was okay and no one else was hurt. "You're right, Harding. It would just open another can of worms and bring more publicity."

"And alert the criminals and we might never find out who is behind all this mess. Now I got a question for you."

"Shoot."

"I know my baby girl is going to want to solve this, especially since it started out as a favor. Are you ready to see this through to the end?"

"I'm ready for this to be over, so we can move on with our lives."

Harding smiled at him. "Well, that wasn't the answer I was looking for, but I like it."

"What kind of injuries does Kam have?"

"She's lucky in that respect. The explosion threw her about twenty feet, but she landed on a car and got the wind knocked out of her mostly. No broken bones, a few bruises, and one hellacious headache. Doc said it could last a few days."

Brayden nodded, listening but not hearing Harding. This little favor of Sandra's was getting stranger by the second. But he promised Kam he'd see it through to the end, and that was what he intended to do.

---

Later that evening, after everyone but Kalyn had gone home, Kamryn let her guard down and cried. Her sister was at her side immediately.

"Kamryn, what is it? Are you hurting?"

She took the mask off again. "No, it all just hit me. We could have died out there today. Just think if Daddy hadn't been there with us."

"I know. But he was there, looking out for us, as usual."

"You got that right. Just think if he hadn't been there when I got hurt. It smelled bad, but I just thought it was because he died in the SUV."

"Kamryn, you can't think about that. I wish we could have found some conclusive evidence that proved it wasn't suicide."

"Poor Jason," Kamryn said. "I wanted to find something so bad, not for Sandra's sake, but for Jason's." She looked at her sister. "You're sure you don't mind staying with me tonight?"

"You don't have to ask me that. You're my sister and I'd do anything for you. Besides, who would cook for me? I'm sure about driving you to your meeting tomorrow, too. You shouldn't be driving until your strength is back. Are you going to tell your boss?"

"No. It'll just give those guys more ammo against me. As long as I can turn my columns in on time, I'm good. I do wonder how many games I'll have to cover for the finals." She took a deep breath.

Kalyn grunted her opinion of that. "You shouldn't have to cover any of the games. You're not a sports reporter anymore, you're a columnist. Just because two good ole boys are mad 'cause you got the columnist job over them, they're whining like babies. Your editor should grow a pair. Then you wouldn't have to deal with those idiots."

Kamryn laughed, which made her cough like there was no tomorrow. The coughing attack brought in the night nurse. Kamryn struggled to sit up, hoping it would ease her pain.

"Ms. Hillcroft, is everything all right?" The nurse checked the computer readouts. "Now you put that mask back on and take a deep breath."

Kamryn did as she was told and slowly her breathing eased. She lay back on the bed, exhausted from the ordeal. "Thank you," she said through the mask.

"You're welcome. Keep that mask on if you want to go home tomorrow. We'll test your breathing capacity in the morning." The nurse gave Kalyn a stern look. "Make sure that mask stays on her face."

"Yes, ma'am," Kalyn said.

The nurse gave Kalyn a sharp look and left the room without another word.

Once the door closed, Kamryn took the mask off her face and told her sister, "I guess she told you." She put the mask back in place and soon went to sleep.

# CHAPTER 14

The next morning Kamryn passed her breathing test and was cleared to go home. While Kalyn had taken some of the flowers down to the car, Kamryn used this free time to call Bray. The team was due to fly to Canada that morning. She hoped she could catch him before take-off.

She was in luck. They were just taking their seats, so he had a few minutes to talk. "Are you sure you're okay?"

She smiled at the concern in his voice. "Yes, Bray," she reassured him. "I'm getting released as we speak. Kalyn is going to spend the weekend with me, so I won't be alone. We're going to watch you guys beat Toronto."

"That's my girl. Call Mom. She's been worried sick. And please promise me no more trips to the wrecking yard."

"That's a promise I can keep."

"Good. See you when I get back."

Later that afternoon Kalyn dropped Kamryn off in front of the *Dallas Morning News* building in downtown Dallas and motored off to the nearest mall. Kamryn walked into her weekly staff meeting at the paper. The sports division normally had monthly meetings, but with Dallas in the finals everything had changed.

Since the playoffs had begun, their department met weekly.

Her editor smiled as she took a seat. "Hello, Kamryn. Good job on that article last week. It was one of the highest ranking articles in *Morning News* history."

"Thank you, Barney. I enjoyed my fifteen seconds of fame," she said sarcastically. "My original story was cut and some of the players' quotes were left out, but the online version ran it in its entirety."

"Yes, uh, we had to cut two inches," Barney said, obviously covering his fat behind. "We had a lot of news that had to get out in that issue. I sent you an email about it."

"After the fact," Kamryn said.

"My apologies, clearly an oversight on the editorial side," Barney mumbled. He cleared his throat. "Okay, guys and lady," he said, nodding at Kamryn. "Since no one saw Dallas getting into the finals, we're going to revamp the schedule and how the games are reported."

Kamryn coughed.

"Except Kamryn. She's been saying since last summer that Dallas would take it all. And it looks like they possibly could this year. The odds, though, lean heavily toward Toronto even with Allen having one of his best seasons ever."

"So, Kamryn," Bill Whitmire, senior sports writer, drawled, "who's the lucky girl ringing his chimes?"

"I'm just his friend, I don't keep up with his chime-ringing schedule," she shot back at her co-worker.

"Besides, if I knew and I told you, you'd get the name wrong anyway."

That got a few chuckles in the conference room. Bill was notorious for misspelling names of athletes and also misquoting them. Most of the athletes wouldn't even let Bill interview them. Kamryn wondered how he kept his job with all the errors he'd made over the years. If she had so much as a misspelled word, Barney was ready to call out the grammar police.

"Okay, everyone, calm down," Barney said, trying to remain in control of the meeting. "I have the schedule for the playoff games. Normally, I let the two sportswriters cover the entire series. Since this is the first time in history for Dallas to get this far, I'm assigning things a little differently. I think it's fitting, Kamryn, that some of the coverage makes it into your column."

Kamryn willed herself not to get upset if she couldn't cover the home games since she was a columnist. But it would be nice to be there when the Mavericks took it all.

"As we all know, the opening game is in Toronto. Second and third games are here in Dallas. The fourth and fifth games are in Toronto. Game six is in Dallas and, if necessary, seven will be here as well. Bill, you've got games four and five, Kamryn will handle the Dallas games, Stewart Maxwell will handle the first game. Any questions?"

Bill cleared his throat, looking directly at Kamryn as he spoke up. "Why does Kamryn have the luxury of covering the Dallas games? Since she writes that column, she never has to go out of town. She's not married, so why doesn't she have to go on the road?"

"Because she just wrote a good, tight story with correct names and no misspelled words. Any more questions?"

No one said a word.

"Good. The meeting is over." Barney walked out without another word.

Kamryn watched as the men quickly filed out of the room. She let out a sigh of relief. The meeting had gone a lot smoother than she could have imagined. And for Barney to actually take her side was truly amazing. She collected her oversized bag and left the room to check her office.

Since she did most of her work from home, she didn't have a large corner office, just a tiny cubicle. The good thing was there were no new messages stuck to the edges of her desktop computer. Her office phone rang just as she sat down at her desk. She answered it as she recognized the caller.

"I heard you were in the office today," Rachel Harris said. Rachel was the editor of the society section.

"Yeah, had a meeting about the NBA finals. The usual."

"Is Bill giving you grief?"

It was no secret around the *Dallas Morning News* office that Bill felt he should have her job. "Of course, but Barney put him in his place today."

"Oh, my God, tell me all about it. Come see me before you leave the office."

"On my way." Kamryn hung up the phone and grabbed her bag, heading for Rachel's office.

As she walked to the large corner office, she smiled. She had known Rachel most of her adult life. Not only had they both attended the University of Dallas, Rachel was also her former sister-in-law.

Rachel greeted her as she rounded the corner. Rachel was pencil thin and stood about five feet, ten inches in her bare feet, but she still loved stilettos. The higher the better. Today Rachel was decked out in a blue suit that clung to her body, and her shoes had to add at least four inches.

"Hey, Kamryn, long time no see." She hugged her. "How have you been?" She guided Kamryn inside her office.

"Pretty good. These games are keeping me hopping, though."

"Don't tell me they're trying to make you cover the games, too?"

"Yeah, I'm covering the Dallas games."

Rachel shook her head. "That damn Bill. He should learn to spell if he wants more responsibility."

"You sound just like Barney." Kamryn took a deep breath and coughed.

"Are you okay?"

"Yeah, just the last few days are kind of getting to me. I was doing a favor for Sandra Woken and it's morphed into a hot mess."

Rachel leaned back in her leather chair. "Oh, do tell."

Kamryn wanted to tell someone outside of her family and Bray, just to see if her suspicions were grounded. She trusted Rachel and valued her opinion. She told her friend what had been going on in the process of doing this little favor. "I just got released from the hospital this morning."

"Wow! I agree with you, Kamryn, something else bigger has to be going on. You think Brayden's near accidents and the attack on him are connected?"

"How do you know about them?"

"Honey, I'm married to a detective inspector of the Dallas Police Department. Every time someone sneezes at the American Airline Center, he knows about it. Although Brayden's attack was not reported, he still heard about it. I'm glad he wasn't hurt."

"Me, too. I don't know if they're connected, but it feels like it. But you know how laid-back Bray is. He thinks it's nothing."

Rachel nodded. "But we both know differently."

"Yes, we do." Kamryn didn't want to talk about Bray anymore. It might lead to her telling her dead husband's sister about the change in her relationship with Bray.

"Kamryn, I don't expect you to mourn Steve for the rest of your days. I've seen the way that Brayden looks at you."

Did everyone know but her? "What?"

"I was at your parents' anniversary party. I saw how that man was watching your every move. I figured he was just biding his time until you were ready to date. I'm glad you stopped wearing your wedding rings.

Don't get me wrong, I loved my brother, but he's gone and he wouldn't want you mourning him this long. I'm glad you're getting out and living."

"I didn't realize I was being such a hermit. Bray and my family told me it was time to get back out there. I don't know, Rachel, I've got some conflicting feelings."

"It's understandable, Kamryn. But you will get over it, I promise."

<hr />

Kamryn thought she was going to watch the first game of the finals alone. Figuring she needed to recuperate from her ordeal days earlier, both Keegan and Kalyn had said they would not join her. She'd just settled on the couch when she heard her doorbell ring. She was surprised to see her parents holding bags of food. Too many bags of food for just the three of them, she thought. "Mom, Dad, what are you guys doing here?"

Her mother walked inside and kissed Kamryn on the cheek. "You look good, baby. I'm glad to see you resting. We couldn't let you watch the game alone. Kalyn and Keegan will be along shortly. Oh, and I invited Janice and James, too. It should be fun, right?"

Kamryn sighed. There went her dream of a quiet evening watching basketball. Her house would soon be overrun with people. "Sounds great, Mom. I'll go get the plates."

Her mother was not to be outdone. "Oh, no you don't. Brayden is not going to chew us out for letting something happen to you. I'll get the dishes and everything else. You just relax on the couch."

Kamryn followed her mother's advice and took her position on the couch. Her dad sat on the loveseat studying her. She still couldn't believe they all could have been killed just a few days before.

"How are you feeling, baby girl?"

"I feel better, Dad. It still hurts a little when I take a deep breath."

"In a few days, you'll be as good as new. Did your boss give you any trouble?"

She shook her head. "I didn't tell him, because I didn't want Bill claiming I couldn't do my job. Barney assigned the games for the finals. I cover the Dallas games."

Everyone in her family knew about the power struggle within the newspaper office for her job. Her father offered his advice on the subject. "I don't know how that Bill idiot can fix his thin lips to say anything about you or your column. I can't begin to count how many times he's misspelled the athletes' names in his stories."

Kamryn nodded. "Barney actually took my side in the meeting yesterday and put Bill in his place."

"About damn time."

"Daddy!"

Harding laughed. "You know it's true. Has Brayden called since he left?"

"No, he hasn't. I figured Greg was going to work them within an inch of their life. I sure hope they win tonight."

"Yes, it would be good to start the series out with a win," her father said. "I wouldn't want to be around Brayden if they don't win."

Kamryn nodded, knowing Bray better than most people. Bray wasn't a gracious loser, especially when it was this important. "Let's pray for a win."

---

Later that night Kamryn, her parents, Bray's parents, Kalyn, and Keegan watched in horror as Dallas lost the first game of the finals by two points. She knew Bray was heartbroken.

"I can't believe they lost," Kalyn said, sipping the last of her wine. "And to lose by only a basket is just ridiculous."

Kamryn nodded. "They had such a solid lead going into the third quarter. Greg is going to blow a gasket. Dallas is going to have to come on strong in the next game if they hope to win the championship. Only about ten percent of the championship teams come back from losing the first game to win it all."

Kalyn shook her head at her sister. "You're like a guy with this sports stuff. How do you know all these facts?"

Kamryn shrugged. "It's dad's fault." She glanced in her father's direction. "That's all we ever talked about. For years, that's all we *could* talk about."

Harding chuckled. "That just helped you in your job."

Kamryn shrugged. "Maybe, but I did have a lot of guy friends in high school and college. Guys love it when you can talk about sports. Well, up to a point anyway." She thought about her one real date with Greg.

"That's just part of your charm, baby," her father said.

Kalyn joined in the conversation. "Kamryn, you knew all along that Dallas was going to the finals, even though every other sportscaster had forecasted L.A./Chicago at the beginning of the playoffs. You still think they're going to win it all?"

"Yes, I do," Kamryn said confidently. "And it's not because of Bray. Well, yes it is. It's because of him, the new players, and Greg. It's quite a lethal combo. Toronto fought just as hard to get to the finals, but I know in the end Dallas is going to take it."

"How many games?"

"Seven."

"You just like drama," Kalyn said. "They could take it in five."

Kamryn smiled and extended her hand to her sister. "Bet. Loser pays for a mani-pedi at the day spa."

Kalyn shook her hand, accepting the wager. "Deal."

---

"Need a ride?" the burly uniformed man asked Brayden as he parked his bags on the sidewalk.

"I got it covered." Brayden glanced around for the car service, but he didn't see it. He pulled out his cell phone to dial the number for the service, when his phone rang. "Allen."

"Mr. Allen, your driver is running about twenty minutes late. I'll give you a courtesy call when he enters the airport."

"Thanks." With time to kill, he sat on a nearby bench and watched the traffic buzz by. His phone rang again. "Allen."

"Don't you use that tone with me," Kamryn teased. "We saw the game."

"We?"

"Yes. My parents, your parents, Kalyn, and Keegan came over and we watched the game here. I'm sorry you guys lost."

"Yeah, me, too," he said. "It was like we just couldn't get it together, and to lose by one lousy basket just hurts."

"I know. It was only the first game. You guys have six more games to kick Toronto's butt. But you need to perfect your game. You guys can't afford many nights like tonight."

"Wow, thanks for the support, Kam."

"You know how much I love the Mavericks, so don't even try to go there, buster."

He chuckled. "Thanks, baby. I needed that. You always put me in my place, don't you?"

"Yes, I do. Now I'm going to bed."

"Good night, baby." He closed the phone and placed it back in his bag. A few minutes later the car service informed him the driver was on his way.

Suddenly a black Lincoln Town Car arrived and the driver jumped out of the car, apologizing for his tardiness. "I'm sorry, Mr. Allen, this won't happen again." He took Brayden's bag and put it in the trunk of the car.

"No problem."

"Thank you, sir." He opened the door for Bray to get inside.

Once they were on their way, Brayden gave the driver a different address. "Are you sure, Mr. Allen? I'm supposed to make sure you're safe."

Since the attack and since they were in the playoffs, the organization wasn't taking any chances. "It's okay."

"If you say so." The driver radioed in the change of address. "Just covering my ass," he told Brayden.

"Right."

They arrived at Kam's darkened home and Brayden took a deep breath. He hadn't taken her spare set of keys with him on the road, but he knew where she kept the spare key for Kalyn. Taking his life in his own hands, he got out of the car, said good night to the driver, and walked up to Kam's front door. After he was sure the car was gone, he located the spare key and went inside the house, hoping Kam would be happy to see him.

Kamryn's eyes popped open at the sound of the front door closing. Someone was in her house. She forced her brain to react. Maybe it was Kalyn. But Kalyn normally called when she was coming over this late. She slipped out of bed and fumbled for something to defend herself with. She wished she kept that blasted gun in the house instead of in her SUV.

She grabbed her laptop, the closest thing to a weapon in the room, and headed downstairs. She noticed the living room light was on. Whoever was in her house was watching TV! The nerve of some criminals, she fumed. *If this is Kalyn, I'm so going to change my locks.* She walked into the living room and stopped cold. "What are you doing here?"

Bray looked up at her. He actually looked like he belonged on her sofa. He was dressed in jeans and a button-down shirt, but he'd kicked off his leather slip-ons. "It's nice to see you too, baby."

She inhaled, calming her tired body so she wouldn't go totally off on him. "Let's try this again. Bray, why are you in my house at three o'clock in the morning? You should be at home resting."

"I had to come see you." He propped his long, bare feet on her coffee table. "You don't mind, do you?"

"Of course not. You just scared the crap out of me. I thought you were a burglar."

"And you were going to hit me with your laptop? Come on, baby. Really?"

"It's all I had in the bedroom."

"Well, I think I can change that."

"I have no doubt about that."

"But?"

"Bray, you're in the middle of the finals. You may not be able to concentrate on … things."

He stood in front of her. "Well, for you I can multitask. I can concentrate on the finals and make love to you. Many, many times." He leaned down and kissed her. He pulled her close against his body, leaving no room for doubt. "Any questions?"

She wanted to say something cutting and sarcastic to him, but he felt too good. Especially after the few days she'd had. She felt safe in his arms. "No, not a one. But I do have a question for you."

"Ask away." He kissed her again.

"Top or bottom?"

———

By Monday Kamryn felt as good as new. Maybe it had to do with the fact that Bray hadn't left until that morning.

Now that her favorite basketball player was out of sight, she could focus on her task. This little favor of Sandra's was fast consuming her life. After not succeeding in getting in touch with Sandra at her home number, she tried her cell. Sandra answered on the second ring.

"Hi, Kamryn, how are you? I'm really surprised to hear from you. We should meet for lunch. How about today?"

Kamryn shook her head in amazement. "I was just about to suggest the same thing."

"Great. See you at Adolfo's at one." She ended the call.

Kamryn looked at her phone. "That woman has a lot of explaining to do," she said aloud. "Well, at least I'll finally get some answer to all these questions."

She walked to the bathroom and decided a bath would soothe her tired body. Kalyn was always talking about the wonders of a good soak in a tub. Her body wasn't as sore as the first time with Bray, but it still objected to all this new activity. Mentally she thought out her day, wondering if she could work in a nap later. It didn't seem possible. After meeting Sandra, she was going shopping with her mom and tonight was game two. Bray had invited her and her parents to sit in the family section with his parents.

After a nice, relaxing bath, she dressed in jeans and a blouse and headed downtown to Adolfo's, a small bistro in downtown Dallas. Sandra was already waiting for her at a table in the corner. She waved at Kamryn.

Kamryn waved back and began walking toward her. This was going to be tricky, she thought. Too bad she wasn't like one of those police detectives on TV, able to wrangle a confession out of Sandra. But a confession to what?

"Hi, Kamryn. Thank you for meeting me." Sandra rose and hugged Kamryn, then took her seat.

Kamryn looked at Sandra. Was this beautiful woman seated across from her one of those women she only heard horror stories about? Sandra was regally tall and thin. Her skin was perfectly tanned, and her brown hair was pulled back in a neat bun. She wore a dark suit, completing the look of a fashion model.

"Have you found out anything?"

"Why don't you tell me about his last day?" Kamryn watched Sandra play with her wedding rings.

Sandra exhaled. "I didn't want this to get out, but he didn't come home the night before. We'd had an awful fight, and he grabbed some clothes, stormed out of the house, and never came back."

"Was that the day the strange men showed up at practice?"

"How did you know about that? He said no one saw them."

*Well, that answers that question.* "How long had Jason been gambling?"

"I don't know. I didn't suspect until right before he died."

"So were you guys seeking counsel for your marital problems?"

"To hear Jason, we didn't have any problems. At least he said *he* didn't. He refused to go to counseling. Did you find anything in his SUV?"

She hadn't mentioned that she was going to check out Jason's SUV to Sandra, not wanting to get her hopes up. Maybe the wrecking attendant had called her, Kamryn reasoned. "No, not a thing. The Range Rover was clean as a whistle." Why did that fact keep bothering her?

"Jason treated that car better than he ever treated me," Sandra said softly.

"So what are your plans now?"

She shrugged. "I've been toying with the idea of opening a tea shop in the upscale area downtown. I did some research, and there's not one tea shop downtown. There are tons of Starbucks, but not one place to have a decent cup of tea. Sometimes when I'm downtown I just want a good cup of tea in a pretty cup. So what do you think of my idea?"

"Sounds like you're really happy about it," Kamryn commented. Sandra had never appeared to be the tea-drinker type to her.

"Yes, since this ordeal with Jason and everything, I finally feel like I can move on with my life."

"What about the girls?"

"Oh, they're with Jason's mother in Chicago right now. I'm thinking about letting them stay with her for a while. They miss their father so much, and there they have their Nanna. It gives them a sense of stability. Dallas has a lot of bad memories for them."

Kamryn wanted to ask Sandra why she wasn't with her kids, like any normal mother would be at this time. They'd just lost their father and were obviously grieving while Sandra was in Dallas contemplating opening a tea shop. What was wrong with that picture? She forced herself to stay on target. "You said you didn't figure out Jason was betting until right before he died. What tipped you off?"

Sandra sat back in her seat and shrugged. "Little things. Money was being transferred out of the accounts. Large amounts Jason couldn't justify. Strange emails started showing up. Weird people were calling the house."

"Maybe it was money he sent to his mother," Kamryn suggested. "How is she? Is she ill?"

"Healthy as a horse. That woman will outlive everyone. Against my wishes Jason bought her a huge house a few years back. He also set up an account for her then. Her money comes out of some other fund. I don't have access to it, and I don't know how much is in it, either."

"Not even now?" Kamryn asked. "It seems odd, since you were his wife. I know the insurance policy won't pay out because his death has been ruled a suicide."

"Yes, the only money I received from Jason's estate was a flat amount a few weeks after his death. I know he was worth more than the twenty thousand I received, but the attorney said it was all in the will."

"Oh," Kamryn said for the lack of anything else to add to the conversation. Well, her avenue of questioning was raising new concerns. Instead of the mystery getting smaller, it was getting larger. Proving Jason was killed was becoming more and more complicated. "Thank you, Sandra." She glanced at her watch. "I've got to run. Are you coming to the game?"

"Oh, no. Actually, I hate sports. I only tolerated them for Jason's sake. Then when the girls came along, they liked watching their daddy play basketball. I'm going to stay home and have a nice relaxing evening. I'm meeting a realtor first thing in the morning. I've got my eye on a building a couple of streets over."

Kamryn stood and grabbed her purse. "I'll let you know the minute I find out something that I can go to the police with."

Sandra stood and hugged her. "Thank you, Kamryn. I just know Jason was a good driver and would never have lost control of his SUV."

"I know," Kamryn said. "I know the truth will come out sooner or later." Kamryn was hoping for sooner.

—∞∞∞—

After Kamyrn left the restaurant, Sandra ordered another glass of wine. While she waited, she took out her cell phone and dialed a number. Getting Kamryn to look into Jason's death had seemed like a logical answer to her problem. Now she was asking too many questions.

"Hello," a male voice said.

"I think she's beginning to suspect something about Jason's death."

"That's what you wanted, right? You said if she looked into it she would add legitimacy to this mess. If she proves it was an accident, you can still get some cash out of this."

"Yes, it's true. It's a small policy, but it's something. I just don't want her uncovering anything I'll regret."

"I don't think that's possible."

"Well, I do."

"What do you plan on doing?"

"Only what I have to." She ended her call as the waiter neared with her drink order. As she sipped the wine, she mulled over a plan that would solve all her problems. Unfortunately, that plan would involve Kamryn.

---

Monday night Brayden was in the zone, or so he thought. The second game in the series had been intense, but they were able to win the game with a ten-point lead. The Center was packed to capacity, and that only fueled Dallas' need to win.

After the game Coach merely told them to be ready for practice in the morning and not to start celebrating after one win. Brayden's adrenaline had been on high alert for the whole game and his body had paid the price. Every muscle he had was sore. He decided on a shower. When he emerged from the stall, just about every player was gone. Tyler, though, was getting dressed by his locker.

"Are you and Kamryn going to Junior's?" Tyler asked, slipping on a pair of jeans.

"No. After her ordeal last week, I told her we could skip it."

"What ordeal?" Tyler asked.

Bray sighed. He'd forgotten he hadn't told anyone about it outside of family. "She was playing detective and searching Jason's car. It was booby-trapped. You know, like someone knew that she was going to be looking through the car. Kam was bruised up, but no broken bones."

Tyler sat down on the wooden bench with a thud. "So he was killed. Man, I wish I'd taken him seriously now."

"What are you talking about?" Bray sat next to Tyler. "If it's something about Jason, you need to tell me."

"Well, a day or two before everything went down, he was looking like he had a major dilemma going on and I asked him what was up."

"And?"

"He told me it was better that I didn't know, but if he turned up dead, the problem was solved. I just thought it was a coincidence, especially when the police said he lost control of the car and then found the note."

Brayden nodded. "Got any idea what it was?"

Tyler shook his head. "No, man. Not a clue."

He would have to tell Kam about this, but he had to hold it until after Wednesday's game. If he told her now she'd want to investigate, and he wasn't ready for that. He needed to stay focused. "Thanks, Tyler. It's something. I wish he had said something to me. Maybe we could have helped him out of his troubles."

"I don't think that would have been possible," Tyler said, slipping on a shirt. "Hey, since Kamryn can't go, how about I go with you? This is the playoffs and you can't break your tradition."

Brayden shook his head. "Not you, too. I normally wouldn't have broken with tradition, but I wanted to make sure Kam was feeling better."

Tyler looked at him. "I know Kamryn is special to you, but I thought Coach was trying to holler at her."

BEST FRIENDS; BETTER LOVERS

Brayden smiled. "Didn't quite work out. Guess they both knew too much about sports. Some men can't handle a woman who knows more about sports than they do."

Tyler laughed. "But you have no problem with that?"

"Not a one." Brayden stood and struggled into jeans and an oversized shirt advertising the University of Iowa. "You want to meet there or what?"

"I'll meet you there. I have to make a stop first."

Brayden nodded. "See you there in thirty." He continued dressing and tried to talk himself out of calling Kam.

He lost, of course. He dialed her as he walked to the parking garage. Since his attack, an escort was normally waiting at his parking level. He listened as the phone rang.

"Hello," she said.

"Hey, baby, where are you?"

"Why?"

"Because, sweetheart, I want to make sure that you don't try to keep our tradition when we both agreed that we wouldn't go tonight."

"Yes, I'm at home. Actually, everyone is here. Your parents followed us here after the game and now my mom and your mom are in my kitchen cooking. Kalyn is here watching over me and the dads are watching the same game we just saw in person."

"Good. Tyler and I are going to Junior's. He didn't want me to break tradition."

She chuckled. "Tell him it only works if I'm there."

"Well, I got something else planned for you tomorrow after practice."

"Oh, my, I can hardly wait. I'll make sure the house is empty."

"I was thinking about making dinner, but I think I like your idea better." He gazed around the parking level. The Mavericks were wasting money paying the escort. The guy was never where he was supposed to be. "I'll see you tomorrow," he told Kam as he looked around the level. All clear. "Don't bother dressing for dinner. I'll just have to take it off you later anyway."

"Smooth talker."

"I try. Good night, baby." He walked to his SUV and unlocked it. He had the feeling someone was there with him. He surveyed his area and didn't see anyone else.

He wondered what had happened to the escort. He threw his bags in the back seat of the Escalade and closed the door.

"Don't move."

Brayden sighed. Not again. He looked in the reflection of the window of the SUV. This definitely wasn't the same guys who attacked before; plus, this time there were three of them. "Look, guys, I don't want any trouble. Take whatever you want."

The older man of the trio spoke. "We want you."

"What?"

He threw a punch, but Brayden dodged it in the nick of time. Unfortunately, the SUV took the hit and the back window was broken.

The man shook the pain from his hand and nodded to the other men. They both rushed Brayden.

The two men got in a few hits, but Brayden emerged the victor and the men scrambled away just as the escort ran to him. "Sorry, Mr. Allen, I was detained downstairs. Are you hurt?"

Brayden took inventory of his body. He was bruised, but nothing that needed medical attention. "I'm good."

"Any idea who those guys were?"

Brayden shook his head. "No. They wanted me, not the SUV. Not my wallet, me." He got into his Escalade and started the engine. "I know you have to report this. I'll tell Coach about it in the morning." He headed out of the parking garage.

He pushed the blue OnStar button.

"Good evening, Mr. Allen. Our records indicate that your back left window has been broken. Would you like a technician to fix it tonight?"

"Yes," he said.

"Would you like us to send them to the American Airlines Center on Victory Avenue in Dallas, Texas?"

"No, send them to this address." He rattled off the diner's address. "I should be there in thirty minutes."

"Thank you, Mr. Allen. Our technician will meet you there. His name is Chris Jackson."

"Thank you." Brayden pushed the blue button again, ending the conversation with his system.

---

"You look like crap," Tyler said when Brayden met him at Junior's later. "I was beginning to think you were going to be a no-show."

Brayden sat at the table and let out a tired breath. "Tell me something I don't know. Some idiots tried to jack me in the parking garage." He waved at the waitress.

"Again?"

"Yeah, that's what I thought. But they didn't want the SUV, or my wallet. They said they wanted me."

"Why you?"

Brayden shrugged. "I don't know. You think it's the opposing team?"

Tyler shrugged. "Anything is possible. This is someone who knows your schedule, and they seem pretty damn persistent about getting you out of the game or something. Maybe someone has placed a major bet against Dallas, and keeping you out is one way to insure they'll win?"

"Well, I don't know about that. I think they're working for someone else."

The young waitress appeared and Brayden gave his order for a cheeseburger and fries and a glass of tea.

"Ms. Hillcroft isn't coming tonight?"

"No, not tonight."

"I think this must be the first time in the three years I've been working here that she's missed a Dallas win. You guys make such a cute couple. It's nice when men actually look past how pretty she is and see the real sister underneath. We're betting on when you're going to pop the question."

Brayden smiled. He was thinking along those lines, as well. "What did you wager?"

She grinned. "I think after you guys win the championship. That would be so romantic."

"I'll see what I can do." He winked at the young girl as she walked away.

Tyler threw a wadded up napkin at him. "I knew it! I knew something was different about you lately. I mean, I knew you and Kamryn had gotten closer, but I had no idea it was like that. So how long have you been thinking about the 'm' word?"

"Not that long. A couple of weeks at the most."

"What does she think of all these accidents you're having?"

"She doesn't know about all of them. I think something is going on. Between her incident at the wrecking yard and these other mishaps, it's starting to look like someone is after both of us."

Tyler nodded, taking in all the information. "You could have her tracked. It would make things easier, and maybe you could find out who was doing this."

He could easily imagine how upset Kam would be at the thought of him invading her privacy like that. But at least he would know where she was and if she was in danger.

"Brayden, you're not seriously considering doing that? Kamryn will kill you for treating her like a kid, not to mention acting like an obsessive boyfriend."

Brayden laughed. "I think we're both too old for the 'boyfriend' term. I'm weighing my options." The young waitress set their food on the table. "Yes, I'm seriously considering it."

Tyler took a bite of his burger. "Man, it's going to hit the wall when Kamryn finds out."

"I'd rather have her mad at me for a day or two than not have her on this earth at all. It's a chance I'm willing to take."

# CHAPTER 15

The next evening Kamryn waited for Bray to arrive at her house. She felt kind of guilty about the date since Bray was going to cook. He'd had a grueling practice earlier that day, but the man still wanted to cook.

Against his suggestion, she had dressed for dinner. Kalyn had come over and picked out a floral dress that hugged her curves. She felt a little uncomfortable in the form-fitting dress as she sat on the couch. It rode up her thighs each time she shifted on the sofa. Should make for an interesting night, she mused. She raised her ring-less hand in front of her face. She'd finally taken off her wedding rings. The only reminder she had of her twelve year marriage was two lines on her finger from where the rings had rested. She didn't feel any different, but somehow she knew she was.

The doorbell rang and a shiver of excitement ran down her spine. "It's go time," she said, rising. She took a deep breath and went to answer the door.

He looked like a dream. His face was freshly shaven and his mustache had been trimmed to a thin, sexy line above his lip. He was dressed in a silk shirt and slacks and looked like a model. "So are you just going to drool over me or what?"

She let him inside the house and closed the door. Then she noticed something missing. "Hey, where's the food? You said you were cooking."

"You took off your rings!" He pulled her into his arms and kissed her. He gently bit her lips, teasing them apart and easing his tongue inside her mouth.

She hated to end the kiss, but she had to know how he felt about her taking off the rings. "It was time."

"Well, yeah," he said. His hand moved down to her hips and he pulled her closer to his body and let her feel every inch of his erection. "In celebration of you finally taking off your wedding rings, how about dessert first?" He led her to the stairs, not giving her many options.

She felt lightheaded and giddy. "Do I have a choice?" She kicked off her stilettos and wrapped her arms around him.

He laughed as he took the stairs two at a time. "You always have a choice." Once they arrived at her bedroom, she sat on the bed.

"Really?" She watched him take off his shirt and slip off his slacks, kicking off his shoes in the process. He stood before her in a pair of silk boxer shorts.

He kissed her before answering. "Of course, you know, like top or bottom." He helped her up.

"Top," she said. She stood on her tiptoes and pulled him down for a kiss. "And bottom," she whispered against his lips. "And maybe a few other positions I've been thinking about."

He unzipped her dress and it fell in a pool at her feet. She stepped out of it and started to take off her panties when he stopped her. "Oh, no, baby. This is going to be my pleasure."

How could mere words put her body on high alert? Her body had responded instantly. She sat down on the bed because her legs were going to betray her at any moment. Bray took advantage of her position and kissed her into submission. Something about the way his tongue mated with hers sent her all the way over the edge.

He took off her panties by simply tearing them apart and ripping them from her body. "Sorry, baby, I couldn't wait." He pushed her legs apart, kissing his way up her thighs.

Each kiss felt like a spark of electricity lighting up her soul. She felt herself melting with each kiss. Panic set in as she realized his destination. But it was too late. She felt his hot breath on her most intimate part. He gazed up at her with those gorgeous hazel eyes, silently asking permission.

She was going to explode if he didn't get the show on the road. She nodded, apprehension building to a thundering crescendo. She moved closer to him, giving him better access. He tasted her gently at first. Kamryn moaned and fell back against the bed. She rubbed her hands through his hair. As his tongue sank deeper into her body, she was seeing the moon and the stars. The sensations roaring through her body were intense. She gave over to the orgasm barreling through her.

"Wow, that was amazing," Kamryn said, trying to catch her breath.

"No, you were amazing," he said, lying next to her and kicking off his boxer shorts. He moved closer to her, unsnapped her bra, and threw it across the room. As they lay facing each other, he nibbled on her neck, enjoying the taste of her skin. She tasted better than chocolate. "You taste so good. I've been thinking about this all day." He hoped she hadn't noticed the faint bruise marks from last night.

"How did you get the bruises? Are they from yesterday's game? You took quite a few hits."

He had two options. He could lie, and Kamryn would send him straight home, erection and all, or he could tell her the truth. "Last night these guys tried to attack me, but I took care of them."

"Oh, my goodness." She sat up instantly, covering her nude body with the bed sheet. "This thing is so out of control. Bray, you need to be careful. Who do you think it is?"

Right now, he didn't really care. He only wanted to make love to her as many times as the night would allow. "I don't know and I don't care. Right now the only person I'm concerned about is you." He moved her on top of him. "You were saying something about being in control."

"Why yes, yes, I did." She reached under the pillow and retrieved a condom. "This is for you."

"Why don't you do the honors?" Brayden thought she'd tell him no. He liked pushing her to the edge.

She moved off his body. "I'd love to." She opened the gold packet with her teeth and got to work.

Kam had a surprise for him. He watched with surprise and excitement as Kam put the rolled condom in her mouth, then leaned over his rigid erection and slid the condom on his shaft slowly, at least as much as she could fit into her mouth. She had to use her hand for the rest. When she finally finished she looked at her handiwork with pride. "How was that?"

It was the sweetest torture Brayden had ever endured in his life. "Baby, that was great. But you started something you're going to have to finish." He pulled Kamryn on top of him and slid inside her in one smooth stroke.

His hands fell to her waist and guided her movements until she caught the rhythm that would satisfy them both. She leaned down and kissed him, crushing her body to his.

Bray thought he was going to go out of his mind. He couldn't get deep enough, fast enough, to satisfy his body. Then he hit the right spot and the heavens opened up and engulfed them both.

"That was better than a massage," whispered Kam. Her eyes fluttered closed.

Brayden stared at the ceiling, trying to get his bearings. Why was sex so different with Kam? They'd been friends for so long, maybe that explained it. There wasn't any awkwardness, and each time they made love, it just kept getting better.

He pulled her closer to his body, slid his hands under the covers and found hers. He'd never taken himself for a romantic or a cuddler, but here he was doing both. This scenario should be scaring the holy crap out of him, but he only felt love and contentment.

---

When Kamryn pried her eyes open again, it was ten o'clock at night and Bray was missing from her bed. Where was he? She sat up slowly, wincing at the pain shooting through her body. She went to the bathroom and took a shower.

After she'd dressed in shorts and a T-shirt, she went downstairs. She heard a commotion in the kitchen, and realized Bray was probably cooking. She walked inside the kitchen and watched him do his thing.

She was expecting … well, she didn't know what she was expecting. Pasta was not her first choice. Bray looked so relaxed as he mixed in broccoli, shrimp, some grape tomatoes, fresh basil, and a squirt of lemon. "Hey, I know I didn't have all that in my refrigerator."

"No, you didn't," he said. "Kalyn was good enough to bring this stuff over for me."

Kamryn snorted. "My sister Kalyn?"

"Yes."

"My sister who has nothing in her refrigerator but a bottle of wine and some orange juice?

"Yes," he said.

"Bray, I know my sister."

"All right. You caught me. I dropped the food off at her place before I came over here. When I gave her the signal she brought it over."

Kamryn sat at the table. "You went to a lot of trouble just to make me think you didn't bring anything with you."

"If it's for you, then it's never too much trouble. You should have seen your face this evening. It was totally worth it." He reached for two bowls and began ladling the food into each dish. "I thought I'd make something light. I've got an early practice tomorrow." He brought the food to the table.

"It smells good." Kamryn picked up her fork and began eating. "Oh, baby, this is so good."

"You called me *baby*," Bray said. "You never use terms of endearment."

She held her head down in embarrassment. "Fallout from my dead husband. He didn't like me to use those kinds of terms, so over time I guess those words just fell from my vocabulary."

He reached for her hand across the table. "Hey, no talk of dead spouses. This is about us."

"You've never been married, Bray."

"Okay, so no talk of other people."

She continued eating and thought about his statement. "What if I want to ask about Jason?"

"Not tonight. This is about us."

"Okay, Mr. Allen. I won't talk about the case or the fact that someone is attacking you."

"I know what you're doing. And since I know your reporter's sense is in high overdrive, you can ask me five questions about it."

Kamryn chuckled. "You know me very well, don't you?"

"This is true."

"Okay, shoot."

Kamryn winced. "Is Brian still in town?"

"I don't know. Do you think Jason and Sandra had a happy marriage?"

"I thought I was doing all the asking?"

"Accident," Bray said. "But since it's out there, what do you think?"

"I think they had a troubled marriage. I don't know who was at fault, though. Did you know that Jason's mother has been keeping the girls since he died?"

"I can see that. She loved those girls. Jason always said that when he retired he was going back to his hometown with his girls."

Kamryn nodded. "Why didn't he say 'family'?"

"According to Jason, that marriage was rocky from the start. Once the kids started coming, things got better between them for a little while."

Kamryn shook her head. "Why do people keep thinking having kids will save a troubled marriage? It will only help for a little while, then that fuzzy feeling will wear off. Do you know she's opening a tea shop downtown?"

"Figures. She'd been wanting Jason to bankroll one for the last couple of years, but he said no. Well, now she can do what she wants."

The tone in his voice raised her suspicions. "You don't like Sandra, do you?"

He reached for her now-empty bowl and stacked it with his, then rose and put the dirty dishes in the sink. "No, she's not my favorite person. In the months before he died, Jason seemed more and more depressed. He said he had been considering divorce, but she threatened to take the girls away and he'd never see them again. So he backed off."

"What? Are you serious? And you just now thought to mention this?"

Bray sat down at the table. "First of all, calm down. Second, it was just married guy talk. Do you know how many of my married teammates say that on a daily basis? If I had a nickel for every time I've heard someone say how sick and tired they were of being married, I would be knee-deep in cash."

After she thought about it as a man would, she could understand Bray's dismissal of the statement. "Okay, but still …."

"I know. I thought about it after he died, but I chalked it up to weirdness. Stuff happens and I can't stop it."

"You think there was any truth to Jason's proclamations?"

Bray shrugged. "Who knows?"

"What about these attacks?"

He stood and took her hand. "Your five questions were up a long time ago. But I do have a question for you." He pulled her up out of her seat and against him.

She was close enough to his body to feel his arousal. Feeling like a seductress, she caressed his erection, squeezing him gently. "Ask away."

He moaned, then pulled her hand away. "I can't talk, walk, or think when you do that." His large hands slid under her T-shirt, heading straight for her breasts.

"No bra, I like it. I created a sex monster," he whispered against the nape of her neck.

He squeezed her breasts and toyed with her now erect nipples. Kamryn whimpered, "No fair."

He slowly slid her T-shirt above her head. "Baby, fair is for amateurs." He bent down and took one of her breasts in his mouth, while sliding down her shorts. "Commando!"

She pulled herself out of her sexual haze, trying to comprehend what Bray meant. Then she looked down. He was as naked as the day he was born, and as rigid as a flag pole. She smiled. Something wicked had taken over her body and she was helpless to stop it. "Race you upstairs."

Before she could make a move, Bray swept her up in his arms and took off for the stairs.

---

The next morning Kalyn decided to visit her sister before she went to work. She had to know how things were between Kamryn and Brayden. While she was out walking her dog, she noticed Bray's Escalade was gone. Once she made sure her canine friend was set for the day, she walked to her sister's house. She unlocked Kamryn's back door, hoping there were some leftovers from dinner. But once she was in the kitchen the picture before her almost made her scream.

Clothes were strewn all over the floor. She recognized the T-shirt as Kamryn's; the larger clothes had to be Brayden's. Where were the lusty owners of these clothes? Not wanting to run into a naked couple, she turned to leave. She so needed to get out of there before someone saw her or, worse, she saw them. Talk about embarrassing. She walked to the back door and thought she was home free until she heard her sister's voice.

"What are you doing here?"

Kalyn was too afraid to turn around. "I thought I could get a little breakfast, but I see you guys are still playing house. So I'll talk to you later." Kalyn opened the door.

"Kalyn, you can turn around. I have on clothes."

She breathed a little easier. "Thank God." She turned and her sister was correct, she had on clothes. Well, kind of; she had on her bathrobe. Her hair was a hot mess, though. "I'm going to have to start taking hints from you if you guys keep this up. This is the most sex you've had in years."

Kamryn sat down at the table, a sign that she wanted to talk. "Sit down."

"Breakfast?" Kalyn could only hope.

"Sorry, Kalyn. I'm so tired I couldn't raise a smile." She covered her mouth for a yawn.

Kalyn couldn't believe her eyes. She grabbed her sister's left hand. "I don't believe it. You actually took the rings off. What the hell?"

"I felt it was time to move on."

"Kamryn."

"Okay, okay. I felt I couldn't give my heart to another man if I was still wearing the rings."

"How cute. Kamryn, those feelings you have for Brayden have been there all along. You just refused to acknowledge them until now. I'm glad you took your wedding rings off." She waited a beat before she asked, "How do you feel about it?"

"That's just it, Kalyn. I don't feel any different. I always felt like the rings were what kept me bonded to Steve."

Kalyn knew where this conversation was going. "Kamryn, Steve died three years ago. He wouldn't want you mourning him this long. It's not healthy."

"I know. You guys have been telling me that, and Bray's been on me for the last year to take them off. At first, after Steve died, it felt like cheating, but today it didn't."

"Because you have finally let him go." Kalyn glanced at her watch. "Since you're not cooking breakfast, I'd better get going. Quit over thinking this, it will be fine. Kiss Brayden for me. Oh, but you already have." She waved at her sister and left the house.

Kamryn let her sister's words soak in her brain. Why was she worrying about still mourning her dead husband? It was time to move on.

---

Dallas lost game three, letting Toronto lead the series two games to their one. After the game, Kamryn took Bray home. Since it wasn't a victory there was no eating at Junior's. In a way it was good that the Mavericks lost, she thought. It would make them want the next game that much more. Bray was quiet all the way home, probably thinking about the game and the mistakes the entire team made. She searched for words that would make the situation better, but there were none.

"Kam, we messed up tonight."

"I know. Your timing was off. You guys have a few days to get it together." She expected him to bite her head off for talking to him like that.

Instead, he chuckled. "You always put me in my place. No matter what I do, you always tell me about myself."

"Yes, you can count on that." She pulled into his driveway to let him out. "Good luck with practice tomorrow."

He opened the passenger door. "How do you know we're having practice tomorrow? Our next game is three days away. Da Money may give us the day off."

"Yeah, right. You guys just lost a game in the finals. You're probably going to practice all day."

"Damn, you know too much about professional sports. Practice starts at seven in the morning, and who knows what time it will end." He leaned toward her and kissed her longingly. "I'd better stop before we get this SUV rocking and Mom comes out here."

That kiss took away her breath and her thoughts. She wanted so much more from him, but, reluctantly, she agreed. "Yes, I can just see Janice coming out here and beating on the windows."

He kissed her quickly and got out of the SUV. After Kamryn was assured he was inside safely, she took off for home.

⊸⊸⊸⊸⊸

A week later Bray ran full speed on the treadmill in his home gym as if the devil were after his soul. And in a way he was. Dallas had lost a heartbreaker in the final seconds on their home turf. Now the team had to focus on the final game, which was also in Dallas. He increased the speed on the machine and continued running.

Yeah, it was three in the morning, but he had too much adrenaline pumping in his body to sleep. The series was tied at three games apiece. It could very well be anyone's game at this point.

Game seven was in two days. After tonight's disaster his parents told him they wouldn't come to the game because they couldn't take the pressure. They'd rather watch them win on TV. He glanced at the large clock on the wall. Had he really been running for an hour?

Most of the other guys went out clubbing to blow off steam. He hadn't wanted to jinx the team's luck by celebrating prematurely. Besides, that was the old Brayden. The new Brayden would rather have been in bed with Kam. He jumped off the treadmill and picked up the cordless phone as he walked upstairs to his bedroom.

He dialed Kam's number, knowing she wouldn't give him the time of day because she was working on her story about the game. Every reporter in town was probably trying to get their story in on time. He knew her deadline was midnight.

She picked up on the first ring. "How are you feeling?"

He heard her typing on her computer. "Resigned, I guess. I can't believe we lost."

"Well, you guys have one more chance. What did Greg say to you guys tonight?"

"Not much. I think he was too upset, or we would have been practicing tonight."

She laughed. "Yeah, that sounds like Greg. I don't envy you guys tomorrow."

"Tell me about it."

"I know you guys will be able to do it. I have a mani-pedi riding on this."

"Don't tell me you bet your sister?"

"Yes, I did. And if you guys don't win, you'll have me to answer to. I'll make Greg look like a kitten."

He didn't doubt her for one minute. "I'll do my best, Kam. Or I'll give you a mani-pedi myself. What is a mani-pedi, anyway?"

"Ask me after you're NBA champs." She ended the call.

He chuckled and threw the phone on his bed. As he slid between the covers of his king-sized bed, he knew the Mavericks were meant to be champs.

# CHAPTER 16

Several days before the final game, Brian knew what he had to do. Well, he had an option, but it wouldn't be good enough. The Mavericks had lost game six, which made him money, but not enough to save his home, his marriage, or the life he'd once known. He needed a sure thing if he planned on resuming the life he loved.

He sat in the rental car outside of Kamryn's house. He just knew Brayden would come by and see her after practice. Maybe she was his way in. Brayden kept bragging about how smart she was. She wasn't too smart if she didn't realize she was being played by one of the biggest playas in the NBA. There was no way Brayden could actually be interested in her. No way, no how. Brayden liked petite women that were knockouts. Women that looked good hanging on a brother's arm, not women that looked like Kamryn. Sure, Kamryn was pretty, but she was thick. What was Brayden's angle with her? His cell phone jangled. He noticed the caller on the display screen and muttered a curse. Damn woman.

"Are you still there?"

"Where else am I going to be?" he asked sarcastically. "Your house?" They thought it best if he wasn't seen at her house. At least not yet.

"How would that look?"

"Yeah, yeah. I know you have to play the role of the grieving widow."

"Has he shown up yet?"

"No. I don't think he's coming. You know game seven is in two days. He might be concentrating on the game, not trying to get a piece."

"We don't have many other options. She's getting close to the truth. I can feel it. If she uncovers the whole truth we're both going to be in a lot of trouble."

Just like her to try to take the high road. "Where's this 'we' stuff coming from?"

"If I'm going down, I'm taking you with me."

Figures. "What else is new? If I wasn't desperate I wouldn't be here with you now. Well, what's your plan?"

"We're going to have to do something drastic. Now that she's investigating this thing fully, she wants to know who those men at practice were. She's not going to stop until she knows the truth."

"You shouldn't have planted that booby-trap on the SUV. You should have known she wasn't going to the wrecking yard alone. How much did you pay that guy to put that stuff in the SUV?"

"A thousand dollars," she said. "All he had to do was put it inside the hood. Once the hood was opened it was supposed to go off, but it had a delay. Wires weren't tight, I guess. You're going to have to get rid of him."

"I know." His heart lurched at the idea of another death. What had he gotten into? But it was all spilt milk now. He was in it up to his neck, and there was no out but death or jail. Death was looking really good right now. "No one on the team is going to mention the Mazolli brothers."

"I'm not worried about that. If she stumbles on that, then they'll take care of her for us. I'm worried about Allen. If he's playing in the game, Dallas has a good chance of winning and there goes my money."

"Oh, so now it's *your* money. What happened to *our* money?"

"Don't start."

"Anyway, I got that covered."

"Really? Is that why he keeps defeating your street thugs? With all the money I'm shelling out for these guys, you'd think they'd be better fighters."

"You just worry about Kamryn and I'll take care of Brayden." He ended the call.

Later that day Kamryn sat at her desk, working on the story that had changed her life forever. Since doing this little favor for Sandra, she'd been in the hospital after being knocked on her butt with a homemade bomb and Bray had been attacked. She didn't know if the events were connected, but it sure felt like it.

The stack of documents related to Jason was quickly growing to an overgrown stack of worry. She sighed and reached for the bulging file. There had to be something she was overlooking.

She needed Jason's attorney. Would he be willing to talk about Jason? Probably not, but she had to try. She couldn't ask Sandra for the attorney's name and number. Talk about a red flag going up …. She knew someone who might have known: Greg.

Their call was short and sweet. He gave her Jason's attorney's phone number, then asked her if she was coming to the game.

"Try and stop me. That place is going to be packed," she told him.

"Yeah, hopefully we'll give everyone a game to remember."

"I know you will. Thanks for the information."

She hung up and dialed Paul Kelly, Jason's attorney. Maybe she'd finally get some answers.

———

The whistle blew and every man in the American Airlines Center groaned. Practice was finally over. Coach blew the whistle and motioned for Brayden and his teammates to come to his side. Practice had been grueling and had lasted way too long. Brayden was the last man to make it to the sidelines.

"Okay, guys, listen up. I know you worked hard today and I need to see that same momentum tomorrow at the game. Got me?"

"Yes, Coach," the men answered in unison.

"Good. Now get out of here."

As Brayden headed for the showers with the rest of the team, he mapped out the rest of his day. He wanted to see Kam, but it just didn't seem possible. After he dressed, he headed for his SUV. Per the general manager, the security guard met him at the elevator and escorted him to his vehicle.

Brayden thought it was funny, considering that the security guard was about five feet eight and portly. After the guard searched his SUV, Brayden was on his way home.

When he arrived at his house, his mother was out by the swimming pool in the warm Texas weather, enjoying a late lunch of sandwiches, potato salad, tea, and chocolate cake. His mother believed in dessert like no other. She gave him a concerned look as he took a seat at the patio table.

"You look tired, Brayden," his mother said, sipping a cup of tea. "You can't burn the candle at both ends while you're in the playoffs. I know Kamryn would understand."

"Mom, I'm a grown man. I know my limits." He reached for a sandwich and took a bite. "I had every intention of coming home last night, but I just couldn't. You know how it is."

She nodded. "Yes, I know, but you've also been attacked several times in the last two weeks. As I said, she'll understand."

"I know. We agreed to put everything on hold until after the game." He devoured the sandwich and reached for another one. "She agreed not to do any more investigating into Jason's death until after the game. I don't know what I'd do if something else happened to her."

His mother nodded. "She's a journalist. Whether she's writing a column or not, it's in her blood to investigate the story and report the truth."

"I know. I need to talk to you and Dad about something."

His mother smiled. "I knew it. You're going to propose to Kamryn! How wonderful. Your father is upstairs taking a nap. But you should be asking Harding first."

"Mom, you're skipping way ahead of the game. Kam and I are just dating for now. What I want to talk about is you and Dad."

"What is it, dear?"

He cleared his throat. "My contract is up after this season. I'm thinking about retiring and remaining here in Dallas. How do you guys feel about that?"

"We want whatever you want," his mother said. "You've been very generous to us. You bought us a house bigger than we could have ever imagined and you've bought our last three cars. We're fine, plus we have our retirement. Whatever you want to do with your money is fine by us, dear."

He knew his parents were set financially; that wasn't his worry. He wanted their blessing to open the restaurant. "Thanks, you guys. I'm considering opening a bistro. It will be open a few days a week. It'll be nice if it made a ton of money, but that's not why I want to open it. I just want to do something that I enjoy."

"That sounds wonderful, and you have our blessing. You're an amazing cook, and I know that place is going to be busy once the word gets out about your food." She rose and began clearing the table. "Now that we have discussed your future, I'll fix you a decent lunch."

Brayden thanked his mother. He had the best parents a son could ask for, and for that he was very thankful.

⟨∞⟩

Kamryn arrived at the law office of Paul Kelly and Associates, which was located north of downtown off Interstate 75 near the Galleria Mall. She was impressed as she entered the three-story glass building. Thank goodness she'd decided to wear a suit. If she hadn't, she would have felt very out of place.

"May I help you?" a mature woman asked from behind a very large desk.

"Yes, I have an appointment with Paul Kelly. My name is Kamryn Hillcroft."

The woman instantly perked up. "Yes, Mr. Kelly is expecting you. Please go right on in." She motioned for Kamryn to walk down a long hall. "Third door on your left."

She followed the directions and arrived at an open door. Timidly, she knocked and was invited inside. He rose to meet her. Paul didn't look anything like an attorney. He looked like a Greek god. Zeus came to mind. He had deep blue eyes, curly brown hair, and a tan that had to be natural.

"I'm so pleased to meet you, Ms. Hillcroft. I'm a fan of your work. You write an amazing column. Please sit down. Can I get you something to drink?"

"No, Mr. Kelly. Thank you for meeting me. I have a few questions about Jason Woken. He was a client of yours until his death three months ago."

"Please call me, Paul." He perched on the end of the desk. "Actually, Jason is still a client of mine. I'm handling his affairs."

"Do you handle things for Sandra as well?"

"No, I don't have anything to do with Sandra's part of Jason's estate."

"So he left a will?"

Paul almost looked insulted. "Yes, of course he had a will. This man was worth millions dead or alive."

"So who gained the most after his death?"

Paul studied her for several minutes. "I'm telling you this because most of the information is public record and I owe him this much." He took a deep breath. "His wife received a flat amount."

"Was the custody of his children specified in the will?"

"How did you know about that?"

"It was the only explanation for the events," Kamryn said simply. "Sandra told me the girls were with Jason's mother. They've been with her since Jason's death three months ago. She didn't seem too worried about them. Why would he make such a stipulation?"

"Because they were entering divorce proceedings," Paul answered.

"Yes, Sandra mentioned that she was going to file for divorce."

"Then she should have mentioned that Jason was the one who was going to file for divorce the day he died. Unfortunately, he made the mistake of telling her the night before."

"Why didn't the cops question her?"

"They did question her. She said they were having marital problems. That, coupled with the note found in his SUV and the rumors of him gambling, insured it was ruled a suicide. She probably flashed those bedroom eyes at the investigating officer and the case was closed."

Kamryn's mind buzzed with the possibilities. Sandra had initially asked Kamryn to investigate Jason's suicide to prove it was an accident, so she could get the insurance money. But if Sandra had lied to her about the divorce, what else had she been lying about?

---

After his mother's delicious meal and a three-hour nap, Brayden felt more alert than he had all day. He glanced at his bedside clock and noted that it was almost six o'clock in the evening. He reached for his cell phone and dialed Kam's home number.

No answer. Where was she? He dialed her cell phone and she picked up on the first ring.

"Hello, stranger," she said. "How was practice? I talked to your mom earlier and she said you were napping."

So she had called. "Where are you?"

"About five minutes from your house."

That perked him up. "Really?"

"Yes, we agreed to no more sex until the finals were over, right? I didn't know that applied to everything, such as conversation or watching a movie together. Or are you telling me to go home?"

"Hell, no. I'll be waiting at the front door." He got out of bed and headed downstairs.

His parents were sitting in the living room watching the news. His mother smiled. "Glad to see you finally decided to get up. How about grilled steaks for dinner?"

"Sounds great. Better add another one for Kam. She's on her way."

"I know," she said. "She called earlier. She sounded excited. Do I have a grandchild on the way?"

"Mom, you know I don't roll like that." He instantly thought of the morning they'd had sex in the shower. They hadn't used a condom. He smiled at the thought. Wouldn't that be something? "I don't know why she's so excited. Guess we'll find out pretty soon." He noticed her SUV approaching the house.

He watched her from his large bay window. She got out and walked to the front door. She was dressed in jeans, a clingy V-neck shirt, and stilettos. His personal favorite. Brayden opened the door and let her inside. He kissed her. "I sure have missed those lips."

"Right back at you. I must be addicted to you or something," she said, leaning in for another kiss. She grabbed his hand and led him to the living room, where his parents were.

"Of course, you already talked to them," Brayden said.

"Yes, I told you."

"I realize that. Now." He sat on the love seat, pulling her down with him. His parents were seated on the larger sofa. "So what has got your lacey panties in a bunch?"

Her cheeks turned a naughty red in embarrassment. "Bray." She lightly tapped his leg. "I'm sure your parents don't want to hear about that."

He liked that he caught her off-guard. She used her practical side way too much. "But I love hearing about just that particular thing."

"Well, right now, I want to talk about Jason."

"Baby, you promised. No more investigating until the game is over."

She sighed. "So now I can't do my job?" But she was smiling at him as she asked the double-edged question. She waited for the answer that would land him in a mountain of trouble.

But Bray knew better. "Please proceed."

"Okay. I visited his attorney and learned a few facts about Sandra, and I need some advice on my next step."

He tried to school his features to reflect indifference. "What did you find out?"

"Like you didn't already know. She lied about the divorce."

Okay, that took him by surprise. "What divorce?"

"Sandra told me that she was divorcing Jason and that's why he hadn't slept at home the night before."

"They were separated?" Brayden sat up and faced her. "How long had they been separated? I knew he hadn't looked too happy the days before he died."

"Bray, just because he didn't sleep at home one night doesn't make them separated," Kam said. "It only means they had a fight and he stormed out, probably went to a motel."

"Okay," Brayden said. "But?"

"What happened on his way to the attorney's office?"

"Well, yeah," Brayden said. "Sandra told the newspaper that he was on his way home when the accident happened. So why file for a divorce?"

"We only have Sandra's word he was actually coming back to the house. What if he was on his way to the attorney's office when he lost control of the SUV?"

He nodded. Kam's brain was spinning with possibilities. "So you think his SUV may have been tampered with so he couldn't file for divorce. But a divorce would have set Sandra up for life."

"Not necessarily," said Kam. "Depending on the wording of the pre-nup, Sandra could be penniless, especially if he was going to demand custody. Sandra could very well be broke."

Brayden nodded. "It just seems off the wall, but when you break it down like that, Kam, it makes a whole lot of sense."

"I know at the beginning of this mess I was totally on Sandra's side, thinking she was the wronged widow, but now, with all this new information, I have begun to question everything she told me."

"You think Jason knew?"

"Yeah, I think in the back of his mind. If he was gambling, as Sandra claimed he was, his thoughts were of his daughters. I don't know why he was going to divorce her."

"Maybe she was having an affair? She was always flirting with the guys on the team."

"You included?" Kam narrowed her eyes at him.

"Me? Hell, no. Jason was a friend."

She looked at him. "Good answer."

He laughed, happy to see that Kam had a jealous side. "So now we need to find out what would drive Jason to file for divorce."

"In a nutshell." She took a deep breath. "I know Jason did everything for his kids. Did you know his mother has custody of the girls? They've been in Chicago ever since Jason's funeral. Sandra is more concerned about starting her tea shop than her daughters' welfare."

"Honey, you can't confront her with this. It's pretty flimsy evidence. Yeah, it's weird that she's given up the kids without a scuffle, but you need more than your journalistic instinct."

"How about the fact that his mother is the recipient of his estate? She's also the beneficiary on most of his insurance policies, except for one. Sandra got a lump sum payout. The lawyer wouldn't tell me how much. She had told me she only got twenty grand, but I think she was low-balling the actual amount to make it look worse than it was. Even so I don't think whatever amount she got was enough to start a tea shop.

"It hurts that she used me like this. I should have listened to you and stayed out of it," she said.

He could tell she was disappointed about the situation. "You can't let one person ruin your spirit. I think this has been a crazy journey for both of us. I don't know why Sandra is lying so much, but we're going to find out."

"Really?" Tears cascaded down her pretty face. "I just knew you were going to tell me that I was overreacting to this. Thank you for believing me."

He didn't know what he'd said, but he was glad he had. "I love you, Kam. There's nothing I wouldn't do for you."

"I love you, too, Bray."

Before either one of them could react, his father interrupted the moment. "Your mother and I are going to go get the grill ready. Come join us when you're done." His parents hurried out of the room, giggling like children.

Brayden shook his head at his parents. They were always one step ahead of them. He laughed and pulled Kam onto his lap.

They kissed until they were breathless.

"We'd better go join your parents, Bray, or I won't be able to keep my promise of no sex until after the final game."

After Kamryn left Bray's house, she headed back home to investigate a hunch. She dialed Kalyn's cell. "Hey, sis, I need a favor."

Kalyn laughed. "What is it this time?"

"I need your brainstorming skills. I'm on my way home. I'll stop and get you some food."

"Call me when you get home," Kalyn said.

Kamryn pressed the end button and chuckled. One day that girl was really going to have to learn how to cook. She made a stop at Callie's Diner to pick up some food.

Kalyn was waiting for her when she pulled into the garage. In shorts, T-shirt, and flat sandals, she was dressed for eating a hearty meal.

Kamryn laughed as she got out of her SUV. "You couldn't wait until I called you? I wanted to heat it up first." She handed Kalyn the bag of food.

"I knew you'd be here pretty quick, so after I walked Sapphire, I came back here."

"Why does your dog have to poop in my yard?"

"I don't know. But you have the greenest yard on the block." Kalyn laughed.

"I can't wait until the pooper law goes into effect. She's going down." Kamryn walked inside her house. Dallas had recently passed the Pooper Scooper law. If anyone's pet, whether on leash or not, was caught doing their business on anyone else's lawn, it was an automatic fine. Unfortunately, the law wouldn't go into effect until the following year.

Kalyn closed the front door and placed the bag on the table. "I know why you like Callie's Diner," Kalyn said as she emptied the contents on the table.

"The food, of course." Kamryn helped set the table.

"You like these eco-friendly bags and the recyclable food trays."

"Well, yeah. I do love that."

They set the food on the table. Kamryn wasn't hungry since she had just eaten at Bray's house, but once that delicious home-cooked aroma attacked her nostrils, she was a lost cause. She grabbed a container and began to eat. She was pondering how to ask her sister to do yet another favor on this case that wouldn't go away when Kalyn beat her to the punch.

"Okay, what's the favor?" She picked up a piece of fried chicken and added it to her plate of corn on the cob and mashed potatoes.

Kamryn looked down at Kalyn's plate. "I don't know where you put all that food."

"I also work out every day. What's the favor?"

"Sandra has been less than honest with me about her marriage. I think the answer is in Jason's paperwork, but I need fresh eyes to look at it."

"Okay, we can look after dinner," Kamryn said. "So what makes you think Sandra is lying?"

"Jason's attorney. I went to see him today and he gave me some insight into Jason and Sandra. It was Jason who was going to file for divorce."

"I can't believe he told you that," Kalyn said, reaching for another piece of chicken. "How about a look at the will?"

"His lawyer wasn't that helpful. He just told me that Sandra only got a lump sum payout, but Sandra had already told me that. I think she's not listed for anything else. She lied to me," Kamryn said, trying to keep the hurt out of her voice.

"I don't know why she lied. You know there are still good people out there. I never understood why she asked you to prove it wasn't a suicide in the first place. If it was me and I was trying to prove my dead husband didn't commit suicide, I'd hire an investigator or a detective, not a sports journalist. It's like she wanted you to prove that he didn't take his own life, but she didn't want you snooping into anything else."

"That just sounds so fantastic, Kalyn."

"As an image consultant, I'm never surprised at the things people have done and then try to cover it up. If Jason had changed his will, his insurance beneficiaries, and was filing for divorce and wanted total custody, something had to have happened to make him react that drastically."

Kamryn knew exactly what. "The wise guys."

"What?"

"Greg told me a few days before Jason died some wise guys came to visit Jason during practice."

"Oh, that's not good. For anyone."

"I know. According to Bray and Greg, the conversation between Jason and the guys wasn't friendly. A few minutes after their heated talk, the men left. After that, Greg said the Mavericks were starting proceedings to get Jason kicked out of the NBA. The NBA has adopted a no tolerance policy on illegal gambling."

"There's your story, Kamryn. What really happened to Jason would be a novel right there. Just think of all that's happened to you and to Bray, for that matter, since you started looking into this. It could be like one of those stories that comes on TV where the wife has run amok and is trying to cover it up."

"I've been thinking about it. I'm almost afraid to think what else is going to happen before everything is resolved."

Kalyn nodded. "You'll make it through, big sister. You always do. Let's look at those papers."

Kamryn rose and led her sister down the hall to her home office, where she kept her work. She handed her sister the overstuffed file folder. The look on Kalyn's face was priceless.

"Seriously?"

"Yes."

Kalyn gave a dramatic sigh and opened it. "I feel like I'm back in the courtroom with this file. This is why I stopped being an attorney and went into image consulting." Her slim fingers flipped through the pages quickly.

Kamryn watched her sister do her thing. But after thirty minutes, Kalyn was still poring over the documents. "Sorry, Kamryn, but nothing is standing out to me right now."

She figured as much. "I'm going to have to get a look at that will."

"Has he been dead ninety days?"

"Yes, it's been a little over three months."

"Anyone's will and testament is public record ninety days after the death. Most people don't know that little fact."

It couldn't be that easy, Kamryn thought. "So I can go to the courthouse and look at his will?"

"Better yet, you can look at it online. Getting a copy of it will cost you money and will leave a paper trail. Sandra might discover that you're doubting her word and retaliate. She may not want you to know what the will contains."

"Won't my ISP show up?" Kamryn worried that Sandra might be technologically smart and able to track anyone who has been accessing her husband's will by their internet service provider.

"Not if you do it like I showed you." Kalyn had shown her sister how not to be tracked when she visited a site.

"You know, you should be a spy or a government agent," Kamryn told her sister. "You have some serious skills and could probably catch a lot of criminals."

"Helping celebrities clean up their hot messes of a life is enough for me. The occasional visit to the courtroom is more than enough. I'm just glad I can help you and we can do right by Jason."

Kamryn followed Kalyn's intricate instructions and was soon on the Dallas County website. She located the inheritance page with a few clicks of her mouse. She gazed at the fourteen-page document, not believing that Jason had been this thorough.

"Wow, Kalyn, this is awesome. Apparently, Jason thought of everything. I can't believe Sandra didn't fight for her kids. What kind of woman doesn't want the children she gave birth to?"

Kalyn shrugged. "I don't know. It's like she was just looking at the money he made and nothing else. You think she realizes the house she's living in is about to go up for sale?"

"What?" Kamryn stared at her sister in disbelief. "They can do that?"

"Big sister, in the legal world, there's always a way. Jason was worth millions of dollars. I'm sure his lawyer came up with something. If he found a way for Jason's mom to get custody of those girls with no fuss, he can find a way to sell the house out from under Sandra. Look at this clause," she said, scrolling down to the bottom of the page. "It's not used often, and most people overlook it because it's buried so deep in lawyer-speak, but it's here."

"So for people like me who don't understand lawyer-speak," Kamryn said sarcastically, "can you please put that in everyday language, or at least some sports reference so I can understand?"

"All right, I'll translate for you. It states in the event that he preceded his wife in death, the house would be put up for sale exactly one hundred and twenty days after his death and the proceeds would be set up in a trust fund for his daughters, with his mother acting as trustee."

"O.M.G." Kamryn shook her head. "Jason, I didn't think you knew what was going on, but I was wrong. You were ahead of the game."

Kalyn continued reading the document. "Yes, Kamryn, he probably saw the handwriting on the wall. But he was still going to look out for his kids, whether in this life or the next."

Kamryn wiped her eyes. "It's just so awful, that one woman could be this evil. She probably thinks she's going to get away with this. I can't wait to see the look on her face when she finds out about the house. It's getting close to the time for the house to go on sale."

"Before you put on your Superwoman cape, Kamryn, this is still pretty flimsy evidence to take to a judge. She could always say that he was depressed before he took his own life and was probably imagining everything."

Kamryn sighed. Life was full of roadblocks. "I know. Statistically speaking, it's hard to get a suicide ruling changed to murder even with concrete evidence. So it's going to be almost impossible."

"Sorry, Kamryn."

"Oh, I'm not giving up. I'll find a way to bring that cow to justice. I have to, for Jason's sake."

"That's my girl."

# CHAPTER 17

On his way to practice the next day, Brayden couldn't help it. He called Kam. At 6 a.m. Yeah, it was a trifle early, but he was so far gone over her, he had to hear her voice before he walked inside the American Airlines Center. He already knew practice was going to be a bear, and hearing her sultry voice would help him through it. As he turned into the parking garage, she finally picked up the phone.

"What?"

He laughed. "Why are you so cranky? I'm the one who has practice for the next six hours."

"I'm cranky because someone is calling my house at this ungodly hour. You're going to pay for this."

"I hope so. I know you're coming to the game tomorrow. Mom and Dad aren't going to be there."

"I thought this was every parent's dream, to watch their son in the playoffs."

"Not mine. Mom said they can't take the pressure because everything hinges on tomorrow's game. She said she'd probably eat everything in sight, and she didn't want to get caught on camera stuffing her face with nachos and beer."

"Understandable."

"I think I'll be too tired to get together tonight. Plus, I want to concentrate on winning tomorrow."

"Like I'd want your mind anywhere else?"

But his mind was elsewhere. The future. Their future. He had to get his head on straight before tomorrow night or he'd let the team down, and he couldn't have that. "Thanks, baby. I'll see you after the game tomorrow."

"Yes, we'll have some celebrating to do. Now go to practice and I'll go back to sleep."

"I love it when you talk dirty." He ended the call and parked his SUV.

Maybe it was because he was still riding high from talking to Kam, or maybe it was because the biggest game of his professional life was on the horizon. Whatever the reason, he let his guard down and, before he could do anything, he was surrounded by four men. Four very large men. He could probably take two, he reasoned, three, if no one knew how to fight. But four guys built like the defensive line of the Dallas Cowboys was going to be a problem.

He carefully catalogued their appearance while he wondered where the security guard was. "Look, guys, I can pay you not to jack me."

As if they hadn't heard one word he said, they began their assault. His last conscious thought was of Kam.

⸺◦⸺

"Coach, Brayden isn't here," Tyler reported. "He's never late for practice, especially when it's this important." He hadn't wanted to rat his friend out, but something felt wrong.

Coach narrowed his gaze at Tyler. "True."

"I'll contact security," Tyler said, glancing around the center, hoping to see Brayden walking onto the court. No such luck. "You have to admit, a lot of strange things have been happening to him lately. Nothing is beyond possibility. He called me this morning before he left the house on the way here."

Coach nodded. "Okay. Call."

Tyler headed for the dressing room and dialed the security office. "This is Tyler Rice. Can you tell me if Brayden Allen's SUV is on the athletes' level of the parking garage? It's a black Cadillac Escalade."

"Yes, Mr. Rice, we just found him."

"What do you mean 'found'?"

The man cleared his throat, the international sign that all was not good. Tyler felt his body tensing up as the security guard repeated the action. "Well, uh, Mr. Rice, you'd better get up here fast."

A cold chill ran down Tyler's spine as he dropped the phone on the desk. He had no idea what had happened, but he had to be ready. Coach met him as he exited the room. "I think Brayden's been hurt. Where's Julian?"

For the first time in a long time, Coach showed emotion. "What? What is it?"

"I don't know. I'm headed up to our parking level."

"I'll meet you up there."

Tyler nodded and took off for the elevator that led to the parking garage. When the doors opened on their parking level, Tyler was blinded by the blue and red revolving lights from the security patrol cars. Four security guards stood next to Brayden's SUV.

Each step he took brought him closer to the scene and Brayden. Nothing in his life had prepared him for the sight of Brayden lying as limp as a wet rag. "What happened?" He kneeled down beside Brayden. His best friend was out cold. His swollen face was barely recognizable, and a black eye was already forming.

The older officer took out his notepad. "As far as we can tell, our guy was clubbed over the head with a blunt object around six forty-five. Mr. Allen entered the parking garage about ten minutes later, according to the access meter. The security guard is supposed to check in every fifteen minutes. When he didn't check in at seven or seven-fifteen, we came to investigate. We've been here about five minutes. We think Allen's been unconscious about fifteen to twenty minutes."

"Coach is on his way," Tyler added for no apparent reason.

"I was afraid of that," the security guard mumbled. "Team doctor coming, too? He's going to need a doctor. Or do you want us to call the paramedics?"

"Yeah, our team doctor is coming. Julian will take care of it if the paramedics need to be called." Tyler glanced at the interior of Brayden's SUV. His wallet was on the driver's seat. "Anything taken?"

"No, that's the crazy thing. He's wearing a watch worth five grand, his wallet, with an ample amount of cash and credit cards, was on the driver's seat, along with his keys. They were definitely after him."

"They?" Tyler stood and faced the guard.

"We got some images on camera and it was four men, pretty big guys. He couldn't have held off all of them. From what we saw on the camera it looks like they hit him initially with a blunt object and then commenced to beating him with their fists. Couldn't make out faces, only shadows," he said, clearing his throat again. "I've seen the reports on the other attacks. You think this is related? We're going to have to report this to the police."

Tyler nodded. "We'd all like to see the person or persons responsible for this behind bars." He watched Coach and Julian approach.

"How's Allen?" Coach asked, surveying the scene. He bent down next to Brayden's body. Julian examined Brayden, and, as he looked for broken bones, Brayden moaned.

Tyler was relieved. At least he was semi-conscious.

Julian looked up at Tyler. "Nothing seems to be broken. I want to x-ray him to be sure." He took out his cell phone, dialed a number, and requested a stretcher.

Tyler was amazed at how fast things went after that. Within minutes Brayden was on a gurney and being transported downstairs. There wasn't anything more he could do, except find the guys who did this to his friend.

———

Kamryn's phone rang at nine in the morning. If it was Bray, she promised herself, she was going to kill him for interrupting her sleep again. Let it ring, she thought.

And ring it did. She listened to that darned phone ring five times, stop, and then start again. When she refused to answer her cell phone, her home phone began to summon her attention again. "All right," she yelled to the room. She reached for her home phone and didn't recognize the number. "If this is a telemarketer, I'm killing somebody." She punched the talk button. "Hello?"

"Hey Kamryn, it's Tyler."

She knew Tyler was Bray's teammate and good friend. She actually liked Tyler. He was good looking, but not in an obnoxious way. "Hello, Tyler. What can I do for you?"

He hesitated. "Actually, this is about Brayden."

Oh, she so didn't like the way this was going. "What about Bray?"

Again with the hesitation. "Well, this morning, he was late for practice. I went looking for him and he was in the parking deck."

She was very close to losing it. "Tyler, cut to the chase."

"He'd been attacked and is in with the team doctor right now. They beat him up pretty bad this time."

She felt her heart constrict with pain at the thought of Bray getting hurt again. "I'm on my way."

"I'm sure he'd be happy to see you, but you should know that his face is messed up. It's swollen something awful. Julian says he doesn't have any broken bones, just a lot of bruises. A whole lot of bruises."

"Okay, I'll call his parents. They might want to come, too."

"Thanks. I didn't want to call them," Tyler admitted.

Kamryn pushed back tears. "Sure. See you in a bit." Kamryn ended the call, pushed back her covers, and went to get dressed.

In less than thirty minutes, she was on her way to Bray's house to pick up his parents. She didn't have to call and tell them the bad news; the team doctor already had. They'd immediately called her.

She had to remain calm, she reminded herself. Janice was very emotional, especially when it came to her children. Kamryn could easily imagine the scene at the Center. Hopefully, no press was there yet. If this got out before the game tomorrow who knew what would happen next? She also knew that this incident would have to be reported to the police. Once that happened, it would be open season with the press. Especially with the series being tied at three games each.

She arrived at Bray's spacious house. His parents were waiting for her outside the front door. They hopped inside her SUV before she could cut the engine.

Janice was a mess. She alternated between sobs and blowing her nose. Finally Kamryn reached for her hand. "I'm sure he's going to be fine."

"I know. My son is too hard-headed to let this get him down. I just wish I knew what was going on."

"Me, too, Janice."

"Thank goodness he's thinking about retiring. At least he'll be away from these fools."

She forced herself to remain stoic. Bray retiring? Had he forgotten to mention that little detail to her? Was he going back to Iowa when he did?

"Kamryn, are you all right?"

"Yes, just thinking." There were a million questions running through her head and no answers. What if this was somehow her fault?

"Why don't we talk about something happy?" Janice blew her nose again. "How's Colleen?"

"Doing fine," Kamryn said absently. "She wants to have you guys over for dinner before you head back to Iowa."

"That sounds wonderful," Janice said.

Twenty minutes later Kamryn pulled into the American Airlines Center parking lot. She gave her name to the guard and, once she was permitted entrance to the parking garage, headed for the athletes' parking level.

She parked the SUV and got out. They all walked to the elevator and she hit the button for the second floor. Greg greeted them as the doors opened. "Hello

Mr. and Mrs. Allen. Hi, Kamryn." He shook hands with everyone, motioning for them to follow him. "I'm afraid that he was attacked. No broken bones, but his face took the brunt of it. He's got bruises and a black eye."

He opened the door to the third exam room and there he was, lying on the table, barely conscious. His face was swollen to almost twice its size. Kamryn noticed the ice bucket and the towels. She made an ice pack and pressed it against his face. Janice did the same. Bray moaned at the slight touch.

James cleared his throat. "Who's doing this to our son? This isn't the first attack, but this one is the worst. I think Toronto is going to a lot of trouble to win a national championship."

Greg shook his head. "No, it's not Toronto. No team would risk expulsion from the league by doing something like this. From the footage on the security tape, and from what Brayden told us earlier, he's been singled out." He looked in Kamryn's direction and then turned his attention back to James. "Any weird women in his life at present?"

"No," James answered. "He's been focusing on the games."

Greg nodded. "Good to know. Until we can get a handle on what's going on, I'd like to assign a security guard to you and your wife."

"No, we're fine. It always happens here or somewhere away from the house. You take care of my son."

"I intend to. He's going to need to be in bed until the swelling goes down, probably a day or two. In all likelihood, he'll miss the game tomorrow."

James shook his head and looked down at Bray. "This is going to kill him. He's been looking forward to playing for the championship for his entire life. Now that the moment is finally here, he can't play because of some criminals who have singled him out."

Greg put his hand on James's shoulder. "I understand your concern, and I know how much he wanted this. I'd love nothing more than to let him play. He's one of my best players, but I don't think he'll be able to."

Kamryn spoke up. "It will kill him if he can't play, but I'm sure he'll understand."

"Like hell, I will." Bray sat up slowly, moaning and groaning the entire time. "I've put up with too much crap to give it all up now." He panted, trying to catch his breath.

"I'll tell you what, Allen," Greg said softly. "You go home and get some rest and we'll let Julian make the official ruling tomorrow. How does that sound?"

<hr />

After Julian gave his blessing and gave Brayden some medication, Kam drove Bray to his house. His parents were following them in Kam's SUV. Julian's orders were very specific. If Bray wanted to play in the final game for any length of time, he was going to need to stay in bed. Bray didn't like it, but there was little he could do about it. His head was throbbing as if those guys were still beating him within an inch of his life.

"Bray, you need to take some medicine? I can stop and get some water for you."

"I can wait until we get home." He leaned against the window. "I just want the jackhammer in my head to stop."

She reached across and rubbed his arm, waking up hormones that would do best to stay asleep. "I know you're hurting. We're almost there."

He looked over at her. The simple act of turning his head caused so much pain an expletive slipped past his lips. "Sorry, Kam."

"That's okay, Bray. I understand." She continued driving. "You can go to sleep if you want. I'll wake you when we get to your place."

"I like it better when you call it home."

———— ∞ ————

When Kamryn parked in front of Bray's house, he was snoring. Whatever Julian gave him knocked him out completely. Now she couldn't wake him.

James came to her aid once he had parked the SUV. He gently shook Bray's shoulders and got no response. He shook his son harder, but nothing. Bray didn't move. Kamryn started to worry that Julian might have given Bray too many meds, but finally he moved. He didn't open his eyes. He just moaned and shifted his position in the seat. She and James both breathed a sigh of relief. "What do you think, James?"

James looked at his bruised up son and let out a breath. "I don't want to leave him out here, but he's bigger than the both of us, Kamryn. We couldn't carry him inside. Maybe some water would wake him enough so we can get him in the house." He turned to Janice, who was watching the proceedings with tears in her eyes. "Baby, get a pitcher of ice water. We have to wake him to get him in the house."

Janice nodded and headed inside the house. James took a deep breath. "Kamryn, call Julian. I didn't want to say this in front of Janice, she worries so much, but I think Brayden might have a concussion. You know how athletes hit their head, think they're fine, and then die. I don't like the fact that it's taking so much to revive him."

Kamryn nodded, took out her phone, and dialed Greg, since she didn't know Julian's number by memory. She knew it wasn't a concussion, since Julian had run all the necessary tests earlier, but something was wrong. Greg answered on the first ring.

"What's wrong?"

All the tears she'd been holding back found an escape route. "We can't wake Bray!"

"Shit."

"Should we just call the paramedics?"

"Already doing it. Stay calm, Kamryn. We're on our way." He hung up the phone.

Kamryn tried to compose herself, but it was pretty useless, considering her best friend was either in the deepest sleep possible or had passed out. James came to her aid and pulled her into his arms. "Now, Kamryn, everyone is allowed a breaking point. You've held up pretty good this morning. What did Julian say?"

"They're on their way."

---

Within twenty minutes Bray's house was flooded with Maverick health personnel. Julian, his assistant, two team trainers, and Greg were assisting Bray. They had arrived in a blaze of glory. In all her years of reporting, Kamryn had never seen the health team in action. They arrived in the Mavericks' private ambulance. The men sprang into action. Julian checked Bray's vital signs and assured Kamryn and Bray's parents that he was fine, just having a bad reaction to the medicine. They loaded him onto the stretcher and took him in the house, followed by Bray's parents.

Kamryn and Greg were left alone outside. "Thank you for reacting so quickly. I don't know what we would have done."

He smiled at her. "That's one of my best players and I know you probably don't believe this, but I do like Allen. He's a team player. And I like you, too, Kamryn. Too bad it couldn't have worked out between us, but then I knew that from the beginning."

"What?"

"Come on, Kamryn. I was giving Allen the push he needed. I knew you guys were close. I know Allen. He might have dated those other girls, but he wanted you. You can tell him to jump and he'll do it. You talked him into buying a hybrid SUV last year, for goodness sake. That's when I knew. He respected you more than any other woman that I'd ever seen him with him. That's not to say I didn't see how it could work between you and Allen as more than friends, but somehow the pieces came together."

Kamryn stared at this man she thought she knew. "You're telling me you had an ulterior motive in asking me out?"

"No, not really. Everything I told you was true. You're a beautiful woman, smart, and not just about sports. But sports are your passion. I enjoyed talking to you, but I had noticed how much Allen watched you when you came to the office to interview me. So I decided to test a theory."

Her head was swimming with all this information. "So you're telling me that you only asked me to make Bray tip his hand, so to speak."

Greg shook his head. "If that's how you have to rationalize it, okay. Let's just say I've never seen Allen act that way over any other woman, and leave it at that."

She digested the statement. With all that had happened that morning, having the knowledge that Greg had been playing matchmaker in his own twisted way wasn't so bad. "Thank you, Greg. I appreciate it. I do admit when he brought up dating, I was a little hesitant. But we both know how persistent he can be."

"He wouldn't be Allen if he wasn't." He opened the front door to Bray's house and ushered her inside.

Kamryn was about to agree when they noticed Julian and the two assistants walking down the stairs with the empty stretcher.

"He's fine. He was allergic to the pain reliever I'd given him earlier. I gave him some Benadryl to offset it. He's going to be woozy for a while, as I explained to Mrs. Allen."

Greg nodded. "So what do you think his chances are for tomorrow night?"

Julian shrugged. "That's going to be up to him. Brayden's pretty healthy, so I believe he'll bounce back quickly. But to be honest, Coach, playing in the entire game would be out, maybe a quarter at best."

Greg nodded. "Yeah, that's what I figured. I was just hoping this one time I was wrong. I'll be right out, Julian."

"Yes, sir. We'll be in the van."

Kamryn knew Greg wanted to talk to Bray alone. "I'll see if I can distract Janice and James so you guys can talk."

"See? I told you you were smart. Shall we?"

Kamryn laughed. "Yes."

---

Twenty minutes after Kamryn had taken Allen's parents downstairs for a tea break, Greg sat there watching Allen sleep. Talking to an injured player wasn't usually this difficult, but Bray kept drifting off. This was the first time he'd been to Allen's house. He glanced around the room while Allen slept. The king-sized bed was raised off the floor by at least three feet. He noticed a picture of Kamryn on the dresser.

Allen's eyes shot open and he stared at Greg as if he were a stranger. "What are you doing here?"

Oh, this was not good. Was amnesia to blame? Did those idiots hit him so hard he'd lost his memory? "I'm your coach. You play basketball for the Dallas Mavericks."

"I know that, Coach. I got hit on the head, but I'm not stupid. What are you doing in my house talking to my woman?"

Relief flowed through his brain. Good, he was just jealous. "Don't worry, Allen. She's all yours. We were talking about you."

"Why?"

"Man, I can't believe you're asking me all these questions. I guess that means that you're on the road to recovery. Don't worry, my lips never touched Kamryn. Julian will be back in the morning to check you over. Most likely you should be able to play. How long is going to depend on you. So please follow Julian's orders to the letter. Stay in bed."

"Got it." He closed his eyes again. "Kam."

Greg assumed he was dismissed and that Allen wanted Kamryn. He headed out of the room and met Kamryn coming up the stairs with a tray holding tea, crackers, and soup.

"He's asking for you."

"Thank you, Greg." She continued up the stairs and into Allen's bedroom.

He also noticed that she didn't knock before entering. All he heard was Kamryn's sultry voice. "Baby, I got some food for you."

Allen mumbled something incoherent and Kamryn laughed.

"Not until after the game," she told him.

Greg could only imagine what Allen was asking.

—∞∞∞—

The next morning Brayden woke up early. It was going to be a big day whether he was allowed to play or not. Julian was coming by to check the swelling in his face. Hopefully he would give Bray approval to play. His head didn't feel as bad as it had yesterday. That had to mean something.

He went into his bathroom to check out his body for himself. There was nothing that could keep him away from the final game, whether Julian released him to play or not.

One glance in his bathroom mirror and he knew he would be able to play. The swelling wasn't gone completely, but he didn't look as if he had been beaten by a bag of coins. Now he looked as if he had a whole can of tobacco on one side of his jaw. His eye was turning into a real shiner. There was no way to hide it, not that he wanted to. This last attack would make the news, he knew. He wondered if the press had found out yet. He was so out of it yesterday, he hoped his parents had held up under the strain of the press. He glanced at his phone on the night table. He hadn't heard it ring during the night, but the red message button flashed, grabbing his attention.

Closer investigation showed him that he had twenty messages and that somehow the ringer had been turned off. He smiled. Kam was the most likely culprit. He flipped through the caller ID and saw some were from his NBA friends. He decided to check a few of the messages. It was as he'd feared. News of the attack had hit the news and his friends were checking up on him.

Following the aroma of breakfast, Brayden walked into the kitchen. His parents were already seated at the table enjoying their meal. His mother rose and hurried to him.

"You look much better," she said, hugging him gently and inspecting his face. "Kamryn called earlier. She's on her way here."

He nodded and kissed his mother on the cheek. "I feel a lot better."

She reached up and touched his face as only his mother could. "That eye is going to take longer though. It looks like you were in a barroom brawl." She smiled and fixed him a plate of eggs, bacon, potatoes, and toast. "This will give you energy for tonight."

"Thanks, Mom." He took the plate and joined his father at the table.

His father studied him. "You think they'll let you play?"

"At least a few minutes, I hope. My head is not hurting as bad as it was yesterday. I'll be sporting this black eye for a couple of weeks."

His father reached for his coffee cup and took a sip. "Compared to yesterday, you look like a million bucks. Any idea who wants to hurt you bad enough not to play, but not enough to kill you?"

"What do you mean?"

"I just thought about all facts surrounding the attacks. Whoever is behind it doesn't know where you live or they would have tried something here. When they attacked you yesterday they could have killed you, but they didn't. Killing you would have made more sense."

He knew his father didn't mean it the way it sounded. "I offered them money and they refused me."

His father nodded, deep in thought. "So many things about the attacks don't make sense. You had your watch, wallet, and the keys to your pimped-out ride, yet they left all that alone. Any crook worth his weight in stolen gold would have taken something, just because you're an NBA player. It would have given them bragging rights if they had some kind of proof."

Bray took a bite of eggs, taking in his father's words. The same things had occurred to him while he was showering. "Those guys said they didn't want anything I had. Who could want me out of the way that badly?"

"I watch a lot of crime shows on TV, and the culprit is never that far from your circle of friends."

He didn't have many close friends. Kam, he trusted with his life, and he also trusted Tyler implicitly. That left his other teammates. But why now? "It could be just about anybody, Dad."

"Well, you can narrow your search to people who don't know where you live. That help?"

"Yes, it does. Unfortunately, not enough to do any good. I still have a pretty long list. At least tonight's game will end it one way or another."

His father narrowed his gaze at him. "What if it has nothing to do with basketball? Anyone popped back into your life lately?"

Brian instantly came to mind. "Yeah, one of my friends I started out playing professionally with, Brian Collins. He showed up when we were in the semifinals." As a matter of fact, Brayden realized, it was right after one of their first losses.

"Is he still in the NBA?"

Brayden shook his head. "Didn't make it past his first season. He's a consultant in Chicago."

"Was he injured or something?"

"No, I don't really know the whole deal of why he was let go. After the first season, Sacramento released him from his contract. No other team picked him up, either. He was nicknamed Hurricane Collins because he blew in and blew out of the NBA. He always said he wasn't cut out for professional basketball."

Brayden had a thought as he finished his mother's delicious breakfast. "You think Brian had something to do with my attacks? Why?"

"I'm just saying look at your options, son. I remember that story about them letting him go after paying such an outrageous price to get him. If a player is troublesome, a team usually trades that player to another team, but never just gets rid of them. There is usually a team desperate enough to put up with some bad attitude. No one ever brought up why he was let go, and I guess no one really asked, either."

"Kam didn't like him. She thought he had another kind of angle going on. In all the years I've known her, I've never seen her openly hostile to anyone like she is to Brian."

His father smiled. "I knew I liked that girl. If Kam thinks there's something strange about this guy, listen to her instincts."

# CHAPTER 18

The night of game seven, Sandra Woken did something she rarely did since the death of her husband. She was going to watch the Dallas Mavericks. After Jason's death she didn't have to watch those infuriating basketball games anymore. But tonight she wanted to see them lose the game for herself.

Brayden's attack had been picked up by every news service in the world, it seemed. Everywhere she looked, his face and that horrible security footage were on the screen. The betting community was buzzing with possibilities, including betting whether Brayden would be playing. According to Brian there was no way that he would be able to play. Not with the beating the thugs had given him. She placed a bet that Brayden wouldn't be playing. It sounded like a sure thing and could triple her money while she watched the team she hated lose the biggest game in franchise history.

She sat back in her leather chair and kicked off her shoes. After pouring a glass of her favorite wine, she turned on the TV. She watched the news and noticed they were talking about Brayden's attack and his probability of playing in game seven.

"How about none," Sandra hissed at the TV. "There's no way that idiot will be able to play."

The sportscaster disagreed with her sentiments. "This is just in. It looks like he's been cleared to play. How long will depend on the coach."

Sandra dropped her wine on the white carpet. "What the hell? How can he be able to play?" She quickly dialed Brian's number. "I thought you had this handled. You'd better hope Toronto runs over Dallas. I just lost twenty thousand dollars betting Brayden wouldn't play!"

"It's kind of too late to do anything now, short of shooting him on national television."

"Stop being so dramatic and think of our next move," she said. The situation seemed hopeless at this point. Kamryn was going to uncover the truth and she could kiss the future good-bye unless they did something.

"Already working on it," Brian said and ended the call.

Sandra glanced at the screen. The game had begun and she noticed Brayden was sitting on the sidelines. He was dressed in his team uniform, but still had on his warm-ups. There was still hope. Maybe Coach De-Morris had changed his mind about letting him play.

The camera panned to Brayden's face. The handsome face was no more. Brian's guys had worked him over, and that black eye was a real shiner. She listened as the sportscaster kept talking about the attacks. With each accolade they gave Brayden, the worse she felt. They kept running the security tape of the assault and went so far as to offer a $50,000 reward for any information. She hoped Brian hadn't seen that or she'd be done for.

---

Later that night Kamryn thought her heart was going to pop out of her chest. Game seven had been intense from the tip-off. She had lost count of how many times the lead had changed. It was do or die for the Mavericks, and there wasn't a vacant seat left in the American Airlines Center.

The story about Bray's attack had hit the news earlier and rumors were sailing around in cyberspace that he might not get to play. The betting world had been crazy that day as many people bet against Dallas because of his injuries.

She and Kalyn were sitting in Bray's family seats. Sitting was a relative term, because they had been on their feet most of the game, along with the rest of the Dallas fans. She probably didn't have any voice left.

Kalyn made the motion for another beer and Kamryn shook her head quickly. It was the fourth quarter with only ten minutes to go. Dallas was down by ten points. She wanted to have a clear head when Dallas won the game.

---

Greg DeMorris had only one option. He was going to have to put Allen in the game. Although the team doctor had given his blessing for Allen to play some of the game, Greg was still hesitant about putting him in. His face was still swollen and he was sporting a black eye. Actually, right now his eye was purple, but it would be black in a few days. One elbow to the wrong place on his face could harm Brayden and he'd be out for more than just a game. But they were down by ten, and this was the championship. Everything was riding on tonight. He nodded to Brayden. As he rose, the crowd went wild and started chanting, "Allen, Allen, Allen!"

Brayden smiled and took off the breakaway pants players usually wore when they weren't in the game and walked over to Greg. He had the nerve to smile.

"Thanks for giving me a chance."

"This isn't about me being nice. This is about us being ten points down. Got me?"

"All ready."

"Music to my ears."

Greg watched him trot out to the floor and join his teammates. With a little luck and a lot of defense, Dallas could take their first National Basketball Championship.

⋙⋘

Kamryn's heart swelled with joy when she noticed Bray was out on the floor. She was glad Greg had finally decided to put him in. She hoped Bray and his teammates would be able to pull off the win. She couldn't imagine them not being champions.

After the ball was in play again, Toronto got possession and headed for the basket. If they made this shot, it would stretch their lead even further. The player tried for the three-point shot; it fell short and was in Dallas' hands. Somehow Bray got the ball. He took the shot from mid-court. The crowd roared when the ball went into the basket. Three points.

The crowd went nuts, which was a pretty short trip, Kamryn thought. Dallas just needed a few good solid plays and they could easily gain the lead. Her mind wandered for just a second until the crowd cheered again. What happened? She glanced to the court and noticed Dallas was at the free throw line. Two more points went on the board. They were now within five points with seven minutes to go.

Now Kamryn could understand Janice's reservation about not coming to the game. It was beyond nerve-wracking to watch them play when the stakes were this high. She prayed the team could make up the five points in seven minutes.

It happened so fast Kamryn knew she must have been dreaming. Dallas now had the lead with one minute to go. Could they hold it until the buzzer sounded in fifty seconds?

One lousy basket by Toronto and it could be a tie game once again. Then there would be overtime, she reasoned. Kamryn didn't think she could endure another quarter. She glanced at the court as Dallas's thirty-million-dollar acquisition rushed down court and made a slam dunk with fifteen seconds left in the game. Dallas was now ahead by four points. Then the buzzer sounded. They'd actually done it. Dallas had won the national championship! She reached for her sister and they hugged. Everyone around them was hugging and crying. Fans tipsy from both alcohol and the emotion of the moment reached for each other in celebration. She could only imagine how Bray and the rest of the team felt at this very important moment.

The crowd made a dash for the floor. Kamryn didn't dare try to find Bray in that mess. Unfortunately, Kalyn wasn't giving her that option. She pulled Kamryn onto the floor. It was worse than being stuck on the New York subway at rush hour.

She didn't have to search hard to find Bray. He found her. He was dripping with sweat, his black eye was gleaming, but he'd never looked happier.

"Baby," he said, picking her up as if she weighed nothing. He pulled her close for a bear hug, then planted a kiss on her lips. "I knew we could do it," he said in her ear.

He took her and her sister by the hand and led them through the growing crowd to the dressing room where some of the other players had retreated. The minute they walked into the boisterous room, Kamryn was hugged by many of the players. Bottles of Dom Perignon were popped open and it flowed freely. There was so much commotion in the dressing room, Kamryn couldn't hear herself think. She wouldn't have missed this moment for anything.

Kamryn yawned as she looked at her blank computer screen. One day she was really going to have to give her editor a lesson in life. Not only had he called her at eight o'clock in the morning after the Mavericks made basketball history, but he had the nerve to assign her an additional story about the game to turn in by noon. Since this was Dallas's first trip to glory, he wanted a story that focused on the emotions of the game from both the fans' and the players' view.

It was the first time in years that they didn't go to Junior's after the game. They'd wanted to, but by the time the press finally left, it was after one in the morning. Junior's was already closed. That was her biggest regret of the evening. They would have to make it up to Junior. Thinking of the hole-in-the-wall diner brought her back to her story.

Normally that kind of story was what she enjoyed writing, but she, like the rest of Dallas, had celebrated into the wee hours of the morning. Now, as her clock struck eleven, she had little time and a lot of work to get done.

She flashed on Jason and his death. She wondered if that had had any effect on the team. The pieces of his death were falling into place, but she could feel she was missing something that was staring her right in the face.

Slowly her focus turned to last night's game and she began to type. The game had been intense, and she wanted to capture the emotions of the players as well as those fans. And since she considered herself one of the biggest fans, the story flowed out of her easily.

———◦◦◦◦◦———

A week after the NBA finals Bray's life started to slow down. His parents had flown back to Iowa days earlier. He could actually relax and enjoy the feeling of being free in his own home. Since the season was officially over, there had been no more attacks and his black eye was healing nicely. Now he could turn his attention to Kam. When he asked her for a date the day after Dallas won the championship, he was sure she would say no, but she surprised him by agreeing. She also offered to cook. She was up to something.

He parked in front of her house and surveyed the quiet neighborhood. It was comprised mostly of elderly people. Very few kids were ever seen roaming through on bicycles. Although he loved his house because of its solitude, Kam's house came a close second.

Along with a dozen red roses, he'd also purchased several of her favorite movies on DVD. He hoped she didn't already have them. He grabbed the vase of flowers and the DVDs and headed to her front door.

He was not prepared for the woman who opened the door. Kam was in a black body-molding dress. That was the only way to describe it. It showed off her cleavage, hugged her curves, and stopped just above her knees. She stood regal in a pair of black stilettos. Her black hair swung loosely just past her shoulders.

"What are you looking at?"

She was smiling at him. It took a moment for his voice and brain to be on the same page. "I'm looking at the most beautiful woman on this earth." He handed her the flowers and the movies.

"Thank you, Bray." She kissed him and led him inside the house after closing the door. "These are some of my favorite movies."

"I know." He took a seat on the living room couch and laughed at her shocked expression. "Baby, you're always talking about those movies and how those women kept their clothes on and were still good actresses."

She set the vase of flowers on the table in front of him and the movies on the shelf by the TV. "Would you like something to drink?"

"Whatever you're having," he told her, watching her every move.

She smiled at him as she straightened her dress. "Be right back." She hurried into the kitchen.

Brayden leaned back on the couch. Yeah, Kam was definitely up to something. Finding out what would be fun.

She soon returned with a silver tray with a bottle of wine, a corkscrew, and two crystal wine goblets. Yeah, something was definitely going on.

"Dinner won't be ready for another thirty minutes. Want to start a movie?"

He opened the wine bottle and poured. He handed her a glass and she sat beside him. "What I'd like is for you to tell me what's going on in that pretty head of yours."

―∞―

She was busted. Kamryn cleared her throat and took a sip of wine. "I have no idea what you're talking about, Bray."

"Baby, I know you. I know when you're hurting inside, I know when you're hiding your emotions, and I know when you're bubbling to tell me something, like now."

Did he really know her that well? "Okay, you win." She really had to work on her poker face. "You want the short version or the long one?"

"Kiss me and find out." He winked at her.

She did as he asked and walked right into his trap. She had meant to give him a chaste kiss, but once their lips touched, Kamryn knew it was all over. Bray took control of the kiss with a flick of his tongue. Just when things were getting good, he stopped.

"Okay, tell me."

"Now?"

"Yes, now."

She sighed. "About six months ago I sent in a manuscript proposal to a publisher and the editor liked it. I've been waiting to hear if they wanted to buy it."

She had his attention. "So what happened? Am I in the presence of greatness?"

"Actually today I finally heard from them. They want a three-book series and they want to print it in hardback."

He looked at her blankly. "I know that means something, baby, but you're going to have to throw me a bone."

She giggled. "I forgot. Hardback books are a big deal for a writer. Three books on my first attempt to get published as a romance writer is pretty good as well. But that's not what I really have to tell you."

"Now you're drawing this out on purpose," Bray teased. "You know there's nothing you can tell me that will make me run out that door."

She had to find the courage to tell him or she wouldn't have a book deal. "You're my hero."

"What?"

"You're my hero. I mean, in the book. You don't play basketball, but I did pattern my character after you. He's kind, arrogant, caring, supportive, and very handsome."

He sat there dumbfounded.

Then she got worried. What if he didn't want to be in a romance novel? "Do you mind that I used you in my romance novel?"

"Of course I don't mind. I feel honored. Is the sex hot?"

"Why is it that your first thought is about sex? Not of the fact that I sold a romance novel with you as the hero. What if the sex is just mediocre?"

"We have hot sex," he said honestly. "You should write about our sex life."

"Bray, really."

"Come on, baby, you know what I mean. Besides, we could always go upstairs and practice." He reached for her just as the oven dinged.

"Dinner is ready!" Kamryn stood, ready for a diversion. "You can set the table and I'll take care of the rest."

"I love it when a woman takes charge."

———

Kamryn didn't know how much better the evening could get. Dinner had been spectacular, and now she and Bray were seated on her couch preparing to watch a movie before the rest of the festivities began.

She snuggled next to him and hit the remote control to start the show. "I'm sure you'll like this, Bray."

He wrapped his arms around her and kissed her on the neck. "And why's that?"

"You'll see."

"Oh, you know, Mom really digs those movies, too. Who do you think told me which ones to buy?"

" 'That Touch of Mink' is one of my favorites. I told you your mom and I are kindred spirits. Not only do we both love food, we both love Doris Day movies."

Bray laughed. "Well, yeah, I guess that's why she likes you so much." He kissed her forehead and grabbed her hand. He kissed it, too.

"What do you think you're doing, Mr. Allen?"

"Loving you."

She wasn't prepared for the in-love Bray, who put his feelings out there for her to see. "I'm glad. I love you, too."

She heard her cell phone ringing. "I hope nothing's wrong."

"I'm sure everything is okay." He looked around for the phone. "Where's your purse? I hear the phone, but I don't see it."

The phone continued making itself known. Somebody wanted her bad. "I think it's on the table."

Bray went and got the phone. It finally stopped ringing and Kamryn breathed a little easier. "At least it finally stopped. Maybe it's just Kalyn."

"Check your caller ID." He handed her the phone.

She did, and it was. "She's probably looking for food."

He chuckled. "You make her sound like a dog. Why don't you call her back?"

"She's got to learn to cook someday. She's an image consultant, for goodness' sake." She put the phone on the table.

"If you say so." Brayden sat beside her again. "It's pretty late. You sure?"

Kamryn nodded. "She's rung my doorbell as late as three in the morning."

"You tell her that if I'm here, she'd better not ring that doorbell past ten," he said.

"You think you're running things?" The phone started to ring again.

"No, I just want to spend every possible minute with you and only you."

She picked up the phone, ready to tear her sister a new one for calling so late. "Kalyn, you've really got to start cooking your own food."

"Sorry, big sis, but this is important. Call me when Bray goes home."

"Why can't you tell me now?" Kamryn moaned as Bray placed tiny kisses against her neck. So this was what she'd missed in her teenaged years.

"No, I hear that man in the background. Take care of him and I'll see you tomorrow. It's about Brian, and it ain't good."

"Oh," Kamryn moaned. She felt Bray unzipping her dress.

Kalyn laughed. "It's nice to hear you so happy. I'll be over for breakfast." She ended the call.

Kamryn's brain couldn't function. Bray's hands were inside her dress and driving her mad. He took the phone out of her hand and set it on the table.

"Should we continue this upstairs?"

Before she could answer, he maneuvered her onto his lap and somehow they were upright and walking to the stairs. She was nestled against his chest. "You sure can turn a girl's head, Bray."

"You're the only girl I want to turn." He entered her bedroom and deposited her on the bed. He then proceeded to take her on the ride of her life.

⋘⋙

The next morning Brayden woke up to an empty bed. He sat up, took a deep breath, and inhaled the aroma of food cooking. Kam must be fixing breakfast, he reasoned. He threw back the covers, padded to the shower, and then dressed. He went downstairs and found Kam in the kitchen busy at the stove. She smiled when she noticed him standing in the doorway.

"Good morning, honey," she said, greeting him with a kiss. "I know I keep saying it, but you were awesome last night."

He wrapped his arms around her. "You were awesome, baby. I don't know what it is about you, Kam, but the more we make love, the more I want to make love."

She giggled. "I can tell." She pointed down at his erection. "Doesn't it ever get tired?"

"Not as long as you're around." He kissed her on the forehead. "I think you've put a spell on me, babe." He released her, walked to the refrigerator and grabbed a carton of orange juice. He sat at the table, waiting on Kam to finish cooking the frittata.

She joined him at the table with the dish. It smelled wonderful. Next to the egg dish, she placed a plate of bacon, hash browns, and toast. "Oh, baby, this makes me almost forget about making love to you again."

"Oh, too bad," she teased as she took her seat. "I was thinking about a little extracurricular morning activity."

"Don't tease me, Kam."

"Who's teasing?"

Before any good foreplay could start, there was a knock on Kam's back door. Bray groaned. "That girl is really going to have to learn to cook something. Or move closer to McDonald's," Bray said, cutting into the frittata.

Kam rose and answered the door. It was Kalyn, but she wasn't dressed for work; she was dressed in shorts and a T-shirt. She definitely didn't looked like a working professional; she looked more like a college student.

"Hey, sis." She walked past Kam and took a seat at the table as if she owned the place. "Hi, Bray. So nice to see you." She winked a makeup-free eye at him. "I'm so glad you guys finally got this party started."

Bray was used to Kalyn's bluntness. He laughed at her comment. "Hey, it was Kam playing hard to get. She thought she was going to get rid of me. She should have known I don't give up."

Kam sat at the table with a thud. "And I'm right here and hear every word you're saying. You guys act like I'm in another room."

Kalyn laughed, reaching for the food and ignoring Kam. "Anyway, as I was saying, I'm very happy that you two are actually dating."

Bray looked at Kam. He'd walk through hell for her if he had to. "Me, too."

<hr />

After trading a few barbs with Kalyn at Kam's expense, Bray left. He got the feeling that the women needed to talk alone. Once in the solitude of his home he checked his messages. His realtor informed him that his condo had sold for the asking price. He quickly dialed the realtor and verified her earlier message. She also wanted to know if he'd completely moved out of the condo.

"Yes, I had a cleaning service in there a few weeks ago. Everything is out."

"Great. I'll get the paperwork going and I'll get back to you in a few days. You should still walk through the property one more time before the closing. Is that possible?"

"Sure. Thanks for all your help selling the condo." He smiled to himself as he remembered Kam's little nickname for his uptown digs.

"It's my pleasure, Mr. Allen. I'll be in touch with the closing date."

Bray looked around the room as he hung up the phone. He was dying to tell Kam, but it would have to wait. He had a feeling Kalyn had big news about Jason's case. How could the condo's sale compare with that? If Kam was able to break Jason's suicide, that was going to be big news. He had chalked it up to Jason walking on the wild side, but Kam had proved that theory wrong.

He decided on dinner. He would make her a meal that would make her eyes pop out of her head. He had to give her a little space with her sister first. He waited two hours before he called and asked for a date.

How much had his life changed in the last couple of weeks? He didn't even recognize himself at times.

Like right now. He was actually giving a woman space. The old Bray was dead.

———∞———

Kamryn looked across the table at her sister. "Say that again."

Kalyn reached for a slice of toast. "You heard me. I ran a background check on Brian Collins." She slathered butter on her toast, then topped it with a mound of jelly.

Kamryn took a sip of coffee, wondering why her sister never gained any weight with her dietary choices. "What was so bad about the background check? Bray says he's some kind of consultant."

"According to the report, he's in serious financial trouble. His wife filed for legal separation and a divorce is pending in Cook County. According to the background check, he hasn't had a job in two years. He's also under FBI investigation for illegal gambling. That wasn't on the report. Inside information."

"What?" Kamryn put down her coffee cup. "He's gambling, too?"

"I think he's doing more than that. He was brought in for questioning a few days ago in Dallas. He's staying in some seedy motel downtown. Does Bray know that?"

"I don't think he knows that Brian is still here. Is he still in jail?"

"No, he was released due to lack of evidence."

Kamryn hadn't thought this story could get worse, but she was wrong. "What kind of crime?"

"You're not going to like this." She took a deep breath. "I'll skip the boring details, but someone fingered him in a hire job."

"You mean like 'murder for hire'?"

"One of the men that was caught on film beating Bray talked. At first he said he had no idea who hired him and his buddies, but with a little digging the police tracked it back to Brian. He's a stupid criminal. He was still using the same cell phone. The police didn't have enough information, and since the guy doing the squealing was a three-time felon, they had to release Brian. The suspicion was there, but there just wasn't enough evidence to hold him."

"Why on earth would Brian pay to get Bray beat up? They're friends, or at least supposed to be friends." Kamryn fought the urge to phone Bray immediately. But, as a reporter, she knew this was only a piece of the puzzle.

"They couldn't prove he was the one doing the hiring since there was no paper trail, but he's the number one suspect."

Kamryn sighed as she sat back in the chair. "This will kill Bray. No wonder I didn't like that guy. And to think he's been paying people to beat up Bray." Then it hit her. "He was betting against the Mavs."

Kalyn nodded. "Most likely."

Kamryn shook her head at the possibilities. "I wish I had never looked into Jason's death. I know one thing has nothing to do with the other, but still ...." She rose from the table to call Bray and warn him.

Her phone rang. If the situation weren't so crazy, she would have laughed at the display screen. Bray. How did he always know when to call? She answered with a sigh. "Hi, Bray."

"Was I really that good last night?"

She laughed. "I'm not that tired," she shot back.

"Really? You want me to come back for a repeat performance?"

"I want you come over, but not for that. I have something to tell you."

"How about dinner tonight? My house. I'll fix you something that will make the clothes just slide off your body. Before they do, you can tell me what you have to say, and we can celebrate me selling my condo."

"You sold the toolshed?" Kamryn was shocked. She'd named the condo as such because of the number of groupies Bray had entertained there.

He laughed boisterously. "Yes, I did. I'm actually on my way over there to check it out. I put it on the market about three weeks ago. See what you did?"

"I didn't tell you to sell it." Secretly, she was glad he had. It was too much of a reminder of the kind of life Bray used to lead.

"I know you didn't, but it was time."

He had grown, she realized. The old Bray was gone. "Did you know Brian was still in town?"

"No, I haven't heard from him. I figured he went back to Chicago."

"He doesn't tell you when he leaves town?" Kamryn didn't think she'd ever understand men.

"Baby, we're guys. We don't do that. Just because he's in Dallas doesn't mean he's going to call me and let me know."

"All right. I guess I understand. Guys don't talk. I'll tell you the rest over dinner." She ended the call.

# CHAPTER 19

Brayden entered the three-bedroom condo and sighed. It was the first thing he bought when he came to Dallas five years ago. But he wasn't going to miss the place one bit. Even though it had been only three months, it seemed as if several lifetimes had passed since he'd actually used the place. He'd purchased his six-bedroom home three years ago and had been occupying the house for the last two. He'd brought his dates to the condo when the occasion called for it. They never knew about his home. The only person who knew about the home was the one person he wanted there. Kam.

He went through each of the bedrooms and saw that the cleaning crew had done a good job. The place was spotless. That red wine stain Kelly caused when he broke up with her four months ago was gone. The spaghetti Taylor attempted to make for him six months ago no longer adhered to the wall in the kitchen. The countless stains other women had left over time had all been erased as if they'd never been there in the first place.

He thought of Kam and her spotless house and how much he wanted to be with her. In just a few short weeks, his life had changed drastically. Sometimes he didn't recognize himself. For so long he'd thought of Kam as only a friend. He shook his head at all the time he'd wasted with all the wrong women when the right woman was standing in front of him all along.

The doorbell rang, bringing him out of his trip down memory lane. He opened the door, half-hoping Kam had come over to see the place one last time. No such luck. Kelly.

"Don't look so surprised to see me," she said, stepping inside the condo without an invitation and handing him a bottle of wine. She was dressed in a skin-tight dress and high-heeled shoes. "You're moving?"

"Kind of," he hedged. "What are you doing here, Kelly? I was very specific the other week when you showed up at the Center. I don't want you. You need to move on. I have."

She waved off his remark. "Yeah, yeah, yeah. You've moved on. I had a feeling you were here in our place. I think you've been punished long enough. I'm ready to forgive and move in."

His heart almost stopped beating. "What?"

She nodded. "I thought that would get your attention. I forgive you for breaking up with me and tossing me aside. I know you're a playa, that's what you do. You know you need a pretty woman on your arm when the press is following you around." She glanced at his face. "Your eye is healing well. Was it worth it?"

Okay, he was seconds from doing something to this woman. He wouldn't hit her. That was not allowed. "What are you talking about, woman?"

She started walking around the vacant living room. "I was talking about moving in here with you. But I assume since your furniture isn't here that you bought us a house. I hope it's in upscale Highland Village. What kind of car are you buying me? I think I'd look hot in a BMW."

"You got about two seconds to explain what the hell you're talking about."

"Duh. All the press you've been getting in the play-offs. You need to be seen with a pretty woman. It's no secret your contract is up this year. The Mavericks will have to pay a lot to keep you here."

"Get out."

She looked at him. "What? You know you want me. Men always want me. Stop playing."

"Out!"

"How can you not want me? Men always want me. Married or not. Do you know how many men offer to leave their wives and families for me?"

"Get out."

"But Brayden, I can improve your playa-playa image. You need to be seen with a pretty woman. All the pictures I've seen of you lately have been either with Kamryn or your parents. People are going to think you're dating her if we don't start dating."

*This woman had lost her mind.* "Get out or I'm calling the police." To make his point he grabbed the bottle of wine she had brought with her and sent it sailing across the room until it connected with the clean wall and splashed on her dress.

Kelly stared at the red liquid cascading down the wall and onto the carpet. Then she looked at the front of her dress. "You're going to be sorry you did that." She headed for the bathroom down the hall.

Brayden knew this woman was not going to leave his condo on her own. He took out his cell phone and dialed security. "This is Brayden Allen. I have an unwanted guest that needs to be escorted off the property."

"We'll be right there, sir."

Brayden pushed the button on the phone and called to Kelly, down the hall. "Kelly, this is your last warning. Get out. Security is on the way."

"I'm cleaning my dress. You spilled wine on it, remember? You're paying for cleaning my dress," Kelly yelled from the bathroom. "I bet Dallas won't look so kindly on you if they knew you have a violent side. That coach doesn't seem like he takes too much foolishness. He might fine your ass or something."

Brayden sighed. The day had started out so well and it had gone straight to the devil. Kelly was not going to leave quietly, and he was sure she was going to run to the press with some kind of lie. This wasn't going to look good, and Kam would probably kick him to the curb for something he hadn't done. The door bell sounded. "Thank goodness, security is here." He opened the door and was shocked to see Kam standing in the doorway.

Her smile slowly faded away. "You don't look too happy to see me. I wanted to talk to you about Brian, and it couldn't wait until dinner and I didn't want to say it over the phone."

He still stood there like a block of cement.

"Are you going to invite me in or what?"

He didn't have many options. He was sunk and he knew it. "Sure, baby, come in."

She took one step inside and that was when Kelly decided to stride into the living room without a stitch of clothing on. "I thought I heard voices," she cooed. Walking up to Brayden, she circled her arm around him. "Hello, Kamryn, it's nice to see you. I realized that you and Brayden are friends and all, but after we move and buy our house, you're going to have to find a new playmate."

"Kam, I can explain." He didn't know what to do to make this scene less horrible.

Kamryn looked from Brayden to Kelly. She took a deep breath before she spoke. "That will not be a problem." She looked at Brayden, then in a calm voice that was quite scary, she said, "Mr. Allen." She turned and walked away.

Brayden broke Kelly's hold on him. "Get your clothes and get out." He ran after Kam just as the security guard finally showed up apologetically.

"Sorry, Mr. Allen."

"Forget that. Get that woman out of my condo now."

"Yes, sir."

Brayden resumed his chase at full speed. Where had she gone that fast? He glanced around the corner, looking for her SUV. As he spotted it, she was backing out of the parking space and preparing to leave. He had one option, and he took it. Taking a deep breath, he started running all-out to catch her. He finally caught up to her just as she was driving away. "Baby, listen." He jumped in front of her SUV to stop her. "Just listen."

She jerked the SUV to a stop and let the passenger window down a fourth of the way. "What? I told you from the beginning you were going to do this and you did. You're a playa, Bray. You can never be satisfied with one person. So go back to your groupie and leave me alone."

Her tires squealed as she drove away.

Bray felt as if his heart had been ripped in two pieces. Now he knew that what his mother always told him about paybacks was absolutely true. He walked back to his condo just as two security guards emerged with Kelly in her hastily-thrown-on dress and handcuffs.

"She put up a little bit of a fight, Mr. Allen," the guard said. "We had to subdue her. We can turn her over to the police for trespassing on private property and you can file a report."

"Fine. I just want her off the property and away from me."

The guard nodded. "You may want to think about a restraining order."

"Not a problem. I'll get in touch with my attorney and he'll handle everything." Bray thanked the guard and went back into the condo to get his keys. He had to make this right with Kam.

---

Kam didn't stop driving until she got to her house. She told herself not to cry, but, in the safety of her garage, she let go and cried. She kept telling herself it didn't matter, but it did matter.

She entered the house and decided to fix an elaborate meal. It was what she did when she was depressed and/

or upset. When her husband passed away, she cooked boeuf bourguignon, the French classic. Unfortunately, every meat she had was frozen, so it seemed like takeout was the order of the evening.

Her phone rang just as she was deciding what kind of dinner she wanted. She didn't want to talk to Bray. Not now. Not ever. It was Kalyn. She really didn't want to talk to her sister, but knew she couldn't hide from her. It wasn't the Hillcroft way. "Hello, Kalyn." She tried to sound upbeat.

"What's wrong?"

"Why does something have to be wrong?"

"Because you left here less than an hour ago to tell Bray about Brian and we both know it takes at least thirty minutes to get to Bray."

"So?"

"Girl, please, out with it."

Kamryn took a deep breath and told her sister about catching Bray with his hand in the cookie jar. "I left after that."

"Did he explain why the woman was there in his empty condo with no clothes on?"

"I wasn't listening. Why are you on his side?"

"Because I know Bray loves you and he's been breaking his neck to show you how much he's changed."

"Really? But she was standing there naked talking about their house they were buying?"

"So she didn't know Bray already had a house?"

Kamryn thought for a moment. Now that she had a moment to review the scene in her head, it started to make sense. "Apparently not, and you know what else? There was wine all over the wall."

"Honey, he's a guy and he wouldn't hit a woman. He had to let out his frustration some way. I bet it splashed on her dress and she claimed she was going to clean it up."

"Why do you think that?"

"Because she's a groupie. Bray's name has been all over the news since the last attack. It's no secret that his contract is up. Everyone is waiting with bated breath to see how much Dallas is going to pay to keep him."

"You think I overreacted?"

"What do you think?"

"That I should talk to him."

"That's my girl."

Kamryn ended the call. Kalyn could always make her do the right thing whether she was feeling it or not. Her phone rang again. She picked up the phone and answered. "Hello?"

"Kamryn, this is Sandra. Any luck on the case?"

"Sorry, Sandra, I haven't had time lately."

"Oh. Why don't you come and look at my new office? I have some information that might help you with Jason's case."

Kamryn was in no mood for Sandra or her lies. She wished for the thousandth time that she had listened to Bray and left Jason's apparent suicide alone. But now she was in too deep, and this thing had to be resolved. She didn't have any proof that Sandra was nothing more than a gold digger. If she wanted to get some real proof she was going to have to meet Sandra. "Sure, Sandra, give me about thirty minutes and I'll be there."

"I'll be waiting."

As Kamryn pushed the end button on her phone, she knew this meeting was going to change her life. She just had no idea how.

———

Kamryn knew she was in trouble the minute she walked into the dark storefront, but she wanted to resolve this disaster and this was her only way. She took a deep breath and surveyed the area.

Looking around the room, she saw there was no furniture, not even a chair, and it looked too small to be a future tea shop. But Sandra had seemed so happy about being able to acquire the building.

Her cell phone buzzed at her. She looked at the display. Bray. She wasn't ready to talk to him right now. Her heart still hurt at the memory of the naked girl.

"Kamryn, I'm so glad you could make it," Sandra said, walking into the room. She was dressed in tight jeans, a tank top, and stilettos. Not the typical tea-shop-owner attire. "I never thanked you for looking into Jason's suicide. I really appreciate it."

"But?"

"I've come to realize that it was just that. I have to let him go and move on. For whatever reason Jason hit that concrete pillar, I have to come to terms with it."

"What about the insurance policy?"

"Well, since it was ruled suicide by the police, the insurance policy won't pay out. So I'm moving on. I suggest you do the same." She rubbed her fingers on her jeans. "I can't bring him back."

Kamryn's reporter's sense kicked in and her adrenaline skyrocketed. Most women would want to clear the suicide stigma from their dead husband's name, but not Sandra. She slowly moved toward the door. "It seems you've had a change of heart, Sandra. You don't want to know what happened to Jason in the last hours of his life? And how about all the information that we found?"

She stopped walking. "We?"

"You don't think I did all this alone? I have some contacts in the financial community that have helped me uncover the information."

"So someone else knows you're here?"

She took another step back. "Why?"

Sandra shook her head. "It wasn't supposed to happen like this."

"It was you, wasn't it?"

Sandra's head popped up. "I don't know what you mean. Are you accusing me of killing my own husband? How dare you!"

"I didn't say you killed him, Sandra. You said you loved him."

She sniffed. "Yes, I did. He was my life."

"I'm sure he was. He was the provider for you and your family. He also discovered your secret."

"What secret? My life is an open book."

"Even flirting with his teammates?"

"Kamryn, I never thought you went in for gossip. What about all that gibberish about the third estate and reporters only writing the truth?"

"It's the fourth estate, Sandra. You started me on this journey, but I'm going to see it through."

"I loved Jason. I love our girls."

"The girls that have been with your dead husband's mother while you remained here in Dallas with no family or support present? I kept wondering why you remained here."

"I don't have any idea what you're talking about. So I let the girls stay with Jason's mother in Chicago for a while. Big deal."

"You know, I used to always see them with Jason. Never with you. Every time he was at a charity function, it was the girls by his side. Not you. You married him for the money he could provide. You were a sales girl at the local mall until you married him. Now you're opening an upscale tea shop with your dead husband's money."

"He refused to help me realize my dream."

Kamryn shook her head. The beautiful woman standing before her made her sick. "So you turned to gambling thinking it would pay off really fast, probably hoping Jason never noticed the missing money. He loved those girls and he even loved you."

"He was going to divorce me."

"Yeah, I know. He found out about your gambling and how much of his money you'd lost and that he was going to divorce you. First you threatened him with his own kids, and he backed off. The deal-breaker was when those guys showed up at practice. But your world had already started to unravel months before. That's when you put your plan into action. Then there was talk of Da Money having him kicked out of the NBA for gambling. He knew he had to do something to save his name. Divorcing you was his only option."

"Too bad you're smarter than anyone gives you credit for. How do you think I got Jason to marry me after two months of dating all those years ago?"

Kamryn didn't want to think about it.

But Sandra wanted to share. "I did just about every freaking thing he wanted done in and out of the bedroom. Nothing was too strange in those days."

Kamryn wanted to hit her, but, more importantly, she wanted to get away from her. She put her hand on the doorknob and discreetly tried to turn it, but it was locked.

Sandra reached behind her back and pulled out a small gun, pointing it directly at Kamryn. "Move away from the door and walk down the hall," Sandra ordered. The soft, sultry voice was gone, replaced by the uncaring voice of a woman who had stooped to murder to attain her dream.

"Sandra, think about what you're doing," Kamryn said, hoping for a little reprieve.

"Oh, I have thought about this since you discovered Jason's SUV. I wanted to burn it, but I just couldn't do it."

Since she was probably going to die anyway, Kamryn just had to know. "What does Brian Collins have to do with you?"

⋘∞⋙

After he made another cleaning appointment and spoke to his realtor to finish the process for him, Brayden's next move was Kam. His cell phone rang. He hoped it was Kam and she'd calmed down and was ready to forgive him, but no such luck. It was the last person he wanted to talk to. Brian.

"What's up, Brayden? You and your woman have a fight?"

"How did you know?"

"I know. Meet me downtown." Brian rattled off an address.

"See you in twenty." Bray didn't like two things about the brief conversation he'd just had with Brian. One, he knew too much about Kam, and second, Brian didn't want to meet at a bar. Brian always seemed to have trouble around him. Did it somehow involve Kam this time? He didn't like that thought.

With all the craziness that had been going on in his life the last few weeks, Brayden had placed a tracking device on Kam's SUV and her cell phone. Heck, he was still sporting a black eye from the last attack.

He pulled over to check her whereabouts. Thank goodness he'd listened to her and bought the pricey cell phone last year. He had her location within a few minutes. Why was she downtown? What was going on? And why was she at the address that Brian had just given him?

Something didn't smell right. Brayden knew his limits. He couldn't face Brian and whatever drama he had in store for him alone. He called in his backup plan.

———

Brayden parked a block away from the address Brian gave him and waited for Tyler to arrive. In the meantime he reached inside his glove compartment and retrieved his pistol and slipped in a clip of ammo. He smiled. Kam's dad had convinced him to get licensed to carry a weapon. He was so glad he had listened to Harding. He wasn't crazy about having to use it, but if Brian had harmed Kam in some way, all bets were off.

Tyler parked his truck next to Bray's SUV and got out. "What exactly is going on?" He nodded at Bray's pistol.

"I don't know. Kam and I had a fight. Kelly showed up at the condo. It's a long story, but let's just say Kam is not happy with me right now. She has some suspicions about Brian, too."

"I think she's right. I didn't want to say anything, but all this trouble didn't start until he showed up. Trouble always did seem to follow him."

"Do you have a gun?"

"Yeah." He opened passenger door and reached inside his glove compartment and retrieved his nine-millimeter. "And yes, I have a license to carry a concealed weapon. So we're not breaking any laws."

They started walking toward the building's back entrance. "So you thought Brian was bad news, too. Why didn't you say something?"

"Brayden, who wants to hear that their friend is up to no good? Plus, I didn't think he would be here that long, but I was wrong."

Brayden thought about his friend's words. "You're right. I've probably seen Brian six times in the last ten years, and each time it's been a phone call in the middle of night and meeting him in some dive."

They approached the back door of the address. Tyler motioned to Brayden to be quiet. "I hear voices," he whispered.

Bray heard two voices, one male and one female. He listened closer. He knew both of those voices, and neither was Kam's.

Brayden watched the couple as they were searching for something in a cabinet. He wanted to take them both right now, but Kam was nowhere in sight. He looked to Tyler and whispered, "I don't see Kam."

Tyler nodded. "Maybe she's in the front of the store," she whispered. "What do you want to do?"

"Wait until one of them is alone. It'll be easier to get them one at a time."

Okay, that made sense. They quietly watched Brian and Sandra. Brian and Sandra's conversation soon became louder and louder. Brayden and Tyler didn't have to strain to hear.

"Brian, I can't believe you were stupid enough to tell that man to come here. Have you lost your mind?" Sandra opened another cabinet door and took out a bottle of

Fiji water and opened it. "You just made matters worse about tenfold."

Brian stood directly in front of Sandra. "You said get him here. I got him here."

She took a drink of water. "That was before. You should have checked with me. You're the same irresponsible idiot I knew in college."

"You would know."

"Yes, I would know." She took another drink of water, then screwed the top back on it, and set it down. "Now what are we going to do?"

"You know, since you keep calling my ideas stupid, why don't you come up with a plan to make all this go away. This was supposed to be simple. We were supposed to make enough for my wife to take me back and you to open that shop you've been talking about for years."

"Your wife isn't taking you back."

"Yes, she is. She said when I got back on my feet. And this would have put me back on my feet."

"How did I ever love you?"

---

Kamryn opened her eyes, but she couldn't focus in the dark room. She must be in a storage closet, she reasoned. From what she'd seen of the shop, she knew it didn't have many rooms. Slowly her eyes became accustomed to the dark room. Yes, it was definitely a closet, and now she had to figure out how to get out of there.

She listened closely to the muffed voices. Sandra and Brian were arguing. Typical. Brian may not have helped her get rid of her husband, but he knew about it. College sweethearts. Who would have ever guessed those two had been at the same college?

---

Brayden listened to the bickering couple for at least twenty minutes. After hearing them confess to just about everything possible, Brayden shuddered at how close to the danger they actually were. Every suspicion Kam had was right on the money. Sandra killed her husband by draining the brake fluid. He couldn't wait to tell her that she was right.

Finally, Brian left the room. This was their chance. He signaled Tyler and they made their move. Brayden tried the back door; he'd expected it be locked, but it wasn't. Maybe it was a trick. He'd find out in about thirty seconds.

# CHAPTER 20

Brayden opened the door and slipped inside the building without being noticed. Sandra was assembling something on the counter. Brayden glanced around the room as he approached Sandra, hoping to spot Kam, but he didn't see the love of his life anywhere.

He stood directly behind her. "Okay, Sandra. The game is up. Turn around real slow and keep your mouth shut."

"I told that idiot that you'd come through the back door, not the front." She did as Brayden directed. "I knew you'd be here."

"Skip it. Where's Kam?"

"Who says she's here?"

"I heard you and Brian, so I know she's here. You can make this easy or hard, the choice is yours."

She smiled. "Well I've always liked things hard, but this is not one of those times."

Brayden relaxed. "Where's Kam?"

"Closet."

Brayden couldn't bring himself to ask the one question.

Tyler did. He'd entered the room without making a noise. "Have you harmed her?"

Sandra looked at Tyler. "Not yet."

"Meaning?" Tyler asked.

"You let me go and I'll tell you where Kamryn is."

"How about you tell us and we don't hurt you?" Brayden searched the drawers for something to subdue Sandra. He located the rope and some electrician's tape.

"At this point, it doesn't matter. This was such a simple plan. And it went to hell. I just didn't want him to divorce me. This seemed to be the only way. When those guys showed up at the Center, Jason was livid. He told me I'd ruined his career. What else could I have done?"

Brayden tied her hands behind her back. "Murder is never the answer. You could have started your life over. You didn't have to do away with Jason."

"He told me he had left everything to me, and he left me nothing." She shook her head.

Brayden shivered at how cold and uncaring Sandra sounded as she recounted the whole fiasco. After Jason's death was ruled a suicide, she started trying to cover her tracks. She had planted that note in his car the day before. It was from a letter written years ago. This was one crazy woman. He covered her mouth with tape. He looked at Tyler. "Now what?"

"I'll look for something to tie her, too, so she won't get away."

Brayden looked at Sandra as she crouched on the floor and began to cry. "I don't think she's going anywhere, but better to be safe. I'm going to look for Kam, then kick Brian's ass."

---

Brayden walked softly down the hall, hoping to get the drop on Brian. He wanted to hurt him in the most elemental way for all the lies he'd told and the attacks he'd orchestrated. He also was still looking for Kam. The store front didn't have that many rooms, and so far he'd come up empty.

Brian was facing the storefront, no doubt looking for Brayden. He looked nervous and fidgety. As if he sensed Brayden's presence, he whirled around to face him.

"Glad to see you could make it, Brayden." Brian smiled at him. "I'm guessing you know the whole story, since you're coming through the back. Should have known Sandra would sing to save her skinny ass," he said.

"That's all you have to say?" Fuming, Brayden walked closer to him. "You pay thugs to beat me up, and that's all you have to say?"

"Don't take it so personal. It was business," Brian said. "You know the deal. I'm broke and I had to get some cash. Toronto was slated to win this year, Dallas was nowhere in the equation. So When Dallas made the playoffs, I had to take matters into my own hands, so to speak. But you wouldn't lay down like you should have. You cost me a mint."

Fury burned through Bray's body at an alarming rate. This … person that he'd known for the last ten years had offered him up like a sacrifice. Brian wasn't concerned about Brayden's welfare, or Kamryn's. Brayden closed the remaining distance between them and threw a right hook that connected solidly with Brian's jaw. "That was for all trouble you and Sandra have caused."

Brian fell to the floor in a heap, dazed and confused. "What the …."

Brayden knew he was out of control, but there was little he could do about it. He jumped on top of Brian before he could get up and pummeled Brian's face until someone pulled him off.

"Hey, man, save some for the cops," Tyler said.

Slowly he came to his senses and realized Tyler was right. "I didn't find Kam." He looked around the room and noticed one door he hadn't checked.

"Tie his sorry ass up. I'm going to check this room. She's got to be here." He strode over to the closet and pulled the door open. There she was, tied to a chair and out cold. "Baby!" He quickly untied her and picked her up. He laid her gently on the floor, checking her for injuries. He noticed a bruise on her forehead. Rage filled him again. He wanted to kill Brian and Sandra, but he had to take care of Kam. He pulled out his cell phone and dialed 911.

After Tyler had secured Brian, he came to Brayden's aid. "How's Kamryn?"

Brayden looked down at the woman in his arms. Kam was still out cold. He could feel a knot forming on her head where she'd been hit. "She must have gotten clubbed on the head. I called the cops. They should be here soon. I can't believe Brian would do this, not only to me, but to Kam. Bastard. He can't get enough time for all the things he and Sandra did."

"I know, man. They're both bad news. I feel sorry for Jason's kids. When all this hits the press, it's going to hurt them."

Brayden agreed. "Yeah, it's awful to know your mother killed your father. Talk about a harebrained scheme. I wonder who came up with the idea, her or Brian? I had no idea they knew each other until tonight. I feel like all kinds of a fool. Kam kept saying she didn't like Brian, but I just thought it was a personality clash."

"Now we know," Tyler said. "I hear the sirens."

Bray looked down at Kam's still form. "Thank God."

She opened her eyes and stared at him. "Sorry."

"Don't worry, baby. It's going to be fine. We're going to be fine. Brian and Sandra are going to jail and we're going to take you to the hospital. I love you, Kamryn." He planned on saying that every day, every hour of every day, for the rest of his life.

"Good." She fainted.

<hr />

Two hours later the doctor walked into the waiting room and went straight to Brayden. "Hello, Mr. Allen. Awesome season." He cleared his throat. "Sorry, big fan. Although you and Ms. Hillcroft aren't related, I know you accompanied her in the ambulance, so I wanted to let you know she has a simple concussion."

Bray wasn't feeling the doctor's careless attitude after all they had been through. He looked the young man up and down. "What do you mean, simple? She could barely stay awake! How much more out of it does she have to be for you to actually care!" Brayden couldn't believe he was yelling at this doctor. The doctor's tanned faced turned red with embarrassment. "I'll have her out of here in five minutes if she doesn't start getting better treatment immediately!"

"Mr. Allen," the doctor said in a calm voice. "Why don't we start over?" He motioned for him to take a seat.

Brayden sat down and waited for the doctor to clarify. "Sorry, doc, but she's very important to me. And it seemed that you weren't taking her injury seriously. I'd be less of a man if I didn't tell you what's what."

The young man cleared his throat and began. "There are two types of concussions, simple and complex. A simple concussion is just as the name implies. Ms. Hillcroft received a blow to the front of her head with a blunt object. The skull wasn't cracked, which is good. Depending on the extent of her injuries, the symptoms will disappear in about seven to ten days. So you're going to need to be patient with her for next week or so. She may have trouble forming her thoughts, experience nausea, dizziness, and occasional headaches. Currently, she's having a CT scan to check the swelling in her brain. I won't be able to assess her injury fully until some of the swelling goes away. We'll discuss that more when her family gets here. Please let me know when they arrive." The doctor left the waiting room.

Brayden wiped his eyes with the back of his hand. He wished for this day to end and for him to be able to take Kam home with him.

"How you holding up?" Tyler sat beside him and said nothing about his tears.

Brayden couldn't speak. It hurt too much to voice his fears. Tears ran full force now. He didn't try to hide them. They were for Kam and all the pain she was feeling at the moment. Tyler handed him a tissue. Bray nodded his thanks and dried his eyes.

"Don't worry, man. I got your back." Tyler sat back in his seat.

Brayden realized Tyler was truly a good friend. Not many people would have come to his aid with the brief explanation he had given him a few hours earlier. Now that was true friendship.

Brayden smiled.

"Oh, dear," Colleen said as she entered the waiting room. She was dressed in jeans and a T-shirt and looked as bad as Brayden felt. Her plump face was swollen from crying. "How is she?" Colleen sat on the other side of Bray. Harding was dressed almost identically to his wife. He walked in and took a seat, shaking Tyler's hand.

"Harding Hillcroft, Mr. Rice. I'm Kamryn's father."

"Nice to meet you, sir," Tyler said. "I've heard nothing but good things about you and your family from Brayden."

Brayden wanted to join the conversation, but his mouth didn't seem to be working. He opened his mouth but nothing came out. Finally, he could choke out a word. "Doctor."

"Where is the doctor?" Colleen glanced around the room and reached for a tissue.

Brayden forced his mouth to cooperate. "I have to tell him you guys are here."

Tyler shot up out of his chair. "I'll do it." He was gone before Brayden could say anything to the contrary.

Harding moved into Tyler's vacated seat, next to Brayden. "It's okay, son. We know you did all you could." He patted Brayden's leg. "Thank goodness you were there for her."

"But she still got hurt," Bray choked out. "I wasn't in time to save her from getting hurt."

"It's all right, son." Harding patted his shoulder. "I know my baby girl had a job to do. She figured it all out," he said proudly. "My child is too hardheaded to let some injury get the best of her."

The doctor walked in and greeted everyone. "Hello, I'm Dr. George Jensen. I'm attending to Ms. Hill-croft."

"Her name is Kamryn," Harding offered, shaking his hand. "I'm her father, Harding. This is her mother, Colleen. Her brother and sister will be here shortly."

Dr. Jensen nodded. "Pleasure to meet you both. I know you want to know about your daughter, so I won't keep you in suspense. Kamryn has a simple concussion. I won't know the extent of her injuries until the swelling has gone down. That should take about two to three days."

"Will she need surgery?"

"Not at this time. She's having a CT scan right now. She's been admitted to hospital and will be in room 345. She'll be here until the swelling goes down in her brain. If you want to wait for her there, that's fine."

Harding nodded. "Thank you, doctor. I appreciate everything you're doing for my baby girl."

The doctor smiled. "You're welcome. She may have problems forming sentences right now, so be patient with her." He left the room without another word.

---

Brayden wanted nothing more than to see the woman he loved, but he knew that her parents were probably anxious as well. He took a deep breath. "Why don't you guys go ahead and I'll wait for Tyler to get back."

Harding looked at him with observant brown eyes. "No, son, you're coming with us. We're family."

"But Harding …."

"No buts. Besides, here comes Tyler anyway."

Brayden knew he was sunk. "All right, Harding. We'll come with you guys."

The four of them walked in silence to Kamryn's room. They arrived just as the nurses were getting Kam settled in her hospital bed. After they made sure all the machines were monitoring her, the nurses made a hasty retreat.

Saying that Kam was awake would be a stretch, Brayden thought. Her eyes were open, but she had a glazed look. Brayden just wanted to take her away from all this. He walked to her bed and picked up her hand. She felt warm.

"Baby," he said quietly.

She stared at him as if he were a stranger. Then suddenly she blinked, smiled at him, and pulled his hand closer to her and kissed it. "Thank you."

Those words were his undoing. He mumbled something to her and bolted out of the room. He couldn't hold back his emotions anymore. He had to go somewhere, anywhere people couldn't see him break down. He didn't want Kam and her family to see him fall apart.

"Where do you think you're going?" Harding asked, stepping out of Kam's room. "She's asking for you."

That stopped him in his tracks immediately. He didn't have the option of running. Kam wanted to see him. He was going to have to suck it up and face the woman he loved. "I'll be right in."

---

Somebody was snoring.

Kamryn opened her eyes and glanced around the room. This looked nothing like Sandra's tea shop. It smelled too clean, and there was an annoying beeping noise interrupting her sleep. She glanced to her left and saw Bray sitting in a chair snoozing. Well, that was one mystery solved, she thought.

Her head hurt like the devil. She didn't like being hooked up to so many machines. She sighed.

"Hey, you're up," Bray said, smiling. "You've been out for two days. Your parents stayed with you the first night. I wanted to stay the first night, but I didn't want the press camped out by your hospital room." He picked up her IV-free hand and kissed it. "Nothing was going to keep me away a second night. I snuck in the back way last night. I made sure there was no press following me on the DL."

She loved him so much. As a friend and as a lover. When he first brought up their relationship, she hadn't thought he would be able to go the distance. Bray had showed her a very different man in the last few weeks. The playa was gone and a mature, responsible man had taken his place. She could count on him when the chips were down. "I'm sorry about what happened. I should have believed you when you said nothing was going on with you and Kelly."

He shook his head. "It wasn't the way it looked. Kelly was an uninvited guest and she didn't want to leave. Security took her away."

She tried to remember the events, but everything was hazy. The image of a naked Kelly was burned into her brain, but little else about their fight remained. She had a thunderous headache. "I don't remember all the details. I remember Sandra and the tea shop." She could only imagine what kind of pillow hair she had this morning. She raised her free hand to finger comb it, but something felt wrong. Very wrong.

"What is this?"

Bray shook his head. "A bandage. You were bleeding."

At least she was alive. "Thank you for being here and saving me. I believe they would have killed me."

"Don't worry about that now."

"What's wrong with me? I feel weird."

The doctor walked in with a metal chart in his hands. "Hello, Kamryn. How are you feeling this morning?"

"Tired. Dizzy. The room keeps going in and out of focus. My head is killing me."

"Understandable. You'll have these symptoms for the next seven or so days. I'm going to release you in a few days. When you go home, I need you to stay in bed for a week. That also means no driving, no working. Will that be possible?"

She opened her mouth, but Bray beat her to it. "Yes, she'll be able to stay in bed. I'll be there." He gave her a look that dared her to challenge him, and she was not fool enough to do it.

"Good," the doctor said. "See you tomorrow."

Once they were alone again, Kamryn pled her case. "Bray, you don't have to stay with me. Kalyn can stay."

He shook his head. "I'm staying with you, or you can stay at my house. The choice is yours. But we'll be together. I love you, Kam. If you want it, and I can do it, you will have it."

She didn't expect him to declare his love right there in the hospital. She was so glad he did. "I love you, too."

With her heart lighter, she went back to sleep.

———

Kalyn came to the hospital to visit her sister. Kamryn had been in the hospital almost four days; she had to face her. Since the night of her accident, Kalyn couldn't take the sight of Kamryn being so out of it or the fact that all she did was sleep.

Now it was time to shake off all that apprehension. After all, they were close, and she owed her sister that much. She walked into the hospital room. Bray was sitting in the chair next to the bed reading the newspaper while Kamryn was sound asleep. He rose as soon as he saw her. "I'm glad you came to see her. She's been asking for you."

Kalyn nodded. Walking inside the room was the hardest thing she'd ever done. "It just hurts me that she was so sick."

Brayden hugged Kalyn. "I know. No one felt as bad as I did, but you can't hide from your fear. She's doing well and should be released tomorrow."

"Thank you, Bray," she said, wiping her eyes.

He kissed her forehead. "Hey, you're important to Kam, which makes you important to me, even if you don't cook."

"Why are you hugging my sister?" Kamryn asked in a soft voice.

Kalyn laughed as Brayden quickly released her. "He was comforting me, Kamryn."

Kamryn smiled weakly. "I know. Isn't he great?"

"Yes, he is."

He leaned down and kissed Kamryn on her forehead. "I'll let you guys talk. I'm going to meet Tyler downstairs."

She nodded. "Bring him up. I'd love to see him."

"Okay, babe." He left the room.

Kalyn sat down in the vacated chair and inspected her sister. Kamryn had always been the strongest of them all. She was the problem-solver. Now she looked frail and helpless. It broke her heart. "First, I want to say that I'm sorry I didn't at least offer to go with you to Sandra's place. I'll do whatever it takes to make it up to you."

"Kalyn, it's okay. It was my choice and my choice alone."

Kalyn knew that, but somehow she still felt guilty. "I'm glad all this mess is over."

"Me, too. I love you, sis."

---

A week later Kamryn had had enough of the house, her family, and Bray. She was ready to get back to her life after all that mess was finally resolved.

Her dull headache had finally gone away, and she actually felt like herself again. Her family had babied her since she got out of the hospital. Her parents had come over daily, along with Kalyn and Keegan. No one would let her do a thing. Bray was no better. He fixed her meals, cleaned her house, and kept her company. He slept with her every night.

Okay, that part she didn't mind, but sleeping was all they had done in the last seven days. Granted she was not feeling too good at first, a little intimacy would be nice now, she thought.

She sat up in bed. All this idle time was driving her nuts. Her boss had been understanding and told her to take as much time as she needed to heal. Now she had too much time on her hands. She had to do something. Usually writing took her mind off her worries. She needed her laptop.

Normally she kept it under her bed when she wasn't using it just in case she had a moment of inspiration. She got out of bed and bent down on her knees to get it. The simple action made her dizzy.

"Hey, what are you doing?" Bray asked, helping her up and back into bed. "You know you're not supposed to do that."

"I was looking for my laptop," she said, resting against the pillow. She waited for the room to stop spinning counter-clockwise. "I thought it was under the bed."

"I came up to ask you what you want for lunch." He was dressed in shorts, a T-shirt, and no shoes.

"Bray, sit down."

He sighed. "This is one of those talks."

"No, it's not," she said. "Don't take this the wrong way. I really appreciate you being here."

"But?"

"You've been here every moment since I came home from the hospital a week ago. I don't want you to regret getting involved with me and thinking you have to be here with me every second of every day."

He pulled her into his arms and hugged her. He kissed her lightly on the lips before letting her go. "That could never happen. This is where I want to be. With you."

She couldn't stop the tears. "I love you."

"You know I love you." He cleared his throat. "Since you're in the talking mood, I do have something I want to discuss with you."

He picked up her hand and laced his fingers with hers. "I decided to retire from basketball. As you know, my contract is up and I wasn't looking forward to another grueling season of running up and down the court. My parents are set, and I've made some good investments over the years."

"W-what are you going to do?"

"I've been thinking."

She hated when he took forever to get to the point.

"I bought a restaurant."

"What? When?"

He laughed. "I wasn't here all the time. Times when your family was here, I had to meet my attorney to finalize the deal. I also officially retired."

She nodded, not knowing what she was supposed to say.

"I've been kicking the idea around for a minute. I want to open a bistro. Open a couple of days a week. I'm doing this for me. If it doesn't make a dime, I'm still set for the rest of my life. If it makes money, terrific, we'll have one hell of a nest egg."

"I think that's wonderful Bray. You love to cook. You deserve to do something you enjoy."

He moved closer to her. "I'm telling you this because you have a stake in this, too."

"I'm not following you."

"I want to marry you. I already talk to Harding and I have his permission."

She was stunned. Bray had actually asked her father for her hand in marriage? Who does that? If she didn't love him madly, this would have done it.

"Kam, an answer is necessary." He had a very serious look on his face. "I know we've been friends a long time, and in that time we've both seen each other at our best and worst, so I know we can make it. You thought I couldn't give up my old ways. For a minute, I didn't, either, but when it came down to it, it was you. And only you."

She wanted to say yes, but her mouth wouldn't cooperate with her heart.

"Kam, baby, please say something." He picked up her hand. "I'm putting myself out there and you're not saying anything." He took a deep breath. "Have your feelings changed?"

"It's not that," she croaked out. "I do love you."

"But?"

"Bray, I'm almost thirty-nine. Children might be a lost cause." She couldn't hold back her emotions. "Every man wants children."

"Honey, I don't care about that. I have nephews, and if you're really feeling that baby thing, we can adopt."

And that was when she realized he really had changed. He was no longer the man who thought only about himself. He was thinking about them. "Yes, I'll marry you." She wrapped her arms around him and kissed him.

"We'll get your ring tomorrow after your doctor's appointment," he said, smiling. He kissed her softly, savoring the taste of her lips.

Kamryn put her hand up to stop those sinful kisses. "You mean you asked me, thinking that I'd say no?"

He moved her hand out of the way and kissed her. "Yeah. Kam, you fought me every inch of the way on this. I'm very happy that you said yes."

"How happy?"

"This happy," he said, easing down in bed beside her and unbuttoning her nightshirt and tossing it aside. He kissed her softly. "I want us to be this happy every day for the rest of our lives."

She helped him out of his clothes and the rest of hers. She laughed as he hurriedly slipped on a condom. "I believe you are a romantic."

He eased on top of her and entered her, sliding deep inside her. "Good thing you are, too."

# EPILOGUE

*Twelve months later*

"Honey?" Bray called as he entered their bedroom. "Are you up here? Is everything all right? I'm sure Mom was kidding about childbirth," he said sitting on the bed. Tomorrow was going to be such a big day for them. He was concerned about her health.

The last year had been anything but quiet. Both Brian and Sandra each got twenty years in prison for Jason's death and assorted charges. Jason's mother had custody of his daughters and the team had officially retired Jason's jersey. After a small church wedding and a honeymoon to Greece, Kam had sold her house and moved in with Brayden.

Kam wrote a story chronicling Jason's death for the newspaper, and now a movie company wanted the story, offering Kam her first seven-figure deal. Which she accepted.

The bathroom door opened and Kam emerged, dabbing her face with a wet towel. At sixteen weeks along in her pregnancy, she positively glowed. Except for times like this, when her normally honey-brown skin paled with nausea. "I'm better." She walked toward him in her lounging attire: a Dallas Mavericks' oversized shirt and a pair of knit shorts, a present from his former coach. "No, your mom wasn't kidding, because my mom said the exact same thing. And let me tell you, you're nuts if you're think I'm enduring a natural childbirth!"

He reached for his wife and guided her to his lap. "Is that how a best-selling author should talk?" Kam's first hardback release, *The Chocolate Hero*, had netted her a position on the *New York Times* best seller list.

"I was number eighty-eight." She leaned against him. "Some days I can't believe the life we have. I'm doing what I love with the person I love and we're going to have a baby. I had given up on the idea of a baby a long time ago." She kissed him. "Thank you. I didn't know what I was missing." She wiped her eyes.

"Now, baby, you promised to ease up on the tears." He wiped her eyes. "You know what that does to me."

"Yes, I do, and I think it's wonderful. And to think tomorrow is the grand opening of the restaurant. It's your dream come true." She rose off his lap and slipped into bed.

He lay down beside her. "You're my dream come true. KamBray's is just a nice side thing. This," he rubbed her tummy, "is what I want." He was being totally honest. If it came down to Kam or the restaurant, the restaurant lost.

She stared at him. "What if I said I needed some attention right now?" Her hand glided over his T-shirt. "You know, we've both been so busy getting ready for the grand opening tomorrow that intimacy has kind of taken a backseat. I don't want that to happen to us."

He didn't either. He slipped off his T-shirt, jeans, and boxers. "Ready?"

She laughed. "I hadn't quite expected you to be that ready, but okay."

He was always eager for her, and that would never cease. "I was waiting for you." He helped her out of her shirt and shorts. "Umm, commando, I like it."

"Oh, I don't know what I'm going to do with you." She caressed his face and brought him closer for a kiss. "I hope you never change." She snuggled closer to him.

He caressed her waist and her stomach, marveling at the small changes in her body so early in the pregnancy. He couldn't believe the miracle of life they'd created was moving around already.

"Now who's the one with tears in his eyes? I hope nothing is wrong." She kissed him. "You can tell me if there's something wrong."

"The only thing that's wrong is that we're talking," Bray said.

"Oh, I can fix that." And she did.

# About the Author

**Celya Bowers** was born and raised in Marlin, Texas, a small town of 8,000. With not much to do, she turned to reading to expand her horizons. She became an avid reader at an early age. Soon she wanted the characters in the books she read to look more like her and she became a closet writer.

After attending Sam Houston State University, she relocated to Arlington. Currently she's completing her bachelor's degree after a 20 year absence from college. When she is not studying, writing or attending meetings, she likes hanging out with her great-niece Kennedy who just turned five.

She joined Romance Writers of America in 2001 and also the local chapter of Dallas Romance Authors where she learned more about the business of writing. She's now on the executive board as Published Author network liaison for the second year. She is also a member of Kiss of Death and The Sizzling Sisterhood Critique group.

When she's between deadlines and final exams, Celya likes to keep up with friends and fans, surf the net and daydream about finally getting to Ireland, her dream vacation.

## 2011 Mass Market Titles

### January

From This Moment
Sean Young
ISBN-13: 978-1-58571-383-7
ISBN-10: 1-58571-383-X
$6.99

Nihon Nights
Trisha/Monica Haddad
ISBN-13: 978-1-58571-382-0
ISBN-10: 1-58571-382-1
$6.99

### February

The Davis Years
Nicole Green
ISBN-13: 978-1-58571-390-5
ISBN-10: 1-58571-390-2
$6.99

Allegro
Adora Bennett
ISBN-13: 978-158571-391-2
ISBN-10: 1-58571-391-0
$6.99

### March

Lies in Disguise
Bernice Layton
ISBN-13: 978-1-58571-392-9
ISBN-10: 1-58571-392-9
$6.99

Steady
Ruthie Robinson
ISBN-13: 978-1-58571-393-6
ISBN-10: 1-58571-393-7
$6.99

### April

The Right Maneuver
LaShell Stratton-Childers
ISBN-13: 978-1-58571-394-3
ISBN-10: 1-58571-394-5
$6.99

Riding the Corporate Ladder
Keith Walker
ISBN-13: 978-1-58571-395-0
ISBN-10: 1-58571-395-3
$6.99

### May

Separate Dreams
Joan Early
ISBN-13: 978-1-58571-434-6
ISBN-10: 1-58571-434-8
$6.99

I Take This Woman
Chamein Canton
ISBN-13: 978-1-58571-435-3
ISBN-10: 1-58571-435-6
$6.99

### June

Inside Out
Grayson Cole
ISBN-13: 978-1-58571-437-7
ISBN-10: 1-58571-437-2
$6.99

## 2011 Mass Market Titles (continued)

### July

The Other Side of the
Mountain
Janice Angelique
ISBN-13: 978-1-58571-442-1
ISBN-10: 1-58571-442-9
$6.99

Holding Her Breath
Nicole Green
ISBN-13: 978-1-58571-439-1
ISBN-10: 1-58571-439-9
$6.99

### August

The Sea of Aaron
Kymberly Hunt
ISBN-13: 978-1-58571-440-7
ISBN-10: 1-58571-440-2
$6.99

The Finley Sisters' Oath of
Romance
Keith Thomas Walker
ISBN-13: 978-1-58571-441-4
ISBN-10: 1-58571-441-0
$6.99

### September

Except on Sunday
Regena Bryant
ISBN-13: 978-1-58571-443-8
ISBN-10: 1-58571-443-7
$6.99

Light's Out
Ruthie Robinson
ISBN-13: 978-1-58571-445-2
ISBN-10: 1-58571-445-3
$6.99

### October

The Heart Knows
Renee Wynn
ISBN-13: 978-1-58571-444-5
ISBN-10: 1-58571-444-5
$6.99

Best Friends; Better Lovers
Celya Bowers
ISBN-13: 978-1-58571-455-1
ISBN-10: 1-58571-455-0
$6.99

### November

Caress
Grayson Cole
ISBN-13: 978-1-58571-454-4
ISBN-10: 1-58571-454-2
$6.99

A Love Built to Last
L. S. Childers
ISBN-13: 978-1-58571-448-3
ISBN-10: 1-58571-448-8
$6.99

### December

Fractured
Wendy Byrne
ISBN-13: 978-1-58571-449-0
ISBN-10: 1-58571-449-6
$6.99

Everything in Between
Crystal Hubbard
ISBN-13: 978-1-58571-396-7
ISBN-10: 1-58571-396-1
$6.99

## Other Genesis Press, Inc. Titles

## Other Genesis Press, Inc. Titles (continued)

| | | |
|---|---|---|
| Blindsided | Tammy Williams | $6.99 |
| Bliss, Inc. | Chamein Canton | $6.99 |
| Blood Lust | J.M. Jeffries | $9.95 |
| Blood Seduction | J.M. Jeffries | $9.95 |
| Blue Interlude | Keisha Mennefee | $6.99 |
| Bodyguard | Andrea Jackson | $9.95 |
| Boss of Me | Diana Nyad | $8.95 |
| Bound by Love | Beverly Clark | $8.95 |
| Breeze | Robin Hampton Allen | $10.95 |
| Broken | Dar Tomlinson | $24.95 |
| Burn | Crystal Hubbard | $6.99 |
| By Design | Barbara Keaton | $8.95 |
| Cajun Heat | Charlene Berry | $8.95 |
| Careless Whispers | Rochelle Alers | $8.95 |
| Cats & Other Tales | Marilyn Wagner | $8.95 |
| Caught in a Trap | Andre Michelle | $8.95 |
| Caught Up in the Rapture | Lisa G. Riley | $9.95 |
| Cautious Heart | Cheris F. Hodges | $8.95 |
| Chances | Pamela Leigh Starr | $8.95 |
| Checks and Balances | Elaine Sims | $6.99 |
| Cherish the Flame | Beverly Clark | $8.95 |
| Choices | Tammy Williams | $6.99 |
| Class Reunion | Irma Jenkins/ John Brown | $12.95 |
| Code Name: Diva | J.M. Jeffries | $9.95 |
| Conquering Dr. Wexler's Heart | Kimberley White | $9.95 |
| Corporate Seduction | A.C. Arthur | $9.95 |
| Crossing Paths, Tempting Memories | Dorothy Elizabeth Love | $9.95 |
| Crossing the Line | Bernice Layton | $6.99 |
| Crush | Crystal Hubbard | $9.95 |
| Cypress Whisperings | Phyllis Hamilton | $8.95 |
| Dark Embrace | Crystal Wilson Harris | $8.95 |
| Dark Storm Rising | Chinelu Moore | $10.95 |
| Daughter of the Wind | Joan Xian | $8.95 |
| Dawn's Harbor | Kymberly Hunt | $6.99 |
| Deadly Sacrifice | Jack Kean | $22.95 |
| Designer Passion | Dar Tomlinson Diana Richeaux | $8.95 |

## Other Genesis Press, Inc. Titles (continued)

| | | |
|---|---|---|
| Do Over | Celya Bowers | $9.95 |
| Dream Keeper | Gail McFarland | $6.99 |
| Dream Runner | Gail McFarland | $6.99 |
| Dreamtective | Liz Swados | $5.95 |
| Ebony Angel | Deatri King-Bey | $9.95 |
| Ebony Butterfly II | Delilah Dawson | $14.95 |
| Echoes of Yesterday | Beverly Clark | $9.95 |
| Eden's Garden | Elizabeth Rose | $8.95 |
| Eve's Prescription | Edwina Martin Arnold | $8.95 |
| Everlastin' Love | Gay G. Gunn | $8.95 |
| Everlasting Moments | Dorothy Elizabeth Love | $8.95 |
| Everything and More | Sinclair Lebeau | $8.95 |
| Everything but Love | Natalie Dunbar | $8.95 |
| Falling | Natalie Dunbar | $9.95 |
| Fate | Pamela Leigh Starr | $8.95 |
| Finding Isabella | A.J. Garrotto | $8.95 |
| Fireflies | Joan Early | $6.99 |
| Fixin' Tyrone | Keith Walker | $6.99 |
| Forbidden Quest | Dar Tomlinson | $10.95 |
| Forever Love | Wanda Y. Thomas | $8.95 |
| Friends in Need | Joan Early | $6.99 |
| From the Ashes | Kathleen Suzanne | $8.95 |
| | Jeanne Sumerix | |
| Frost on My Window | Angela Weaver | $6.99 |
| Gentle Yearning | Rochelle Alers | $10.95 |
| Glory of Love | Sinclair LeBeau | $10.95 |
| Go Gentle Into That | Malcom Boyd | $12.95 |
|    Good Night | | |
| Goldengroove | Mary Beth Craft | $16.95 |
| Groove, Bang, and Jive | Steve Cannon | $8.99 |
| Hand in Glove | Andrea Jackson | $9.95 |
| Hard to Love | Kimberley White | $9.95 |
| Hart & Soul | Angie Daniels | $8.95 |
| Heart of the Phoenix | A.C. Arthur | $9.95 |
| Heartbeat | Stephanie Bedwell-Grime | $8.95 |
| Hearts Remember | M. Loui Quezada | $8.95 |
| Hidden Memories | Robin Allen | $10.95 |
| Higher Ground | Leah Latimer | $19.95 |
| Hitler, the War, and the Pope | Ronald Rychiak | $26.95 |
| How to Kill Your Husband | Keith Walker | $6.99 |

## Other Genesis Press, Inc. Titles (continued)

| | | |
|---|---|---|
| How to Write a Romance | Kathryn Falk | $18.95 |
| I Married a Reclining Chair | Lisa M. Fuhs | $8.95 |
| I'll Be Your Shelter | Giselle Carmichael | $8.95 |
| I'll Paint a Sun | A.J. Garrotto | $9.95 |
| Icie | Pamela Leigh Starr | $8.95 |
| If I Were Your Woman | LaConnie Taylor-Jones | $6.99 |
| Illusions | Pamela Leigh Starr | $8.95 |
| Indigo After Dark Vol. I | Nia Dixon/Angelique | $10.95 |
| Indigo After Dark Vol. II | Dolores Bundy/ Cole Riley | $10.95 |
| Indigo After Dark Vol. III | Montana Blue/ Coco Morena | $10.95 |
| Indigo After Dark Vol. IV | Cassandra Colt/ | $14.95 |
| Indigo After Dark Vol. V | Delilah Dawson | $14.95 |
| Indiscretions | Donna Hill | $8.95 |
| Intentional Mistakes | Michele Sudler | $9.95 |
| Interlude | Donna Hill | $8.95 |
| Intimate Intentions | Angie Daniels | $8.95 |
| It's in the Rhythm | Sammie Ward | $6.99 |
| It's Not Over Yet | J.J. Michael | $9.95 |
| Jolie's Surrender | Edwina Martin-Arnold | $8.95 |
| Kiss or Keep | Debra Phillips | $8.95 |
| Lace | Giselle Carmichael | $9.95 |
| Lady Preacher | K.T. Richey | $6.99 |
| Last Train to Memphis | Elsa Cook | $12.95 |
| Lasting Valor | Ken Olsen | $24.95 |
| Let Us Prey | Hunter Lundy | $25.95 |
| Let's Get It On | Dyanne Davis | $6.99 |
| Lies Too Long | Pamela Ridley | $13.95 |
| Life Is Never As It Seems | J.J. Michael | $12.95 |
| Lighter Shade of Brown | Vicki Andrews | $8.95 |
| Look Both Ways | Joan Early | $6.99 |
| Looking for Lily | Africa Fine | $6.99 |
| Love Always | Mildred E. Riley | $10.95 |
| Love Doesn't Come Easy | Charlyne Dickerson | $8.95 |
| Love Out of Order | Nicole Green | $6.99 |
| Love Unveiled | Gloria Greene | $10.95 |
| Love's Deception | Charlene Berry | $10.95 |
| Love's Destiny | M. Loui Quezada | $8.95 |
| Love's Secrets | Yolanda McVey | $6.99 |

## Other Genesis Press, Inc. Titles (continued)

| | | |
|---|---|---|
| Mae's Promise | Melody Walcott | $8.95 |
| Magnolia Sunset | Giselle Carmichael | $8.95 |
| Many Shades of Gray | Dyanne Davis | $6.99 |
| Matters of Life and Death | Lesego Malepe, Ph.D. | $15.95 |
| Meant to Be | Jeanne Sumerix | $8.95 |
| Midnight Clear | Leslie Esdaile | $10.95 |
| (Anthology) | Gwynne Forster | |
| | Carmen Green | |
| | Monica Jackson | |
| Midnight Magic | Gwynne Forster | $8.95 |
| Midnight Peril | Vicki Andrews | $10.95 |
| Misconceptions | Pamela Leigh Starr | $9.95 |
| Mixed Reality | Chamein Canton | $6.99 |
| Moments of Clarity | Michele Cameron | $6.99 |
| Montgomery's Children | Richard Perry | $14.95 |
| Mr. Fix-It | Crystal Hubbard | $6.99 |
| My Buffalo Soldier | Barbara B.K. Reeves | $8.95 |
| Naked Soul | Gwynne Forster | $8.95 |
| Never Say Never | Michele Cameron | $6.99 |
| Next to Last Chance | Louisa Dixon | $24.95 |
| No Apologies | Seressia Glass | $8.95 |
| No Commitment Required | Seressia Glass | $8.95 |
| No Regrets | Mildred E. Riley | $8.95 |
| Not His Type | Chamein Canton | $6.99 |
| Not Quite Right | Tammy Williams | $6.99 |
| Nowhere to Run | Gay G. Gunn | $10.95 |
| O Bed! O Breakfast! | Rob Kuehnle | $14.95 |
| Oak Bluffs | Joan Early | $6.99 |
| Object of His Desire | A.C. Arthur | $8.95 |
| Office Policy | A.C. Arthur | $9.95 |
| Once in a Blue Moon | Dorianne Cole | $9.95 |
| One Day at a Time | Bella McFarland | $8.95 |
| One of These Days | Michele Sudler | $9.95 |
| Outside Chance | Louisa Dixon | $24.95 |
| Passion | T.T. Henderson | $10.95 |
| Passion's Blood | Cherif Fortin | $22.95 |
| Passion's Furies | AlTonya Washington | $6.99 |
| Passion's Journey | Wanda Y. Thomas | $8.95 |
| Past Promises | Jahmel West | $8.95 |
| Path of Fire | T.T. Henderson | $8.95 |

## Other Genesis Press, Inc. Titles (continued)

## Other Genesis Press, Inc. Titles (continued)

## Other Genesis Press, Inc. Titles (continued)

# *ESCAPE WITH INDIGO !!!!*